IT WASN'T THERE . . .

"Damn! They took my communicator!" Riker struggled to his feet, cursing the sick weakness that made his knees shake, and stumbled over to the nearest body.

It was Dr. Crusher. She lay facedown, arms flung out as if she were embracing the earth. As he rolled her over, she moaned. A small, ragged hole at the breast of her uniform showed where her communicator had been ripped away.

"Oh, hell," Riker exclaimed.

He felt the tension knot tighten in his stomach. "Dr. Crusher . . . Captain Picard and Counselor Troi have been kidnapped."

Look for STAR TREK Fiction from Pocket Books

Star Trek: The Original Series

Star Trek: The Next Generation

#21

STAR TREK®
THE NEXT GENERATION™

CHAINS OF COMMAND

W. A. McCAY and E. L. FLOOD

POCKET BOOKS

New York   London   Toronto   Sydney   Tokyo   Singapore

An *Original* Publication of POCKET BOOKS

POCKET BOOKS, a division of Simon & Schuster Inc.
1230 Avenue of the Americas, New York, NY 10020

ISBN: 0-671-74264-7

First Pocket Books printing April 1992

10 9 8 7 6 5 4 3 2 1

POCKET and colophon are registered trademarks of
Simon & Schuster Inc.

Printed in the U.S.A.

CHAINS OF COMMAND

Chapter One

As THE AWAY TEAM winked into existence on the planet's surface, the luxuriant undergrowth stirred, riffled by a gentle breeze. Commander William Riker saw the leaves shiver in the gust, but he couldn't feel it through his atmosphere suit.

He glanced around. There was no sign of animal life in the pristine landscape. "No bugs," he muttered. "Paradise for picnickers."

A laugh crackled in his ear. Riker turned and gestured impatiently at the other members of the team. "Let's get on with the readings and samples." He shifted uncomfortably in the suit. "Move, people, unless you want to spend your entire time planetside in these blasted things."

The young crew members burst into a flurry of

activity, none of them eager to appear slow in front of their commander.

"Tricorders show sixty-five percent nitrogen, thirty percent oxygen, trace amounts of other gases —not too different from the air aboard the *Enterprise.*" Yeoman Janet Kinsolving, a trainee biologist, continued her enthusiastic observations, which she must have known had already been determined by the ship's scanners.

"The air seems breathable," she said eagerly. "I think it would be all right to try it, sir."

"Not Starfleet procedure, Yeoman," Riker reminded her. "Let's do it by the book." He cut his helmet communicator and sighed. A milk run, he thought. Just what I need. I already broke one date to run a training session with this team. This makes two—and Marla isn't the kind of woman to wait around for a third chance. His expression was half-sour, half-amused. Don't these kids know what they're doing to my love life?

Irritation with himself mingled with his annoyance at the unexpected and inconvenient mission. He knew his presence on Amon-4, as they'd dubbed this planet, was important. Though Riker's style of command was perhaps a bit more freewheeling than Captain Picard's, he was a staunch proponent of the captain's rule that no away mission should ever be conducted in the absence of an experienced senior officer.

No matter how many holodeck simulations of planetary exploration the crew members had been through, when they were doing the real thing there was always the possibility of some dangerous variable, a wild card even the *Enterprise* computer's vast processor hadn't anticipated.

If only this mission hadn't come up *today,* he thought.

He felt a tickling on his upper lip and reached up automatically to scratch it, arresting the motion only at the last moment, when he remembered his helmet. Amon was a G-type star, and its planet had a terrestrial atmosphere. The atmosphere suits were merely an extra precaution—an aggravating one, in Riker's opinion. Somehow whenever he closed the faceplate on an atmosphere suit an inexplicable but fierce itch began under his beard.

It was intensifying now, but there was no hope of relief. As commander of the expedition, he couldn't disobey his own order and open the helmet, even though he knew there was breathable air on the other side of the clear plastic.

"Commander? Kinsolving here," came that high, breathy voice again. Riker thought he detected a hesitant note in it. "I've found something you might want to look at. A single-cell creature. It's the first animal life we've found."

Amon-4 had no dangerous fauna. In fact, it had seemed to have no fauna at all—at least nothing large enough to register on shipboard scanners. The yeoman's find was unlikely to be very dramatic. Still . . .

"Good work, Yeoman." Riker made an effort to sound encouraging. "On my way."

He started toward Kinsolving. The rich native flora—a little too purple to pass as terrestrial vegetation—stirred again. Leaves parted to reveal a fiercely orange blossom, petals spiking outward in riotous splendor. Riker paused to eye it. Hmm. Maybe an exotic bloom or two would take the edge off the delectable Marla's pique. . . .

It was then that he heard the screams. They weren't coming through his communicator, and for a second he couldn't figure out where they had originated. Then he realized that the horrible bubbling cries were reaching him through the atmosphere itself. The sound was muffled by his helmet. Even so, Riker recognized Yeoman Kinsolving's voice.

He ran over the small rise she'd disappeared behind. The yeoman stood with her back to him, clutching her helmet with both hands. As he watched, she fell to her knees. Riker ran forward, bent down, and grasped her heaving shoulders. Her head fell back so that she was facing him.

"Good God!" Riker exclaimed. With an effort he stopped himself from thrusting her away from him.

Apparently, having tested the air, Kinsolving had cracked her helmet open to take a sniff. And she was paying for it.

The first time he met her, Riker had classified the young woman as a bland blonde: wide forehead, snub nose, frankly plain features. Now he gazed helplessly down at her as the skin literally boiled off her face. The screaming stopped as a bloody froth poured from her mouth. The bones of her skull were already showing through.

Gingerly Riker lowered Kinsolving to the ground. He could see at a glance that there was

4

nothing to be done. She was already dead—lucky, in a way, to have died so quickly.

But whatever was devouring her wasn't finished. Kinsolving's suit twitched on the ground in a grotesque parody of life as muscles, ligaments, even bone, bubbled away.

Riker looked up and saw that he'd been joined by the other members of the team, their questions cut off by shock as they took in Kinsolving's rapidly dissipating form. He rounded on them fiercely. Slapping his communicator into life, he ordered, "Back over the hill—now!"

He contacted the *Enterprise*. "We've run into trouble. Beam us back to a quarantine section for decontamination. Inform sickbay as well."

"Five to return?" Engineering asked.

Riker stared down at the now still form at his feet. The suit was ominously flat—empty.

"Four still alive. Lock on to Kinsolving's suit."

We can't even bring her body back for a funeral, he thought bleakly. There's nothing left.

It took the science and medical techs three days to discover what had killed Yeoman Kinsolving. At last the report came in: the air she had taken in was fatally different from the *Enterprise*'s atmosphere in that it harbored something that hadn't shown up on the tricorder. That something had seized on the luckless Kinsolving in seconds.

In a ghastly way the yeoman's death explained the lack of fauna on Amon-4. When Dr. Beverly Crusher finally isolated the killer, it turned out to be a subviral body that the tricorders hadn't even identified as a life-form. It attacked animal protein, explosively reducing it to nutrients and carbon dioxide. The only animals on Amon-4 were single-cell creatures, too small to arouse the subvirus, which had simply remained dormant—until Kinsolving opened her helmet.

The away team members had to stay in quarantine during the investigation, trapped in their suits unless they wanted to court the same fate that had taken Kinsolving so horribly. Three days in an atmosphere suit, with its limited water supply and sanitation, unable to wash, unable to eat. . . .

Riker watched the bright faces of his team grow pale and gaunt and berated himself for the tragedy of Amon-4. If only he had stated the rules more clearly. If only he hadn't delayed responding to Kinsolving's call. If only . . .

But all the reproaches in the world wouldn't change what had happened. Sighing, Riker leaned back against the wall and shut his eyes, trying to ignore the sour smell of his unwashed body and the fierce itching beneath his beard.

The void stretched beyond the hull of the USS *Enterprise,* punctuated with a few flyspeck stars and planets. Though huge to a man's eyes, its engines pulsing with power, in truth the starship was merely an infinitesimal bubble of life plunging silently through stark vacuum.

The *Enterprise*'s first officer rarely dealt in such musings. But at the moment, his cheeks still sunken from his ordeal in the decontamination unit, Riker was feeling less than usually optimistic. And the universe kept offering little reminders of its emptiness, reminders like the world on the viewscreen in front of him.

The planet's sere brown surface was marred by a stretched-out collection of craters describing an arc on one side of the globe. But what force had created that scarred visage?

"Report, Mr. Data," Riker ordered, leaning forward in the command chair.

"A terrestrial planet, sir, similar in mass and density to other terrestrial planets we have encountered in this sector," announced Data. The android's tenor voice was perfectly modulated, revealing nothing but polite interest. He bent his sleek head over the readout on the Ops panel, then straightened again before going on. "No life readings. However, soil analysis indicates the planet had a nitrogen-oxygen atmosphere in the past."

"What happened to it?" Riker demanded.

Data blinked, his golden eyes as guileless as a child's. "It dissipated, sir."

Riker sighed at Data's literal answer. "I meant, Data, what do you think *caused* the atmosphere to dissipate?"

"Unknown, sir."

"Speculations, anyone?"

The bridge crew's only answer was silence, stretching until frustration tightened the corners of Riker's bright blue eyes. They'd encountered six earthlike planets in as many star systems while

7

charting this seemingly empty sector. And all were dead, though the signs suggested they hadn't always been that way. What had happened to them?

Four of the planets were scarred wastelands like the one that filled the viewscreen now. The fifth one . . . Riker tried to repress the memory of Kinsolving's face.

The turbolift doors swished open, and Counselor Deanna Troi glided in to take her seat next to Riker. She neither spoke nor looked at him, yet Riker was intensely aware of her presence. Is she keeping an eye on me? he wondered.

The night before, when he'd gone to Ten-Forward to celebrate his release from quarantine, he'd seen Deanna and Beverly Crusher with their heads together at a corner table. When he approached them, they'd immediately stopped talking. Riker had made a joke about doctor-counselor confidentiality, but he couldn't help thinking he'd barged in on something he wasn't meant to hear. And a tiny corner of his psyche had wondered if they were talking about him.

He knew he was being paranoid. A doctor and a psychologist were likely have any number of confidential conversations about any number of topics. But ever since his return from the Amon-4 catastrophe, Riker had had the feeling that Crusher was paying special attention to him. Now he wondered if she had recruited Deanna to do the same.

Troi gave him a single startled gaze from those inky Betazoid eyes of hers, reminding him that his feelings were as clear to her as if he had spoken them aloud. Riker sighed and pushed the useless thoughts away.

"Take a look at that." He nodded toward the viewscreen. "What do you think happened down there?"

Troi's delicate brows drew together in a frown. "Impact with an asteroid, perhaps," she suggested.

"Doubtful," Data commented. He swiveled in his chair so that he faced Riker and Troi. "An asteroid would essentially fall into the planet, not having the velocity to escape its gravitational pull. Its impact would have made a single large crater, not a long trail of them such as we see here. And besides, this area is remarkably free of space debris."

Riker nodded. Data was voicing thoughts he'd had himself.

The android cocked his head to one side. "It is theoretically possible that something of substantial mass, traveling at extremely high velocity, approached the planet at a tangential angle, breaking up in the atmosphere and thus producing a pattern of craters."

"Moving tangentially," Riker said thoughtfully, "the body might have executed an orbit through the planet's atmosphere. What effects would that have?"

Data considered. "Friction with the atmosphere would have heated the outside of the object to temperatures in excess of eighteen thousand degrees centigrade."

"Whoa." From the engineering console, Geordi

La Forge added, "That's more than three times the surface temperature of your average G-type star. That planet was pan-fried."

"Geordi is correct, sir," Data concurred. "The effect on any life-forms on the planet would have been catastrophic."

Riker frowned, staring at the continent-long swath of craters. One of them had to be a good hundred kilometers wide. "What size body are we talking about here? And what sort of velocity would it require, Mr. Data?"

"Without knowing the mass involved, I can only conjecture," the android said slowly. "From the amount of devastation, I would postulate a body with a diameter of approximately ten-point-seven kilometers—roughly the size of the Martian satellite Phobos. As for velocity, it would require a significant percentage of light-speed."

"Going like a runaway freight train, it blew away the planet's atmosphere and pulverized the entire surface. I sure wouldn't want to run into a thing like that in a dark alley," Geordi muttered.

"Unlikely," Data advised him. "Our readings indicate the impacts occurred at least ten thousand years ago."

"War." Lieutenant Worf's voice was a rumbling growl.

Riker and Troi both turned from the viewscreen to stare at the towering figure of the Klingon security chief. Worf's massive ridged features were contracted in a scowl. He stood ramrod straight, his gaze directed firmly at an imaginary point about a meter in front of his nose. "Sir, this was war. No natural force made those craters. The odds of an ordinary asteroid striking the planet at so great a speed and at that angle are almost infinitesimal. Obviously it was done by intelligent beings using unknown advanced technology. But an event of such destructiveness could only be an act of war."

Troi shook her head. "I don't agree. Look at the readings. There is nothing on that planet—*nothing*. There aren't even any ruins! That means this war destroyed not only all life but also all structures."

"An impact like that would have mangled the planet's crust," La Forge said. "Earthquakes, tidal waves . . ."

"And the debris trail takes in the main landmass, right in the temperate zone." Riker frowned at the planet's scarred face. "That was probably the area of greatest population density."

Pushing himself up out of the captain's chair, Riker strode closer to the viewscreen and studied the image for a long moment. "What about Amon-Four?" He whirled to face the bridge crew. "Could we explain the situation there as the aftermath of war? A biological weapon tailored to eat up the population? Suppose it was a one-two punch: a virus to kill anything that contained animal proteins and an engineered life-form like the Nanites to eliminate the technological infrastructure."

"It is difficult to say," Data replied equably. "On the evidence we have, it seems as probable as any other theory."

"But there were no signs that any civilization ever flourished on Amon-Four," Troi objected.

"Nor does nature create situations like the one

on Amon-Four," Riker responded. "Nothing we've ever seen, nothing in any of the science or history banks, can explain an M-class planet of that age with lush vegetation and a nitrogen-oxygen atmosphere but no significant animal life."

"I know little of biological warfare," Worf growled. "Klingons fight with *real* weapons. Nonetheless, Commander Riker, I say someone fought a great war in this quadrant."

"But surely there is also the possibility that some sort of massive natural disaster occurred," Troi countered.

Worf's broad nostrils flared. "Such as . . . ?" he asked skeptically.

"I don't know. Perhaps a supernova in a nearby system." Troi twined her fingers together. "It would have released intense radiation and caused great devastation for light-years around. That could explain the dead planets."

"If there had been a supernova as recently as ten thousand years ago, our sensors would have detected signs of it," Worf said. "No, Counselor, that"—he aimed a finger at the viewscreen—"is a battle scar."

Sighing, Troi raked a hand through the heavy black mass of her hair. "I hope you're wrong, Lieutenant," she said softly. "Because the existence of a race that could inflict destruction on that scale is a terrible thought."

In his quarters Jean-Luc Picard started from a fitful sleep as the *Enterprise*'s engines powered down. Through the hull the sound was no more than a tiny decrease in the intensity of the pervasive hushed hum of the ship's systems. To Picard, though, it was a ringing trumpet.

He sat up in bed, his lean features alert. We're in orbit, he thought, and his hand went to the small gold chevron on the breast of his uniform, which hung over the back of a chair near the bed. Then he stopped himself. No need to call the bridge. Riker knew what he was doing. And Picard was under doctor's orders to get some rest.

Easing back down, Picard shut his eyes and attempted to sleep once more. What had Dr. Crusher suggested? Counting sheep? What kind of damn-fool remedy is that? he wondered, annoyed.

After ten minutes he gave up. "I'm not even tired," he muttered, pulling on his uniform and boots. Straightening up, he surveyed himself in the recessed mirror over the old-fashioned oak chest of drawers where he kept his clothes.

The face that gazed dispassionately back at him was a study in lines and angles. Two deep creases made parallel tracks across the high, ascetic forehead. Two more, vertical, trisected the space between the eyebrows. The mouth formed the base of a triangle whose sides were etched lines that met somewhere above the nostrils. Keen slanting eyes made obsidian slashes on either side of a hawk nose.

He strode over to the viewscreen and pressed a button to draw back the shutter. The planet that met his gaze was yet another lifeless ball of rock. Picard contemplated it, absentmindedly smoothing the silver fringe of his hair.

Starfleet would recall the *Enterprise* from this charting run if the crew didn't find something soon, he realized, and was surprised to find the idea vaguely appealing. With the growing number of member races in the Federation, the time Starfleet was able to allot for simple exploration kept shrinking. Picard accepted the need for all the diplomatic and courier missions the *Enterprise* was increasingly sent on, but his first love had always been investigating the unknown reaches of space. To push outward the limits of knowledge, to witness the unimaginable vastness of the universe—these were the enticements that had drawn Jean-Luc Picard to the stars.

But this sad, desolate field of ravaged systems depressed even him. It had an air of abandonment that was almost tangible. "'"My name is Ozymandias, king of kings,"'" he quoted softly. "'"Look on my works, ye Mighty, and despair!" Nothing beside remains. Round the Decay of that colossal wreck, boundless and bare, the lone and level sands stretch far away.'"

A pang of melancholy made him turn away from the dark window. He shook his head as if to clear it, then tapped his communicator. "Picard to bridge. I'm on my way."

When he strode onto the bridge moments later, Riker stood up, vacating the command chair. The first officer gestured at the forward viewscreen. "Have you seen this?" he asked.

The captain nodded. "I see no reason to send an away team down, Number One, do you?"

"No, sir," Riker said. "I doubt there's anything there."

"Ensign, lay in a new course: bearing three-point-seven, mark four." Picard sank into his chair.

"Course laid in." The ensign at the conn looked up at him for the command.

For a moment the captain's eyes remained on the dead planet wheeling in its endless dance. "Take us out of orbit," he said at last. "Warp six."

The next G-type star was only six light-years away—a neighbor on the same astronomical block. The *Enterprise* reached it later that day and cruised toward its one M-class planet at a sedate 25 percent of impulse.

"Long-range scans, Lieutenant Worf," Picard ordered.

"An arctic world, sir," Worf said, examining the sensor array. "No sign of habitation. There is also evidence of a major impact such as we discovered on the last planet."

The planet appeared on the viewscreen, a glittering ball with enormous white ice caps covering much of what would normally have been temperate zones. An enormous scar angled across one continent, then disappeared into the ice mass.

"It appears that this planet is undergoing a period of major glaciation," Data spoke up. "An ice age."

"One large scar, as opposed to many smaller ones. . . . It looks as if this world suffered a more direct impact than the last one," Riker said. "There would have been tremendous volcanic activity and enough dust and debris clouding the atmosphere to lower the planet's mean temperature and trigger glacial growth. It's just gone on for millennia."

"Sir!" Surprise made Worf's voice even more resonant than usual. It boomed through the bridge like a drum. "We're being hailed from the planet!"

"On screen," Picard commanded instantly.

The voice, obsequious yet insistent, came through before the picture. "What ship is that, please? We have sent for the regent Drraagh. No ship is expected for another three years. Please, what ship is that?" The words were heavily accented, yet recognizably English.

"What ship is that?" the voice repeated. It faded for a moment, and then the picture suddenly came through to show a plump, sallow-skinned face.

"Human!" Troi exclaimed.

"A lost colony, maybe?" Riker wondered aloud. "But how'd they get here? This area is parsecs beyond the range of old Earth technology."

For about a second the plump man's face maintained its anxious, servile expression. Then his cold little eyes seemed to focus on Picard in the command chair. They popped wide open.

"What—" He fumbled for words, finally blurting out "A human crew! What gang are you? Where are your masters?"

"What do you mean? This is the USS *Enterprise*, representing the United Federation of Planets," Picard responded. "Who are you people? And who are these masters you refer to?"

Pandemonium suddenly raged behind the plump

face on the screen. "No masters? They're free humans? Help us!" a voice yelled. "Help us, brothers!"

"Quiet, slag!" Fat-face hurled the order over his shoulder. He never saw the bulky, deadly-looking instrument aimed at his back. But the bridge crew did.

For an instant Riker considered warning him. But the instant was gone and the weapon flashed. The last thing they saw was the plump man's death. A blinding beam tore right through him and into the communications gear he was using. Everyone on the bridge flinched back from an intolerable blast of light.

Then the screen went blank.

Chapter Two

"Mr. Worf, can you reestablish contact?" Captain Picard snapped out the question.

"Negative, sir," the Klingon replied after a moment. "I am attempting to hail the planet on a broad range of frequencies, but so far there is no response."

Picard's nostrils flared in irritation. "Damn! What was that all about? Counselor"—he turned to Troi—"what impressions did you get from that scene we just witnessed?"

"Nothing very clearly defined." Troi's face was a little paler than usual, but her manner was composed. "I sensed fear, anger, hatred, but there was such a jumble of personalities that I can't be more specific."

"Mmm," Picard said, nodding. "Gangs . . .

masters." He looked up at Riker, who was standing by Data at the Ops panel. "Number One? Speculation?"

Riker spread his hands. "Not without more information," he said. "The contact was too brief."

"Agreed." Picard leaned forward and addressed the officer at the conn. "Ensign, get us into orbit. Lieutenant, can you establish the location of that broadcast?"

"Yes, sir," Worf rumbled. "Sensors have traced an energy discharge that matches the output from the beam we just saw. It seems to have come from an underground complex located near the north end of the impact scar."

"We've been handed a mystery—and a cry for help," Picard said. "At the very least we have to investigate the situation in that complex."

"I recommend placing an away team near the energy discharge site but away from other life-form readings," Worf said.

"Make it so. Assemble an away team, Number One," Picard said crisply to Riker. "I want to know what the devil's going on down there."

Riker suppressed the flutter of anxiety he felt at the thought of leading another away team. He'd known the order was coming, and he knew it was the logical course of action to take. There was no point in worrying. The surest way to invite another tragedy like the one on Amon-4 was to let worry paralyze him.

"Aye, sir," he replied. After thinking for a moment, he added, "Riker to Engineering. Mr. La Forge, I need you in Transporter Room Two as soon as you can get there. I'm taking a team down to that ice planet."

"Anything you say, chief," came the voice of the irrepressible chief engineer. "See you there."

Riker allowed himself a small grin. He was always glad to include Geordi La Forge on an away team. Geordi's enhanced vision and thorough knowledge of engineering and physics were valuable assets in a strange environment. And besides that, his perpetual high spirits were infectious.

The first officer beckoned to Worf. "Lieutenant, come with me."

Worf followed Riker into the turbolift. Riker was a big man, but the security chief still topped him by inches, and his large chest seemed to strain the fabric of his fitted red and black uniform. Looking at him, Riker felt dwarfed.

"Deck eight," he ordered, and the turbolift began its smooth descent. Riker eyed Worf again. The Klingon stood—hands behind his back, legs slightly apart—as relaxed as a Klingon would ever be, Riker guessed.

"Shall I issue hand phasers, sir?" he enquired.

"Yes, do that," Riker said. "And add a security detail as well. I have a feeling we might find a hot situation down there in spite of the cold climate."

"Agreed." There was a note of anticipation in Worf's voice.

The doors slid open at deck eight, and the two strode down the corridor toward the transporter room. Pausing at a comm panel, Riker touched it lightly. "Riker to Dr. Crusher."

"Akihiko here," came a male voice. "Doctors

Crusher and Selar are involved in an emergency procedure at the moment. Can I help you, Commander?"

Riker frowned. "I just wanted to alert sickbay that an away team is heading into a possible combat zone."

"We'll be standing by, sir," the doctor said.

"Good. Riker out." He turned away from the comm panel, feeling again a little tug of foreboding. He shook it away. "Lieutenant, let's get this show on the road."

As the familiar tingling of the transporter beam swept over him, Riker strained his eyes. It was useless, he knew. The process was instantaneous. But through all the years he'd been beaming from place to place, he'd never given up trying to *see* what it was like in between.

He had no more success this time. One moment he was standing on the transporter platform looking at Chief O'Brien. The next instant, with no discernible shift, he was staring into frigid twilit darkness.

The place was silent and still. At Worf's nod the two security officers spread out to defensive positions. Riker stepped forward. Worf was beside him in an instant, one huge hand resting lightly on the phaser at his belt. In the other hand he held a tricorder, with which he swept the room slowly. "No life forms other than our own in the immediate vicinity," he reported.

Riker's eyes were adjusting to the feeble light. He glanced around with interest. They'd beamed into a large, shabby room that seemed hewn out of the frozen soil and bedrock of the planet itself. On closer inspection Riker saw that the rock walls had been sealed with a clear plasticlike substance, though not very well. Streaks and viscous globs testified to a job clumsily done. The floor was coated with the same stuff. Insulation, he guessed.

Tall stacks of crates and boxes marched in rows into the deep gloom. The only illumination came from a single glowing metal strip set into a track running across the ceiling. Two doorways led to unlit, unwelcoming tunnels. The air held a stale, musky tang of dust and unwashed flesh, as if the place hadn't been ventilated for years.

"Brrr. Chilly in here," Geordi La Forge remarked.

It was an understatement. Riker pulled his parka more closely around him and watched his breath puff out in a cloud of vapor. Good thing the away team had donned cold-weather gear before beaming down. The air was near freezing, if Riker was any judge. Which raised a question: if it was this cold inside a shelter, how cold was it outside?

He touched his insignia. *"Enterprise,* this is Riker."

There was no response. Frowning, Riker tried again, striking his communicator more sharply. "Riker to *Enterprise.* Riker to *Enterprise.* Come in, *Enterprise."*

"Let me try mine," Geordi suggested, tapping his insignia. But his communicator, too, proved to be dead.

Stroking his beard, Riker cast an anxious glance at the chief engineer. "What's your assessment?"

Geordi's dark-skinned face, dominated by the prosthetic VISOR that served as his eyes, was impassive. He shrugged. "Could be anything from an ion storm to some sort of unintended interference from the planet."

"Yet we beamed in without interference," Worf pointed out. He unhooked the phaser from his belt, his brow ridges drawn together in fierce concentration. "I don't like it. In my experience it is always best to assume—" He broke off abruptly. "Sir! Someone's coming!"

Worf wasn't looking at the tricorder. There was no need to. The sound of rushing footsteps told the whole story. A voice snapped, "Through the store-room."

Riker saw a cluster of figures burst from one tunnel entrance, mostly grim-visaged men in gray uniforms, like that of the man he'd seen die on the viewscreen. A few others in patched, baggy mud-brown coveralls stumbled along with scared, mutinous expressions.

For a brief instant the new arrivals stared at the away team. Riker was able to note that the gray-clad men carried small weapons. Then a stone-faced man in gray said simply, "Kill them."

Riker snatched up his phaser. Worf and his man both had their weapons out; they took out two of the strangers. But there were too many of them. A snarling buzz erupted as the men in gray fired and charged.

Fat bluish sparks shot from their weapons. Riker saw one strike a security man in the arm. He reeled back with a scream, his phaser clattering to the floor as he clutched at his wound. Another bolt caught him in the chest. His scream—and maybe his breathing—stopped as he fell.

Riker ducked behind a crate and snapped off a shot. One of the brown-clad men dropped. Worf and Geordi also took cover, then attempted counterfire as a fusillade of bolts tore at them. Reflexively Riker tapped his communicator. Still dead—and the security officer needed treatment. So much for alerting sickbay.

Another cry rang out, and Riker saw the other security man pitch against a crate, his face pale, a smear of blood trailing down the rough plastic container.

Numbers had always been on the side of the attackers, but now they were drawing in for the coup de grace. They had enough people to keep the *Enterprise* team pinned with covering fire and still advance. Riker managed to hit another target, but his stomach was tight with dread. Can't retreat, can't call for help, he thought. The away team that didn't get away.

He was debating standing up to take a few more attackers with him when the far wall of the chamber suddenly exploded outward in a blinding ruby flash. A man stood outlined against the gaping hole, something bulky over his shoulders, a tube snaking around to a blunt rod in his hand. He whipped the wand toward the gray-clad attackers, and a needle of red stabbed out. It scored across a wall of crates, filling the air with the acrid stink of melted plastic. The man behind the barricade fell backward, his uniform smoldering, his flesh burned. A mining laser, Riker thought. An antique.

The man stepped from his newly created entrance followed by a flood of others in patched brown burlap. With the laser for cover fire, they advanced, most of them armed with heavy hand tools—picks, hammers, sharpened chisels. A couple carried the mysterious weapons the gray-clad men had used—captured in combat, Riker guessed.

One of the newcomers—a lithe, swift shadow of a man—held a bolt-firer at the ready as he took his place to cover the laser wielder. He stepped up just in time to hurl a bolt at a gray-faction sniper who'd come up from the side.

The new arrivals called and shouted to one another as they charged into action, in contrast to the deadly silence of the others. Now the gray-clad men and their followers began to retreat, but an additional force of men in brown burlap filled the tunnel they'd come from.

Riker saw the stone-faced leader of the gray faction, his expression now bitter. The leader plunged forward, weapon extended in both hands, trying to reach the man with the laser. The red beam clipped him, as did a blue spark from the man beside the laser wielder. The man fell back, and Riker saw a roughly clad figure in silhouette bringing down a pickax.

The rest of the fight was brief but vicious, the gray faction fighting like trapped rats, giving no quarter and receiving none. Riker saw no wounded, no survivors in gray, especially after the brown-clad men engaged them hand-to-hand.

The snarl of the gray faction's weapons died away as their owners died. Now a mob in brown faced the *Enterprise* team. The man with the laser stepped forward. "Good work, keeping them from their escape tunnel until we could block it. But where did you get those weapons?"

He stepped closer, peering through the semidarkness until he was close to Worf. Suddenly Riker saw him recoil.

"What in God's name *are* you?"

The rod of the laser came up to aim as Worf, growling, targeted him with his phaser.

The man who'd guarded the leader's back was beside him in one supple movement. He was dark and lithe, with lines of suffering and hard life carved into his bony cheeks. Black hair and brows overhung the brooding, hooded eyes of a perfect killer. Riker could clearly see the pistol in his hand, its long, thin barrel swelling into a cylindrical charge chamber. Oddly dainty grips made the weapon appear too small to be effective. But Riker had seen the guns at work. Now it was aimed point-blank at Worf.

"Hold it!" Riker shouted. "We want no more fighting."

The laser-carrying leader turned to him, and Riker had to keep down his own gasp of surprise. In the dimness, he'd seen the man only in profile— pale hair, noble brow, high-arched nose, a young, commanding, handsome face. Full-front, he confronted a wreck. Half of the face, from the left hairline to the point of the jaw, looked as if its skin had been flayed away. An expanse of scar tissue—dead white, steel gray in patches, with an occasional purplish tint—gleamed in the wan light. Yet the piercing blue eyes that glared at him from deep-set sockets were feverishly alive. Those eyes seemed to devour Riker's face and the uniform he wore.

The man's heavy lips quirked in an unexpected smile. "You! You were on the screen in the control room with the man who asked what masters were." He glanced at the weapons in the *Enterprise* crewmen's hands. "You heard me! And you came to help us!"

"We came to investigate," Worf said.

"Ah." The man's gaze flicked back and forth between Riker and Worf; then he gestured at the body of one of the gray-clad men. "But you fought these."

"We had no choice," Riker said. "They attacked us."

The blond leader dismissed that as if it were axiomatic. "I'm Koban. Who are you?" he demanded, focusing on Riker. There was an urgency in his tone, as if he already knew the answer but wanted it confirmed by someone else. Riker lowered his phaser cautiously.

"I'm Commander William Riker of the *Enterprise,* a vessel of the United Federation of Planets." Riker said. Then he furrowed his brow, suddenly unsure of himself.

Koban was leaning forward, a hungry, hopeful look on his ravaged face.

What's he thinking? Riker asked himself. Does he know what the Federation is?

Then, to Riker's immense surprise, Koban threw his arms around him. "So it's true. I never dared hope this could happen!" he exclaimed. "Vossted always said you were out there somewhere, but I never really believed anyone had survived. And now this—to actually see you here! Damn, but this is the best news I've ever had. Welcome them, men! Welcome the free humans to Koorn!"

Koban's companions raised a cheer.

Despite himself, Riker couldn't help feeling some of Koban's enthusiasm. "Thanks," he said, smiling.

"Do you have your own ship?" Koban asked eagerly.

"Well, it's not exactly his," Geordi murmured.

Koban's face darkened for a moment, but then he laughed. "Oh, I see. You have a superior officer. But no master? You're free?"

"Free?" one of the brown-clad men echoed, looking awed.

There was a faint groan from the security man sprawled on the crate. Riker strode over to the man's side and peered down at him.

A usually ruddy face now had a greenish cast. The man's eyes were glazed and unsteady. "I think I'll . . . live," he croaked. "But I'm . . . afraid I'll be . . . no use to you, Commander."

A remorseful Riker wheeled to face Koban. "Look, two of my men are injured. Can you help? They need medical attention now."

"Chu." Koban gestured to his companion, who

unslung a backpack and went over to the conscious security man.

"A touch of neural disruptor," he reported after a second. "This gash in the head is long but shallow." He took out some strips of cloth and a jar of some evil-smelling salve and went to work. As he did, he gestured with his head at the other security officer, the one who didn't move. Riker's heart thudded dully when he said, "I'm afraid there's nothing I can do for that one. He's alive, but . . ."

Riker nodded dumbly.

"Chu Edorlic," Koban explained, introducing his lieutenant. "He knows a bit about treating wounds. We in the gangs don't have doctors. There was one on the planet, but he was with the overseers." He gave a grim smile. "Not anymore, though."

"Who are these overseers?" Riker asked.

Edorlic spat.

"They're slave drivers," Koban said. His mouth twisted in contempt. "For profit they force other men to labor here and rebuild this hellhole of a planet—"

"They *did*," Chu Edorlic cut in. "Now we're taking over. And the bastards are all going to die."

"I get the feeling we walked in on the middle of a revolution," Geordi said.

"A slave society," Riker murmured. "That's where all the talk about masters comes from."

"But it ends now," Koban said. "Today our enslavement ends." Those piercing blue eyes held an unnerving intensity, an almost hypnotic power that transcended his ruined face. Suddenly Riker

29

understood exactly how he had become the leader of this ragged band.

"Uh, Koban," Geordi suddenly said, staring off at a wrecked row of crates. "I think your laser left something smoldering in there. I can see some heat."

"See heat?" Koban frowned. "How?"

"With this." Geordi tapped his VISOR. "This serves as my eyes. It lets me see the entire electromagnetic spectrum. Heat shows up as red patches." White teeth flashed in a grin as he added, "On a planet as cold as this one, it's pretty easy to catch the hot spots. That crate is definitely hot."

Koban took a step closer. "This is fantastic!" he exclaimed. "You mean you have no eyes of your own?"

"Oh, I have eyes, all right," Geordi explained. He'd stopped being sensitive on the subject years ago. In his opinion, most of the time his VISOR more than compensated for his lack of optic nerves. "They just don't work. I was born that way."

"Yet they let you live," Chu Edorlic said wonderingly, "in spite of such a defect." He stared at Worf. "And you. With a facial deformity like that . . ." He shook his head.

Worf's eyes widened slightly as he realized what Chu was saying. Then he growled low in his chest. "I am *not* deformed," he said emphatically. "I am—"

"Worf," Riker warned. He thought it might not be a bad idea to keep Worf's Klingon identity a secret. These people had obviously been in this desolate region for generations. Why, if they really were a lost colony from Earth, they could even have been here since before humans discovered other intelligent races! If they thought Worf was human, it was probably best to leave it that way until he was sure they were ready for the truth.

"Chu didn't mean any insult," Koban said to Worf. "It's just that your ways are new to us." His eyes took on a wintry look. "Here, when a child's born . . . defective, the overseers have it killed. And workers who can't go on . . ." He abruptly ceased, a muscle twitching in his ravaged cheek.

In spite of himself, Riker was appalled. How could they have sunk to such barbarism? How had Koban survived? He wondered if, in Koban's place, he would have been able to maintain such dignity in the face of such brutalization.

He wasn't at all sure he would have.

"Who are you people?" Geordi asked. "Where are you from? And how did you end up here on this ball of ice in the middle of nowhere?"

Koban braced his foot on one of the crates and leaned forward, resting a forearm on his knee. "We're taught that our ancestors came from the planet Earth," he said. "They left it almost four hundred years ago during a terrible war. We believed that the human race destroyed itself in that conflict."

"Is that so?" Geordi nudged Riker discreetly.

Riker nodded, excited. Four hundred years . . . That meant Koban's people must have been refugees from the Eugenics Wars. What an astonishing find!

"As to how we got here . . ." Koban paused as

the sound of running footsteps echoed in one of the tunnels.

"Koban!" a man's voice called. "We've got them!"

A moment later a gnarled man hurried into the room. When his eyes landed on the *Enterprise* crew, his mouth fell open.

"They're friends," Koban said quickly. "You'll hear all about them soon. Now, what's the news?"

Obediently the man turned to face Koban, though he kept sneaking awed glances at Worf as he spoke.

"We've got them," he repeated. "Both of them—Vossted and that damned chicken. We found them in block nine."

Koban's breath escaped in a long sigh. "Alive?"

The man nodded.

Chu Edorlic's dark eyes glittered with hate. "Koban, leave the chicken to me," he begged.

"Chicken?" Geordi repeated. "You mean a coward?"

Chu let out a snorting laugh. "A coward! Yes, that's a good word. Exactly right."

"Take me to them," Koban ordered. He turned to Riker. "If I'm going to ask your help, you should know something about those who have oppressed us for so long."

Riker nodded. "Let's go."

Leaving some brown-clad followers to watch over the injured crewmen, the group began to wind its way through a warren of rough-hewn tunnels.

As they walked, Geordi tugged on Riker's arm to slow him down. "We're going to help these guys?"

he asked when they were some way behind Koban and his men. "We're going to intervene in their dispute with these overseer guys?"

"That remains to be seen," Riker admitted.

"Uh-huh." Geordi rubbed his close-cropped hair. "So, Commander," he said after a second, "how does the Prime Directive fit into this mess?"

Riker shrugged. "We've been asked. They're human. At least we can investigate. And I hope we can mediate. I'd like to be able to help these people."

"I know what you mean," Geordi agreed. He grinned wryly. "I don't especially care for the notion of slavery myself. It's hard to come up with a cause that seems more just than these people's."

"Right." Riker shrugged. "Well, all we can do is hope for the best."

They emerged into another rock-walled room, slightly smaller than the one they'd beamed into. At one end a seething mob crowded around something that Riker couldn't see. Suddenly there was a short, sharp, effervescing noise. Then a shout: "No!"

All at once the air rang with panicked cries and choking noises. Several men near the front of the crowd began clutching their throats, gagging.

Riker froze in his tracks as a ghastly stench hit him. Then he reeled, seized by sudden faintness. "My God, what is that smell?" he gasped.

Koban bared his teeth as he brushed past. "That wretched *Drraagh!*" he growled. He put a hand up to cover his nose and mouth. Riker saw the glint of glass or metal on his finger—a ring, perhaps.

Pushing men out of his way, Koban made straight for the center of the disturbance. Riker followed, holding a fold of his parka over his mouth and nose to block the smell. Even so, acrid fumes made his eyes sting. Everything became blurry. Or was his brain out of focus? He felt as if he were struggling to wake up, and his limbs began refusing to obey him. The sensation was disorienting and rather frightening.

But then he reached the front of the mob—and promptly forgot his discomfort as he stared at the two personages who were the object of the crowd's raging fury.

One lay on the pitted cement floor, unconscious. He was a small, thin man with a leonine head of gray hair and deeply hollowed cheeks. And the other . . .

The other was a chicken. Literally. A birdlike creature, about the size of a ten-year-old child, with soft down in hues of yellow and green. It had flipperlike wings that ended in slender clawed hands.

As Riker stared, it turned toward him. Its gaze was unmistakably intelligent.

A sentient alien, Riker thought, and unless there's some expedition I don't know about, the Federation's never even heard of this one. It's definitely not a member race.

The tight worry that had attacked Riker's gut right before he beamed down suddenly returned. He had a feeling his job had just become a lot more complicated.

Chapter Three

BEVERLY CRUSHER pushed a syringe against her patient's arm and pressed the plunger. In went the mexolodin.

A moment later the child turned huge eyes on Crusher, eyes that held the memory of fear. "Am I all better?" she said, and tried a tentative smile.

"Not quite *all* better." Crusher tapped the girl's arm, which was encased in a molded cast. "This'll have to stay on for one week."

In fact, the bones were already knit back together. True, they needed time to heal completely, but the cast was there mostly as a reminder to the child to be careful.

"W-will Jeremy get better?" the girl asked. "You and Dr. Selar were with him for so long."

Crusher brushed back a lock of hair from the child's wide eyes. "Jeremy was hurt worse, so it will take him longer to get better. But he will. Don't you worry." She glanced at Selar for confirmation.

The Vulcan nodded gravely. "Indeed, Doctor."

Crusher felt tension drain from her neck and shoulders. She went into her office and got a cup of hot tea from the replicator. What an afternoon it had been!

The chaos had set in two hours ago when a frantic call for help came from one of the holodecks. Three ten-year-olds on a school assignment had decided to test the limits of the holodeck programming. Young Jeremy discovered a reference to parameters forbidding death or serious injury. Unfortunately the parameters applied to combat simulations. When Jeremy pulled his friends off a cliff, he paid for his miscalculation with a shattered femur. It had taken an emergency team composed of Crusher, Selar, and four med-techs to repair the damage. For a while it had been touch and go with Jeremy as his femoral artery spouted bright blood everywhere. At least his classmates had suffered less serious injuries. Save us from young would-be geniuses, Crusher thought. Children are so reckless.

Well, at least these three had survived their recklessness. Not everyone was so fortunate.

Against her will her mind turned to Yeoman Kinsolving, the eager young woman who had died on Amon-4. Kinsolving had been someone's child, too. She was only twenty-two, just a bit older than Crusher's son, Wesley. And once again Crusher was unable to silence the little voice that said, Next time it could be Wesley.

"Stop it, Beverly," she muttered aloud.

Since Wesley Crusher had begun his training at Starfleet Academy, his mother had missed him intensely. Even so, she'd been unprepared for the wave of frantic helplessness that assailed her when Kinsolving met with her tragic accident. It *could* so easily have been Wesley; that was the problem.

There was an infinity of accidents in a vast universe, all waiting to happen. And not every commander was as competent, as careful of his charge, as Will Riker. Under another officer, the entire away team could have perished.

In choosing Starfleet, Wesley had chosen a dangerous life. Beverly Crusher knew that from painful experience. Her husband had died on a Starfleet mission. She'd had nearly twenty years to adjust to that loss, and she had thought the time had been enough. But with Kinsolving's death, all the old fears had come flooding back, and all the old pain had reawakened. *Next time it could be Wesley.*

Crusher had taken her distress to Deanna Troi the night before, in Ten-Forward. When she told Deanna of her fears, the counselor said only "I understand how you feel, but you're only making it harder on yourself. You cannot watch over your son forever, Beverly. You have to let go sometime." Then Will Riker had joined them, and the conversation turned to other topics.

Let go, Crusher thought now. What kind of mother can let go of her child, stop caring, just like that?

Of course Crusher knew that the counselor hadn't meant it that way. And she still didn't know what to do.

On the bridge Jean-Luc Picard sat back in his command chair, waiting with leashed impatience for the report of the away team. What would Riker find down there?

Short-range scans had found traces of a settlement along with heavy energy discharges. If there was indeed a retrogressed Earth colony, it had retained some technology. How much? What sort of culture had arisen? It was a tantalizing mystery, but the view from orbit was still clouded with unknowns. Riker and his people on the ground would have to sharpen the picture.

Picard turned from the image of the scarred planetary face on the screen to the officer manning the security console. "Any communication from the surface?"

"None, sir." The officer shook his head, glaring at the console as if he could force some additional information from it. His fingers flashed across the board. "Wait. There's some sort of broadcast, but it's not coming in on our communicator frequency."

"Perhaps the ground station that originally contacted us has been repaired," Data suggested.

"This is on a different frequency than the ground station signal," the man objected. "Doesn't even seem to be aimed at us. It's some sort of pulsed beam, in machine language." Suddenly his voice tightened. "Captain! There's energy activity on the outer moon. Energy readings rising. Sir! There's a silo opening on the surface of the moon. And I detect some sort of projectile inside."

"Red alert," Picard said crisply. "Shields up, phasers on full—"

His voice was drowned out by the wild hooting of alarms. Before him the viewscreen turned a brilliant white, then went blank.

"Scanners dead," the security man reported tautly. "We can't even see what hit us."

"Are the phasers working?" Picard rapped.

"Yes, sir, and they're trained on that silo."

"Fire on it. We don't know what else may come at us."

"Phasers fired, sir!" the security man reported.

Picard, however, had moved on to the next step of the program. "Engineering!" he demanded. "Damage reports!"

The voice that answered him was Dr. Crusher's. "Sickbay," she said in weary tones. "What's going on?"

Picard's lips tightened. "I'll explain later, Doctor. Computer! I want to be connected with Engineering. Now!"

After two more communications slipups—one with hydroponics, another with a very confused weapons officer in the armory—Picard finally got in touch with the engineering section. Chief O'Brien answered the call. He sounded harried, and there was considerable background noise.

"I'm sorry, Captain," he said apologetically. "Just arrived here myself with a repair party. Whatever knocked out our scanners also made a dog's dinner of our internal communications. And it hasn't helped reports of damage."

"Can you outline the situation?" Picard asked.

"The shields failed for an instant, but they're back up. The outer hull appears to be intact, with no collision or blast effects evident so far as we know."

"So far as we know?" the officer on the security console repeated. "That doesn't sound encouraging, Chief."

The noise level rose behind O'Brien. "Try to operate it manually!" someone cried.

O'Brien sighed. "The computer misroutes most of our sensor data, so we have to inspect the hull physically. And the automatics are sealing off decks that are absolutely undamaged, reporting that hull integrity has been broken." He paused. "Besides these problems, all external scanners are out of service. Communications, both long-range and with the planet's surface, are impossible. And all our transporters are knocked out."

The away team is trapped, Picard thought. *We can't talk to them, can't beam them up, can't even see what's happening to them.* He frowned. *Is that why our systems were blacked out? What's happening down on that planet?*

"I'd be very careful about using any computer equipment up on the bridge, sir," O'Brien warned. "Systems close to the hull are crashing all over the place."

"Awr."

Picard glanced toward the forward helm consoles. Data had turned in his seat, his mouth hanging slack.

"Mr. Data!" Picard came half out of his chair, alarmed.

Data's mouth remained open as he fell out of his seat and crashed to the floor. The ensign at the conn abandoned the useless board to kneel by the android. Picard joined her.

"Data! What is it?"

The fall seemed to have jarred the android back into operation. "The interference—awr, hawr." Data lapsed into silence, his mouth half open, staring at the captain with unblinking eyes. He looked drunk. For Picard, the scene was oddly unsettling. It made Data seem like nothing more than a glassy-eyed robot.

After easing Data back into his seat, the captain took a deep breath, then called Engineering again. "Chief O'Brien, our priority is restoring scanners. We can't risk moving blind." Picard cleared his throat, darting another look at Data. "We'll also require an engineer on the bridge—someone who's familiar with positronic computer circuits."

Picard willed his face to remain impassive as he returned to the command chair and assessed the situation: We're orbiting blind after an apparent attack. We can't see if another attack is being planned or what our phasers did to that emplacement on the moon. Damn it, we don't know if the phasers even worked.

The minutes passed, and the captain forced back the frustration seething within him as he waited for reports on the crew's efforts. With so many circuits out, he might as well have been working in a mechanical womb.

His lips tightened. The people reporting to him were competent officers, but in an emergency like this, he'd rather have depended on Worf and La Forge, both of whom were unavailable, trapped on the surface facing who knew what?

"Captain!" O'Brien's voice cut through the background murmur.

"You've restored scanners?" Picard managed to keep the eagerness out of his voice.

"Not yet, but we know what happened to them."

"Don't keep me in the dark, Chief. We're in enough of that as it stands."

"Our shields and all the exterior scan equipment were overwhelmed by a wave of ionization. The scanners burned out, and the other equipment closer to the hull suffered from ionization interference."

Picard glanced over at Data, slumped in his console chair. An engineering tech had peeled artificial flesh and hair back and was delicately manipulating an electrical probe in the positronic brain. Again, Picard wished that Geordi were still aboard to take on that most sensitive of repairs. If the away team was in danger, the ship would be all the more dependent on the android officer. "Have you replaced the damaged scanner units?" Picard asked O'Brien.

"Yes, sir, but until the ionization effect dissipates, they're unusable." The viewscreen came to life, but the image looked like nothing so much as overilluminated fog.

"There is no way we can navigate through *that*," Picard said grimly, "much less see what's coming at us."

"Ah, yes, sir." O'Brien sounded distracted. "Patch Three to the bridge."

A fuzzy view of the planet's surface suddenly appeared. "Captain, this is the view from Ten-Forward," O'Brien said. "We've managed to arrange visual recording, but as you can see, the resolution isn't very high."

"Sir," the security officer began, but Picard anticipated him.

"Give us a view of the outer moon's surface."

The picture shifted jerkily. "It has to be moved manually," O'Brien explained.

The moon seemed to sweep crazily across the screen, then steadied in the center. Even in the fuzzy picture, they could make out traces of fresh destruction on the face of the small satellite.

The security man's fingers danced over the console. "Phasers did the job, sir. Those are the coordinates where the missile silo was located."

"*If* it was a missile silo." Picard pursed his lips in thought. "We assumed the projectile was hostile."

"Sir?" the officer said. "It's left us blind. We're still close to being a sitting duck."

Picard rose from his seat. "It penetrated our shields and neutralized our scanners, and yet no warhead exploded. Why?"

"Because the object launched was not intended

as a weapon," Data's tenor voice entered the discussion.

Picard was glad to see the android sitting up straight at his station, in command of himself again.

"I suggest, sir," Data said, "that we experienced a near-brush with a tachyonic missile. The damage we experienced came from the drive, not from any sort of warhead."

"Tachyonic missile?" the security officer scoffed. "A projectile with a tachyon drive? No Federation scientist has ever succeeded in making a tachyonic *anything.*"

"I do not believe this is the work of any Federation scientist," Data pointed out mildly. "Moreover, laboratory experiments in creating tachyons cite the ionization effect we have experienced, though not on such a large scale."

The security man's tight face gained color. "Do you expect us to believe a colony of non-Federation refugees could develop such a technology?"

"Oh, no," Data explained. "I do not believe they built the missile. But they may have found it."

Picard felt his own face growing tight. "You're suggesting that the missile was an alien artifact?"

Data advanced his hypothesis almost diffidently. "We have already noted that planets in this sector have shown evidence of great destruction, possibly inflicted by beings using extremely high technology," he said. "True, we have found no traces of an alien civilization so far, but this planet has suffered less destruction than the others. And I might point out that what little we have seen of the human colonists' technology does not equal that lunar silo—or the missile."

"Humans who've stumbled onto highly advanced technology." Picard considered the possibility. "A very dangerous combination, it seems. Mr. Data, can we do anything to protect ourselves if another missile is launched?"

The android was already at work on his board. "Certain changes in the harmonics of the shield patterns should protect us more fully from the ionization effects, though the haze would still interfere with scanners, communicators, and transporter beams. That, however, might be a moot point."

"Why?" the captain wanted to know.

Glancing at his screen, Data entered more variables. "I do not believe the ship would have survived a direct hit from the missile. But it was not targeted on us. Apparently it was aimed out of the system—perhaps as a message pod."

The android faced Picard. "Consider, sir, the damage came not from any attack but merely from the tachyon drive. We happened to be close to the outer moon and to the programmed trajectory of the missile."

"And even a near-miss effectively crippled us!" The security officer looked sick.

"An attack by a weapon imperfectly understood and controlled?" Picard wondered. "An attack aborted by an uprising?" There were still too many questions that couldn't be answered from orbit. The *Enterprise* was flying blind in more ways than one. And the only crew members who might shed some light on the situation were out of reach on the planet's surface.

The star field in the window of the meeting room was clear and unwinking, an infuriating contrast to the viewscreen, which was still clouded with ionic haze.

Captain Picard scowled at the screen. "We've waited nearly an hour," he said, "and our scanners still seem to be operating through a thick fog." He glanced around the conference table. Troi, Data, and Beverly Crusher were at their usual places. But there were also less familiar faces—O'Brien representing Engineering, and the ranking security officer taking Worf's place.

And, of course, there was no Will Riker.

Chief O'Brien began his report. "Repair crews have restored all damaged internal circuitry."

"Excellent, Mr. O'Brien." Picard understood that O'Brien's matter-of-fact tone covered frantic labor by the engineering and science sections. However, some big questions still remained. "Can you estimate how soon we could regain contact with the away team?"

O'Brien had to shake his head. "The tachyonic ionization outside the ship has been another matter. We've been trying to boost the gain from our transmitters, but we still haven't been able to pierce the interference. The same situation holds with the transporters."

"Nor have our scans been able to lock on to the team members' communicators," the representative from security admitted. "We could send a security team by shuttlecraft to their last location to search—"

"With respect, Captain," O'Brien interjected, "a shuttle would be navigating under the same unfavorable conditions as the ship. Perhaps worse, since shuttle systems can't be shielded as well as our circuitry."

Picard frowned. "In other words, not only would they be out of communication, but ionization could make the controls fail."

"Yes, sir." O'Brien nodded.

"We've targeted the two moons, even though we can't scan them for additional missile emplacements," the security representative reported. "We should consider ourselves lucky that the people down there apparently didn't have anything to back up that first launching."

"As I said, I believe the missile was launched as a message pod," Data pointed out.

"Which indicates the existence of other worlds —perhaps other colonies," Picard said. "Quite an achievement for a group of lost terrestrials, even with discovered alien technology." He grimaced. "Another question: what are they doing here? This sector is at the far reaches of the Federation's present technical ability. How could pre-Federation technology have gotten these people here ahead of us?"

No one answered. After a moment Picard turned to Troi. "Counselor, can you add anything to our present knowledge? Who are we dealing with?"

Deanna Troi merely shook her head. "I've

opened myself for any possible impressions." She shuddered. "The best description I can give you is cacophony. Feelings are running very high on the planet. Fear, hatred . . ." She trailed off, her face troubled.

"Sickbay is on standby," Beverly Crusher reported. "Judging from the activity on the surface, we'll be busy as soon as contact is reestablished." She suddenly seemed to fumble for words, glancing over at Troi. "I mean, there'll be a lot of people down there in need of medical attention."

Possibly even the away team. Picard had caught the implication. And Will Riker.

The meeting wound to a conclusion, but Troi stopped at the door. "Captain," she suddenly said, as the others left the room, "may I speak with you?"

"Certainly, Counselor." Picard watched the conference room door hiss shut. "There seems to be little we can do at the moment *except* talk."

"When we can operate on the planet again, we may find another unanticipated variable." Troi raised a hand to her brow. "During the meeting, I felt something . . ." She paused. "Something *else* down on the planet's surface. It's difficult to pinpoint against such an outpouring of emotion. But I don't believe it's a human thought pattern."

Picard frowned, trying to fit a new variable into the equation. "So we may not be dealing merely with a lost human colony. This is a possible alien contact as well."

Troi's dark eyes showed uncertainty. "It was just the merest touch. That's why I didn't mention it at the meeting. As soon it's feasible, though, I'd like to beam down."

Picard frowned. "I'm not sure I like the idea of sending another senior crew member down there," he began.

"Putting all your eggs in one basket?" Troi asked, her eyebrows rising.

"As events proved, Worf and La Forge might have been more useful if they'd stayed aboard the ship."

"Other officers handled their functions quite well, I thought," Troi said.

"There's a difference between fulfilling a function and bringing imagination to the job. Perhaps I shouldn't have let Commander Riker take so many of our"—Picard glanced at Troi—"grade A eggs."

"Because you're afraid he might crack them?" Troi's face seemed to cloud. "He's commanded too many away teams for you to doubt him."

"And I don't," Picard acknowledged. "It's not a question of his ability."

He was silent for a moment. Then he looked uneasily at Troi. "Every alien contact has its risks. Are you sure there's a live alien down there?"

"Until I see the situation up close, I can only speculate," Troi told him.

Picard sank into a chair. "Then we'll both have to wait until Commander Riker contacts us."

Chapter Four

"WELL, SIR," Geordi La Forge said in a choked voice to Riker, "I'd say we're looking at a problem."

"Thank you, Mr. La Forge," Riker replied glumly. Then he doubled over, racked by a paroxysm of coughing.

The birdlike alien curled up into an even tighter ball on the floor and emitted soft, cooing clicks.

Geordi wiped away the tears streaming from his blind eyes and concentrated on bringing order to the jumble of visual distortions assailing his VISOR. What's the matter with this thing? he wondered dimly. Then his knees buckled.

"Hold on," he heard a deep voice say. A hand clamped itself firmly around his biceps and hauled him upright. Geordi gazed at a pulsating two-tone image that a curious mottling marked as the face of Koban. The rebel leader's eyes phased from an interesting orange to urgent red. "Don't let it get to you," Koban urged him. "Resist it!"

As the moments passed, the miasmic odor that gripped the chamber seemed to grow less intense. All around Geordi, men began to sit up, dazed and coughing. Worf slumped against one of the dingy gray walls, his eyes gyrating in a wild dance, the rest of his face oddly lax with stupor. Geordi inhaled and coughed. The lingering vestiges of the scent gave every breath the bite of a knife's edge.

And that wasn't all it did, Geordi guessed as his thoughts began to clear. Some chemical in the scent apparently attacked the sensory input centers of the brain. That was what Koban was telling him to resist. Easy for him to say, he thought.

That chemical also explained the apparent malfunction of his VISOR. The prosthetic device hadn't scrambled data; his brain itself had been at fault. "Wow," he said weakly. An involuntary shiver made goose bumps rise on his flesh. It had never occurred to him that he could be so vulnerable.

Riker straightened, his face red with the effort. He steadied himself with a hand on Geordi's shoulder. "Koban, the smell . . . Where is it coming from?"

Koban gestured at the downy ball of yellow and green feathers on the floor. "It produces the odor as a defense—or a weapon."

"That little thing made such a big stink?" Geordi marveled.

"What is it?" Worf rumbled in a strangely gentle voice. He came up next to the first officer and gazed down at the bird creature, bemused.

Koban shrugged. "The regent of Koorn. Its name is Drraagh." He pronounced the word with a rising inflection that made it sound like the harsh squawk of a bird.

"Their name for themselves is Tseetsk. We call them the chickens." Koban spoke in flat tones, but a shifting pattern in the mottled purple under his facial scars betrayed his emotion. "They're the real slave masters. The overseers are just their tools. The chickens found our ancestors two hundred years ago on a nearby planet where we'd set up a colony. They used the stink to subdue us, then sent us out to terraform new worlds for them. We were expendable slave labor."

"So the overseers aren't the enemy," Riker said.

"Oh, they're bastards, right enough—humans who betray their own kind in exchange for a few luxuries. But the chickens flung us down on this ice ball, expecting us to turn it into a paradise. They're the ones who kill us, one part at a time." He touched his ravaged face. "One man at a time." His jaw worked as if he could physically taste his hate.

"Is this the only—" Riker began.

But his question was drowned out by a cry from dozens of throats. "Kill it!" the crowd of brown-clad rebels roared. "Kill the chicken! *Kill it!*"

"Status report, Captain." Chief O'Brien's voice held equal parts of irritation and triumph. "The tachyonic interference has finally cleared enough so that, if we boost the power, we can restore communications and transporter ability."

"Excellent. Make it so." Picard felt the tense knot of muscles in his back loosen. Hastily he set his empty teacup on the desk in his ready room. "Picard to Riker."

After a moment of silence came a slightly fuzzy reply: "Captain, this is La Forge. Am I glad to hear your voice!"

Instantly the knots were back. "Mr. La Forge, where's Commander Riker?"

"The commander asked me to speak to you. He's a little . . . ah . . . occupied at the moment."

"What's going on down there? Are you all right?"

"Uh, yes, Captain," Geordi said. He was speaking in a subdued, even furtive tone, Picard noted. "We came down into a firefight. Two wounded—one seriously. I suggest you have Chief O'Brien lock on to their communicators and beam them to sickbay."

"Stand by." Picard tapped his communicator again and gave a terse order to Chief O'Brien. Then he switched back to Geordi. "Now, Mr. La Forge, what's the situation?"

"Well, sir, there's a revolution going on down here. It's a slave culture. Right now the gangs, as they call themselves, are fighting it out with the overseers," Geordi reported.

"A human slave culture?" Picard mused out loud.

"There's also an alien presence here," Geordi added. "I guess you know we couldn't reach you on our communicators."

53

"I do," Picard replied grimly. "We were having our own troubles up here. More about that in a moment. Please continue, Mr. La Forge."

As Geordi spoke, the doors to the ready room chimed, then swished open. Troi glided in. Picard waved her to a seat across from his own as Geordi continued.

"It's an avian race, they call themselves the Tseetsk. The gangs are—were—their slaves, used for heavy labor. We happened to arrive just as the gangs rebelled. Now the overseers have been routed, and the gangs are in control." Geordi paused. "Or maybe I should say out of control. Right now Commander Riker is trying to talk them out of murdering one of the Tseetsk. The rebels really hate them, sir."

"Captain, let me go down there," Troi broke in urgently. "I can sense the alien's mind more clearly now. It's terrified!"

"Sir, I second that," Geordi agreed. "I think the counselor could do some good down here."

Picard leaned back. "Perhaps, but I have some questions I'd like your opinion on." Tenting his fingers, he outlined the *Enterprise*'s brush with the tachyonic missile.

"Whew. I didn't think those things were feasible." Geordi sounded awed. "Is the ship all right? I'll bet the systems went haywire under that barrage of ionization."

"They did," Picard agreed dryly. "The situation is stabilized, though we missed your expertise, Lieutenant. My question: do you think the humans down there—the people you've made contact with —might have launched that missile?"

"Not the gangs," Geordi replied promptly. "Maybe the overseers, the guys in the gray uniforms. But they certainly weren't expecting us. The sight of us 'free humans' on their viewscreens apparently touched off the revolt. But even the rebel leader only half believed we really existed until the away team showed up. If the overseers launched that missile, it'll be hard to find out why. Most of them are either dead or missing."

"Can you ensure Counselor Troi's safety if she joins you down there?"

"I think so. The rebels seem to feel we're the guys in the white hats. I don't see any problems."

Picard met Troi's dark gaze, and nodded at her. "Go, then," he said.

"Bundle up. It's cold here," Geordi advised.

Troi laughed. "Easy enough. I'll see you soon."

"Kill the chicken!" the brown-clad rebels roared.

Riker cudgeled his still-foggy brain, seeking an argument that would carry weight with Koban and his people. Looking at it from their point of view, though, he couldn't marshal any compelling reasons *not* to kill the chicken. He'd already tried pointing out that it would be cold-blooded murder, but Koban had merely shrugged. "We could tell you about the thousands of humans the chickens have murdered in colder ways."

The slight gray-haired man next to the bird creature moaned and stirred. Heavily veined eyelids fluttered up to reveal dark, mournful eyes.

Riker noticed that the man wore gray overseer clothes.

"Vossted." Koban bent over the man on the floor. "Your side is losing."

Vossted coughed. "I wasn't aware I had taken sides."

"Bah, kill him, too, for lying." Edorlic's slanted dark eyes glittered with hate. "He's an overseer, isn't he?"

"Peace, Chu." The unmarked side of Koban's face actually softened as he knelt, slipping off his dusty outer tunic to make a pillow for Vossted's head.

Watching him, Riker realized that, for whatever reason, Koban loved that old man, that overseer. It was the only chink in his armor that Riker had seen so far. Then he looked at Chu Edorlic's scowling face and said to himself, If Koban's not careful, that weakness could bring him down.

"Vossted," Koban said, "I know in your heart you're with us. You don't have to be afraid to admit it anymore." He waved an arm at the assembled rebels. "None of *these* men are likely to report you to the chickens." His laugh ignited a responding chuckle from the crowd.

"You mistake me greatly if you believe that's what I fear," Vossted said dryly.

Koban's face tensed. He sat back on his heels. "Times are changing, old man," he said in a low voice. "Neutrality is no longer a viable option. Listen to me, Vossted."

The crowd stirred, restless. "Kill the chicken!"

someone yelled again. Koban's hand went to the wand of his laser.

Vossted struggled up to lean on one elbow. "No!" He put out a hand to Koban, and Riker saw anguish in the older man's eyes.

"Now is no time to parade your love of chickens," Koban whispered coldly.

Words tumbled from Vossted's mouth. "It's a question of placing blame correctly. Why kill Drraagh? Has she, personally, done anything to you? She's always been a good regent; you know conditions on Koorn are better than most places. No, Drraagh's only fault is that she's a product of her world." His lips quirked with bleak humor. "And we're products of this one."

"Overseer talk," Chu growled.

"Overseer tricks!" an infuriated rebel cried. "Don't listen to him. Kill Vossted, too!"

"Kill Vossted!" More voices joined the cry.

Riker knew he had to do something. He pulled his phaser from his belt and fired at the ceiling, creating a rain of dust and debris. An instant hush fell.

Chu Edorlic's weapon was half out of its holster before Koban held out a hand to stop him. The rebel leader folded his arms, aiming his intent eyes at Riker. "You have something to say?" he asked quietly.

Riker's stomach knotted. He was treading on thin ice, and he knew it. But Vossted's plea had given him an idea. Maybe if he appealed to their pride . . .

It was a dangerous gamble, but he had to try it. "Yes, I do." Riker raised his voice so that all the men in the room could hear him. "You want to be like the chickens?" he demanded. "Killing people just because you're stronger? Oh, that's brave, all of you against this one lone chicken. Forget the trial, forget any defense Drraagh might have, forget any notions of justice. But remember that if you do, you'll never be truly free."

Riker glared, waiting for the reaction.

The silence continued another moment, during which Riker spotted Koban staring at him with a strange appraising look on his ruined face.

"Who *are* you?" cried someone in the crowd.

Koban raised his arms. "This is one of the men from the starship."

"Kill him, too!" another voice said.

"Yeah! Kill the starmen!" It was the cry of a mob frustrated in its bloodlust.

Worf bared his teeth angrily.

"Quiet!" Koban said sharply. "These are our friends. They've promised to help us." Again he turned that appraising stare on Riker.

"We have?" Worf muttered in Riker's ear.

The noise subsided a little, but not much.

In spite of the cold, Riker felt droplets of sweat beading his forehead. I've botched this, he thought with a burst of futile anger at himself. Unless I can finesse this situation fast, I'll just have to call for help and hope the *Enterprise* can get us out of here—assuming nothing happened to the ship during that odd communications blackout. Geordi managed to talk to Captain Picard; he should know what the status was by now. Riker craned his neck, looking for the chief engineer.

And saw, with dismay, the column of iridescent blue as it sheeted down from the ceiling and swiftly coalesced into a human form. Troi's form.

"Damn!" Riker swore. "Not now!"

Deanna Troi beamed into utter silence and a din of bewildered thoughts—confusion, terror, awe, and over all a residue of rage and hatred. Then came something else—a growing surge she couldn't quite identify. . . .

She looked out at the sea of stunned faces and took a step forward.

Someone broke the silence. Hesitantly, a voice said: "Is that . . . is it a *woman*?"

And the "something else" she had sensed suddenly gained in strength, and converged. Troi staggered as the full force of the feeling struck her. "Oh!" she cried, gulping air that suddenly felt thick and repulsively musky.

Her head swam. The outpouring was like nothing she'd ever felt before: ugly, raw, scaldingly violent, charged with almost unendurable greed, anticipation—and shame. Then came the images. Countless versions of herself, her face blurry, her nude body absurdly overblown, writhing, coupling, collaborating in innumerable obscene acts.

It was lust, she realized in a fleeting instant of lucidity. She was being bombarded by the frustrated lust of a hundred men at once.

Troi groaned, shrinking into her bulky parka. Her hands fluttered indecisively. Her nervous system was unable to decide whether to try to shield her mind or her body from the hideous assault.

"Counselor? Are you all right?"

The dark blur of a face loomed in front of her. Geordi. She focused on the cool, comforting wash of sympathy and concern that flowed from him. "Help," she croaked, reaching out to clutch his sleeve.

"Hold on," Geordi told her anxiously. "Just hold on, Troi. We're here. Sir, I don't know what's wrong with her."

Others had pushed forward now and were holding back the throng of sharp, greedy faces and reaching hands. There was Worf; she could see his towering bulk through the tears that blurred her vision, and she could feel his belligerence against her attackers as he took up a protective stance in front of her. And there was Will Riker—

Oh, no. Not Will. She couldn't face him right now, feeling so raw. Couldn't endure his compassion, his worry, his love—especially not his love.

Troi hid her face in Geordi's sleeve. Waves of hot and cold coursed through her. She drew a deep breath. "Please get me out of here," she enunciated carefully. "I have to get away from these people."

"Koban, where can we take her?" That was Will's voice, deep and urgent.

"Move back, all of you!" a new voice commanded. "Clear out. I'll take care of everything."

"We want the woman!" came a cry.

"She's with our new friends," the commanding voice said sternly. "She's a friend, too."

"Hey, that's all right, Koban. We just want to be friendly!" someone shouted. The crowd burst into raucous laughter.

Troi winced as the press of lust assaulted her mind with renewed vigor. The images began to seep in again, in sharper focus this time. More urgent, more real, somehow. Her flesh crawled from the onslaught of sweaty phantom hands. . . .

"Is this what we've fought for?" The fury in Koban's voice cut through the noise like a whipcrack.

"Can the starman be right about you after one look? Are you animals?" Koban never raised his voice, but the crowd caught his cold disdain. Their reaction was like that of a scolded dog. "I thought I was leading men."

Troi heard the sound of shifting feet, while in her mind the heavy fog of hunger and frustration began to dissipate. She began to perceive the men as individuals, even the one who called out defiantly, "Men need women."

"Wrong! Only an animal or a slave is driven by need. We're free men—that's what we fought for today. Now we control our own lives. We don't *need* anything but freedom."

As the men took that in, Troi felt the pounding hunger abate just a bit and, with it, the counterpoint of her own racing heart.

Koban seemed to know he'd won them over. "You can't distract yourselves with this," he declared. "Our mop-up isn't done. At least fifteen overseers are still unaccounted for. I want the squads to regroup and finish the sweep of the outer sectors. Squad leaders, report to me in the armory when you're done."

Muttering, the men began to move toward the doorways. "What about Vossted and the chicken?" someone asked.

"I'll handle them, Chu. Get going."

As the tramp of booted feet faded away, Troi at last dared to lift her head and release her death grip on Geordi's sleeve.

"Deanna, are you all right?" Riker was at her side in a flash, a solicitous hand on her elbow.

A hot, shameful blush made her cheeks burn, but she forced herself to look into his concerned eyes. "I'm fine," she said shakily. "It was just . . ."

A tall, muscular man with back-swept blond hair and a horribly scarred countenance stepped forward. She saw him wince at her reaction to his appearance, but still he offered her a deep and courtly bow. "I'm Iarni Koban. Accept my apologies on behalf of my men."

As he spoke, Troi apprehensively opened her senses. His mind was positively aboil with strong emotions, pain at her response to his ruined face uppermost, anger, and a formidable resolve deeper down. To her relief, though, there was barely a trace of sexual desire.

Reassured, she returned the bow. "Deanna Troi. I'm ship's counselor for the *Enterprise*. Thank you for your intervention; I'm deep in your debt."

"What the hell happened?" Riker growled.

Koban said flatly, "Something out of the ordinary on this planet. You have to understand that none of us have seen a woman, let alone touched one, in more than five years."

"Whew!" Geordi let out a low whistle. "You mean . . . ?"

"That's right." Koban nodded. "There are no women on Koorn. The slagging chickens keep the gangs on all the planets segregated. When the men saw this lovely lady"—again he bowed to Troi— "well, their reaction was understandable. Though, of course, not acceptable," he added hastily.

"It's part of the chickens' plan." Under Koban's neutral tone, Troi felt curdled rage as he went on. "The gangs are sent for seven-year stints on the work planets. Then we're shipped to the breeding planet for six months to rest up and breed a new generation of slaves. Of course, during the seven years we're segregated, the men build up a lot of aggression." His smile was a twitch of the lips, bare of mirth. "When Gang Fourteen landed, there were a thousand of us. Now we're down to seven hundred twelve. On top of all the accidents that happen out in the field, we simply kill each other off. It's the perfect genocide plan." He added bitterly. "No work for the chickens, and no risk to their own stinking hides."

"That isn't true."

Troi spun around, startled. She hadn't noticed the two figures in the shadows at the other end of the room. Her empathic sense, which would have picked up their presence under normal circumstances, was still numbed from the emotional onslaught she'd just endured.

She extended her senses. Immediately she felt the

presence of the alien mind. Its terror was much abated now. It seemed to possess a cool intelligence, but she could gather little else from it.

Curious, she walked a few paces forward and peered at it. Orange eyes stared solemnly back at her from twin rings of bright blue down. The creature's face was gently rounded, coming to a short, snubbed point at the beak. Its head and body were yellow with black markings, shading into a green ruff around the neck. Except for its coloring and long, muscular legs—and, of course, the hands that sprouted rather absurdly from its flipperlike arms—it reminded Troi very much of a penguin.

"Doesn't look like a member of a conquering race, does it?" Koban's voice dripped irony. "Counselor Troi, this is Drraagh, regent for the Tseetsk race on the planet Koorn."

"How do you do?" Troi said softly. The pleasantry sounded inane to her own ears, but what was one supposed to say in this rather unusual situation?

Drraagh made no reply, nor was there any indication that the creature had understood Troi's words. Orange eyes flicked from Troi to the other humans, paused fractionally on Worf, then returned to scanning the group.

"This," Koban went on, waving at the man who sat propped against the wall next to the birdlike creature, "is Josip Vossted: overseer, sometime teacher, and apologist for the Tseetsk."

Vossted climbed to his feet. He was slight, shorter than Troi, with big sad eyes and a lined face. He smiled crookedly around a swelling purple bruise on his jaw.

"Pleased to meet you all, star people," he said in a soft voice. "I've often wondered if free humans might still exist. And I must immediately explain that my young friend Koban is mistaken. I am not an apologist for the Tseetsk. I can't deny that they've greatly wronged my people. I do maintain, however, that they are not inherently evil, nor are they trying to kill us off." He sighed. "I'm afraid it's a good deal more complex than that."

"It would seem foolish for a conquering people to destroy its labor pool," Worf commented.

"Exactly!" Vossted leveled a finger at Worf. "I can see that you're a practical man. So are the Tseetsk. Why kill slaves who have proved so useful? The single-sex rule is not intended to make us kill each other. That's a by-product I'm sure the Tseetsk never intended."

"But they don't seem to object when it happens." Koban whipped around to confront Vossted, his blue eyes the only live thing in his scarred profile.

"They may not see a connection. The Tseetsk have a rather unflattering notion of the human capacity for violence." Vossted's eyes gleamed with wry amusement. "And I doubt it would ever occur to them that sex and violence could be linked. Their sexual drive works quite differently from ours. No, the single-sex rule is intended merely as a control. The Tseetsk want to ensure that any rebellion on one of the work planets will last no longer than one generation, since there will be no children to carry it on."

Riker stroked his beard, a troubled look on his face. He said to Vossted, "This control plan of the

Tseetsk doesn't sound all that different from genocide to me. Allowing an entire planet's population
to die just because they rebelled against slavery? I'd
like to know how you can condone such policies."

"I don't condone them." Vossted shook his head
vigorously. "All I'm saying is that the Tseetsk are
not monsters. They are a people driven to extreme
measures by extreme need."

"Just what kind of need would drive them to
become slave masters?" Geordi asked.

"Overpopulation. Their home world is strained
to the limit of its resources. They desperately need
more room, but certain . . . factors make it next to
impossible for them to do the full-scale exploratory
work and the heavy labor necessary to make a
planet like this one habitable.

"Their needs and ours may be in conflict, but the
Tseetsk are not evil. There must be a way for us to
reach an understanding with them."

"Impossible," Koban snapped. "The chickens
have made it clear that they have no wish to coexist
peacefully with us. Vossted, you're deluding
yourself."

Vossted cast a quick glance at Drraagh. "I know a
Tseetsk whose dearest wish is to bring our races
into harmony. She and I have discussed how it
might be done."

"Aaah." Koban threw up his hands in disgust.
"Drraagh feeds you lies to keep your brain in her
service. How can you be so blind?"

Suddenly Drraagh let out a low twitter. Startled,
Troi looked at her. Something in the alien's eyes
made her focus on Drraagh's thoughts.

After a moment she turned to Riker. "I can't get much from Drraagh—her responses are unfamiliar to me—but I can tell you this: she hasn't been lying to Vossted. She's extremely indignant at the suggestion."

"She would be," Vossted interjected. "I'm an honorary brood brother to Drraagh. The Tseetsk have strong taboos about loyalty and honesty, especially within families." He stroked the bridge of his nose, gazing thoughtfully at Troi. "Now, just how could you tell she was upset?"

Troi cast a glance at Riker. He gave her a slight nod. Might as well let them know the whole story, he thought.

Troi turned back to Vossted. "I'm an empath," she explained. "I have limited telepathic powers, which come through my mother's genes. I'm half Betazoid."

Koban's face was blank. "Betazoid?"

"A humanoid race from the planet Betazed." Troi half extended her hand as she saw Koban's jaw drop. "My father was human," she added.

"Your father . . ." He faltered, staring at her. "You mean you're not human?" he said at last.

"Not entirely."

Riker stepped forward and gestured at Worf. "Neither is Lieutenant Worf, actually. Worf's facial structure is not a deformity; it's the way his race, the Klingons, developed. You see, Koban, we've established relations with many nonhuman cultures, to our mutual benefit."

"I . . . see."

Did he really? Riker watched Koban with

narrowed eyes, but except for some tension in the set of his shoulders, the rebel leader's mien was neutral. Riker questioned Troi with his eyes. She shrugged.

Riker drew a deep breath. Good, he said to himself. Maybe we're finally making some progress.

Chapter Five

IARNI KOBAN, former slave turned rebel leader, stared at the bearded face of a man from the stars. It had been hard enough to believe that Riker existed. But the things he had just revealed about his people's origins went beyond unbelievable, straight to frightening. Not that Koban showed any fear. But then, for most of the past five years, half of his face had been a mask. And now, it seemed, he'd have to try to mask his thoughts as well, at least around that unnerving woman, Troi.

He watched as Riker conferred in a low voice with the black man wearing the metal band over his eyes—the one called Geordi. There was another alien element: what kind of culture went to such lengths to help the . . . He tried to find another word for "defective," but that was the only one in his vocabulary. Koban had heard it often enough as he struggled to recover from the accident that had destroyed his face. No one had thought he'd survive.

His thoughts were interrupted when Riker spoke again. "Our ship detected a missile fired from Koorn's outer moon into deep space. Can you tell us anything about it?"

Koban shook his head, turning to Vossted. "It's something the overseers must have launched."

The older man's pale features became even more drawn. "The beacon. They must have launched the completion beacon. The Tseetsk know it's not possible for the work to be done yet. They'll come to investigate—and they'll be prepared to punish."

Koban, Riker, and Geordi exchanged glances. "When will the Tseetsk arrive?" Riker asked.

"We have never been told where their homeworld is," Koban said, "though Vossted's been there."

Vossted shook his head. "I know how long it took to reach Tseetsk-Home from our planet, Foothold. And I know the length of our voyage from Foothold here to Koorn. It would certainly be no more than seven days."

Koban spoke up grimly. "That means we have a week at most to prepare Koorn for defense. A week is no time at all. There's only one thing to do: your people must help us take the war to the chickens."

Riker stared at him. "What?"

"Make no mistake, Riker, this is a war—a

Human-Tseetsk war." Koban pinned Riker with his eyes and spoke quickly. "The Tseetsk will view all humans as enemies. They won't make any distinctions between rebellious slaves and free humans. If anything, your spaceship and your people will impress them as a much greater threat than my people. As soon as the Tseetsk ships arrive, they'll try to blow you out of the sky. Believe me, I know them."

Riker shook his head.

Koban gripped Riker's arm hard, staring into his eyes, willing him to forget the ruined face in front of him, hammering with his words. "Our only hope is to strike first, before the Tseetsk know about your ship. We can find the Tseetsk homeworld. All I ask is transport for my men and myself. We'll take care of the rest."

Riker finally found words. "Koban, the *Enterprise* is not a military vessel. We're explorers and ambassadors for the Federation. Our mission is to learn, to greet others in peace. We have a week to learn everything we can about the Tseetsk, how their society works—"

"It works on cowardice and death!" Koban burst out. "Their cowardice, and *our* death!" He turned the scarred side of his face to Riker. Emotion spread more purple mottling under the dead tissue. *"Here* is my understanding of the chickens. Let's call it an ugly truth."

Riker winced. "That doesn't have to be," he insisted. "The Klingons were once deadly enemies of the Federation, but we've overcome that hostility. Now we're allies. As you've seen, Worf serves with me."

"So you think you can befriend the chickens? You're dreaming, Riker. And when you wake up, you'll be digging thermal taps alongside me. Because the Tseetsk have only one conception of humans—as slaves."

They stared in silence for a moment; then Koban stepped back, composing his features. Bleakly he realized it was a futile argument. Riker with his machines and spacecraft had had it too easy. He believed that reason would always prevail, that no dark force could ever really threaten. How could he be shown that the Tseetsk didn't belong to that ordered universe?

Koban shook his head. "If you want to study the chickens, we'll give you all the help we can. But I'm afraid my people and I understand them better than you can hope to. You'll have one week. We've had two centuries."

He started off, then turned. "I'll make arrangements for your people to have access to the computers and whatever other Tseetsk technology we have." He gave Riker a half smile. "It is true that one should know one's enemies. I'll also have Drraagh made available to you."

Chu Edorlic appeared, his high-cheekboned face expressionless as he surveyed the off-worlders. He spoke softly to Koban, who nodded. "Our control center has been repaired, and we're in communication with your ship," Koban told Riker. "Excuse me. There's a lot to be done."

He beckoned to some brown-clad guards, who

closed in around Vossted and Drraagh and followed their leaders.

Geordi gazed after them. "I think we've been dismissed."

"Koban's a busy man, who's already spent a lot of time with us," Riker said. He tapped his communicator. "Riker to *Enterprise*. Four to beam up."

They materialized in the transporter room to find fevered activity. Medical personnel were packing up what looked like half of Sickbay's equipment, while a six-person team, led by Beverly Crusher and Selar, slipped into parkas.

"What's going on, Dr. Crusher?" Riker asked as he stepped off the transporter stage.

"Emergency medical aid for the people down there," Crusher responded. "We're ready to go down as soon as you've reported."

Worf frowned. "Not without at least twenty security officers," he said.

"And after a *long* talk with the captain." Riker hit his communicator. "Riker to Picard. Sir, I think we should discuss the medical mission." He glanced at Troi. "With the counselor as well."

"Very well, Number One. In my ready room."

The meeting was predictably stormy. Crusher was interested as she listened to the away team's report, but her interest turned to incredulity and then fury when she discovered that Riker wanted the mission canceled. "There are people down there who need medical attention!" she said, the color rising in her cheeks.

"There are more than seven hundred men down

there who haven't seen a woman in five years," Riker pointed out. "Their response to Counselor Troi . . ."

Deanna shivered at the memory. "I'm sorry, Beverly, but the situation down there is highly explosive."

"I'm sure Worf has enough security people to see to our safety," Crusher argued. "I understand the only doctor on the planet is dead. What are they doing for the wounded?"

"From my glimpse of the fighting, I got the impression that there were lots of dead but not many wounded." Riker sank tiredly into a seat. "I think the medical mission should be part of a much larger effort to study the Tseetsk and give aid to the humans on Koorn. Until we have a secure base, however, I would not advocate sending female crew into those tunnels."

"I would have to second that opinion," Troi said.

Crusher stared as if a trusted ally had turned on her.

"I agree, too, Captain." Worf scowled as he considered the situation. "Protecting the study team and the medical personnel would overextend our security resources."

"Very well," Picard said. "Until we have a comprehensive plan—which will be tomorrow morning, I estimate—we will send no female crew members down to the planet. Dr. Crusher, you wish to say something?"

"If I can't send the team, can I at least beam down some supplies and a couple of—ah, appropriate med-techs to survey the situation?"

Picard nodded. "I think that could be arranged. Now, regarding this study of the Tseetsk . . ."

"Koban, the rebel leader, has given his approval. We can make arrangements through the colony's control center." Riker rubbed his eyes. "I thought perhaps Data—"

"Lieutenant Data could make a preliminary survey tonight," Picard said. "But I want you in charge of this study, Commander Riker. I needn't tell you it might be of paramount importance."

Riker nodded, Koban's words echoing in his mind: *Know your enemy.*

Picard ended the meeting, but as the others left, he beckoned Riker back. "I want to hear more about the situation down there, Will. You reported that the rebel leader asked for military aid against the Tseetsk."

Riker nodded. "Koban knows the rebels are in a spot, trapped on the planet. He can't hold his ground, and he can't retreat. I'm not surprised that he'd attempt to shift to the offensive."

"You seem to sympathize with his situation," Picard sat very still, eyes on his subordinate.

Riker hesitated. "It's just that, without knowing it, we precipitated the revolt," he said at last. "Things were pretty awful down there. The appearance of a shipload of 'free humans,' as they call us, ignited the fighting in their control center that spread through the installation."

"We couldn't have known that," Picard pointed out.

"No, but that's what happened. I feel— responsible."

Picard leaned back in his seat. "What's your assessment of Koban?"

"The rebels couldn't ask for a better leader. He commands from the front line, and his men will do almost anything for him." Riker remembered how Koban had dispelled the ugly scene around Troi, how he'd argued for the *Enterprise*'s support. "The man has incredible charisma. I've seen enough politicians and planetary leaders, but I've rarely encountered anyone to match him. It's like meeting a Washington, a Lenin, a Yaffour."

"That's an impressive group to put him in," Picard said, giving Riker a level look. "Seminal leaders in great movements. But Lenin's revolution led to millions of deaths, and Yaffour's Planetary Union collapsed in chaos after his death." His voice grew softer. "Personalities who ride the forces of history are best admired in history books, Will."

Riker's shoulders stiffened.

"Perhaps you'd like to get some rest. There are challenges enough to face tomorrow."

"Yes, sir." Wearily Riker pulled himself upright and headed out of the ready room. He marched across the bridge to the empty turbolift and stepped inside. Only when the door had closed on the compartment did he sag against the wall.

It's bad enough that I kept questioning my own judgment while I was down there, he thought. Now I've got the captain doing it. He thinks I'm too impressed with Koban. Riker raised a hand to massage his forehead. I've been around long enough not to have stars in my eyes, but at gut level I feel that Koban's cause is right.

He took a deep breath. What if he's right about the Tseetsk, too?

Lorens Ben, the youngest human on Koorn, peered carefully around the rocky entrance of the equipment room that the rebels now used as an armory. Even in slave societies boys were expected to go poking and peering into areas where they didn't belong. And besides, Lorens's father had been an overseer. A head overseer, in fact. That had made Lorens an invaluable spy for the rebel movement.

Now the rebellion was an accomplished fact, and his father lay dead on the junk pile of history, but Lorens still used the skills he'd developed—to catch a glimpse of his hero.

Iarni Koban was the reason Lorens had become a rebel. Koban was everything the boy's father was not. Coming to Koorn had been a stunning revelation for the boy. After being pulled from the crèche school on Foothold, he'd been included with Gang Fourteen for the Koorn terraforming project, thanks to his father's influence. Shakra Ben had believed that work in the field was a better education than any theory learned in school.

Instead, Lorens had learned to hate his father. Gang Fourteen, which in his youthful imagination had been a colorful outfit of devil-may-care adventurer-builders, had been revealed as a haggard collection of driven slaves. And his father, whom he'd always pictured as a leader of men, was a slave just as driven as the others. He'd seen Shakra Ben turn into a cringing toady at the first word from the regent Drraagh. Then Shakra had tried to regain some self-respect by beating men who couldn't fight back.

Shakra Ben would talk to his son about the future, but Lorens saw only the same existence ahead of him: becoming a clone of a man he despised.

He'd been out where he shouldn't have been when he first saw Koban. An overseer was working his gang too close to one of the huge pit-diggers when the heavy machine ran across an ice cavern. The ground beneath its treads cracked, sending the heavy machine slewing around. An enormous hole opened, sucking in the machine and many of the men working nearby. The overseer ran to safety. It was Koban who organized the rescue.

Lorens had found a hero.

Slowly but surely he'd become one of Koban's followers despite the gang members' distrust of his traitorous father. And the boy had proved his usefulness by scouting out places no slave could hope to penetrate. Thanks to him, no secret tunnels had been available for fleeing overseers.

Koban had changed the world, because he had a view of the future.

Now Lorens watched his leader disassemble a laser drill, his hands large and strong, but surprisingly deft. Even while he was doing that, Lorens knew Koban was planning the next step in the revolution, deciding how the rebels would fight on with the help of the new humans from the stars.

Lorens's foot scraped on an irregularity in the sprayed plastic floor, and Koban looked up, his intense expression turning to a smile as he recognized the intruder. "Lorens," he said. "For a second I thought you might be a skulking overseer out to kill me."

"He'd never come close," Lorens said with the fierce loyalty of a twelve-year-old for his hero. "Not while I'm here."

"All right, bodyguard." Koban kept his face straight as he nodded. "Take a position down the corridor. Chu is coming, and the security of our meeting rests with you."

As the boy started purposefully down the hall, Koban turned back to the work at hand. He detached the laser drill's flexible hose from the power pack and peeled back the casing. A bundle of slender, shimmering fiber strands glinted up at him.

A shadow flitted across the weak wintry light that slanted in through the room's small skylight. Without thinking, Koban spun around and dropped to a crouch. The newcomer was no attacker, though; instead, Koban found himself gazing at Chu Edorlic's sardonic face.

"I'm glad to see you don't put all your trust in that overseer's boy," he commented.

"You won't find many more loyal than Lorens," Koban said without heat.

Chu grunted. "I trust him as far as I can throw

him—which is far enough, for the moment. So, now that we've got a minute: what's the news on the starship people?"

Scowling fiercely, Koban began to extract the bundle of fibers from the hose. As he worked, he told Chu the highlights of his discussion with Riker. He didn't go into just how resistant Riker had been to the idea of war with the chickens. He wanted to keep that discouraging news to himself until he figured out what to do about it.

"So that big, dark fellow is some kind of alien, eh?" Chu's face contorted in a grimace of disgust. "Ugh. I knew there was something odd about him. He smelled . . . different. Made the back of my neck all prickly."

"Mmm." Koban knew what Chu meant, but he couldn't let on that he felt the same way. If any of the men got wind of his discomfort, they'd get nervous themselves, and that would be disastrous to the revolution.

He held up the bundle of fibers to the snow-filtered light. His practiced eye detected a subtle flaw in the refraction pattern. Cracked, of course. The cold played havoc with the lasers. Equipment didn't last on this damned refrigerator of a planet. And it looked as if all too soon the humans on Koorn would need every weapon they could get.

"I don't like it," Chu burst out. He started pacing back and forth. "We can't trust these people, Koban. Those freaks they work with, live with, *breed* with—it isn't right."

"Chu," Koban said, "we don't know anything

about the aliens. Maybe they aren't so terrible. After all, they look like humans, more or less."

"That makes it even worse. It's just *wrong!*"

"Whether it's right or wrong doesn't concern us. It isn't even a question of trusting them. We *need* these people." Koban cocked an eyebrow at his lieutenant. "And one way or another, I'll find a way to handle them."

Chapter Six

THE WAN MORNING SUNLIGHT of Koorn had brief competition as ten shafts of light pulsed on an ice-covered plain, resolving into the human forms of a party beamed down from the *Enterprise*. Cold struck Captain Picard like a physical blow. Ice crystals scudded along on a wind from the taller glaciers on the heights above.

Picard turned his attention to the structure before them, hoping to get inside quickly—though Will Riker had reported that there was precious little warmth to be found within. The bunker before them was a strange combination of solid yet slapdash construction. The low, sloping walls were obviously thick, but they'd been built of some sort of textured concrete that made the installation seem unfinished. An entrance bay large enough to accommodate two shuttlecraft abreast was guarded by an articulated metal door. To the groan and whine of machinery, the metal curtain jerked slowly upward.

Behind it stood a tall, muscular man with a ruined face flanked by men in patched but clean brown coveralls. An honor guard, as best they could arrange one, Picard thought.

He turned to speak softly to Commander Riker. "So that's the leader of the revolutionaries." He cast a discreet eye over Iarni Koban, who stepped into the cold without any sign of feeling it. "Rather young, isn't he, Number One?"

Riker's tone was neutral as he responded. "Maybe, sir. But don't forget that his life span is probably considerably shorter than ours. These people are worked to death at a fairly early age."

"Quite so." Picard's left eyebrow quirked. Will sounded a bit defensive. The captain suspected he was reacting to their conversation the previous night.

Simple curiosity had brought Picard to Koorn, over the strenuous objections of the *Enterprise*'s chief of security. A lost colony of humans! And from all Riker had reported, it seemed that these people had been marooned in this desolate sector of the galaxy since the very dawn of human interstellar travel.

And then there was the matter of this new race, these avian bipeds whose expanding population had led them to enslave another race. The little Picard had heard so far intrigued him immensely.

He glanced over at Dr. Crusher, thinking of her

report on the away team's medical evaluations. From samples of their blood and saliva she'd been able to determine that the psychoactive scent they'd encountered was actually a repellent phero-mone of sorts. "It's almost unheard of to encounter a primitive defense mechanism like this in a highly evolved creature," she'd told Picard. "These Tseetsk sound like a strange race to me. I'd love to see one."

Now perhaps they would get the chance, Picard thought.

Koban stepped up to them with a smile as Riker undertook the introductions. "Koban, this is Cap-tain Jean-Luc Picard, commander of the *Enter-prise*. Captain, this is the leader of the freemen of Koorn."

"I appreciate the chance to meet you, Captain Picard. We have much to learn from each other." Koban ushered the group past the honor guard, then turned to a lithe, high-cheekboned man at the end of the line who aimed a suspicious gaze at the group. "My right-hand man, Chu Edorlic."

Riker went on to introduce the other members of the team, including Data and Beverly Crusher.

"I understand you were active all night, arrang-ing your studies," Koban said, his gaze studiously avoiding the android's odd skin tone and yellow eyes. "And we must thank the doctor for the help of her medical team."

"I'd like to offer more," Crusher said. "My team noted a lack of medical supplies, decent food, and warm clothing, so I took the liberty of arranging a delivery of such supplies."

For a moment Koban looked taken aback. Then his square jaw relaxed imperceptibly. "Whatever you can spare would be much appreciated," he said.

Handsomely accepted, Picard thought with a touch of admiration. It was obvious at a glance that the rebels' needs were great, but so far Koban had asked for nothing.

Crusher touched her communicator. "Chief O'Brien? Activate the cargo transporters, please."

A moment later pallets laden with heavy parkas and containers of all kinds winked into existence on the ice outside the door. Koban had already called workers to help bring the loads inside. Brown-clad men swarmed outside and slipped into the coats. Then they formed bucket brigades to pass the items down to storerooms, their faces glowing despite the frigid air being blown into the open bay.

As Beverly Crusher's eyes swept over the scene, they inevitably focused on the shortest link in the human chain—a boy with clear, pale skin and straight black hair that flopped over his eyes.

Wesley! For an instant the name echoed in her mind.

Then common sense intervened. Her son was at Starfleet Academy, not on a grubby world of marooned slaves. And as she looked at him she saw that the boy was obviously *not* Wesley Crusher. There was some similarity, but this boy was much younger. Yet she felt a tug on her heart as the all-too-young man stumbled under the weight of a canister of field rations.

"I thought the slaves had been freed," she said to

Picard. "But that one there"—she pointed to the boy, now passing with a big pile of parkas—"is no more than a child. Why is he being forced to do this heavy labor?"

The boy's cocky grin immediately turned to an expression of outrage. "Forced?" he repeated, angrily passing on his load. "I *volunteered* for this!"

Crusher stared at him. He even sounded like Wesley—always intent on being a man. "Well, if you volunteered, I guess there's nothing I can say."

The boy nodded brusquely, grabbing his next load. But then, seeing her smile, he gave her an uncertain grin.

Beverly continued down the line, overhearing more comments. "Clothes, medicine, food . . . everything we need!" she heard one man say.

"Well, almost." From the corner of her eye, she could see the next man in line staring hungrily at her. Color rose to her cheeks.

She went redder as she realized Picard had heard the exchange. So, however, had Koban, who stared the man down.

Picard observed the look. If Koban's glare had been phaser fire, that fellow would be ashes by now, he thought.

"I must apologize for my men," Koban said. "But they raise a legitimate concern. If your people intend to study the Tseetsk, the women will have to be nearby." He lowered his voice. "But it may be best if they aren't *too* near."

"I understand," Picard said.

"Let me suggest an appropriate location," Koban said. "There's a small installation in the heights above us, a punishment barracks built above the ground. None of my men would want to go there, but with your capabilities, I'm sure you could make it a comfortable base." He hesitated for a moment. "I'm keeping the chicken—the Tsectsk—Draagh there for now. Perhaps you'd undertake custody of her as well. That would remove a temptation from my men, frankly."

Picard nodded. "Understood. I appreciate your suggestion and your help, Koban. The research team will be fairly numerous: geologists, biologists, computer specialists, and so forth. Your base holds a treasure trove of information about this sector and the Tseetsk."

"I imagine it does," Koban agreed, with a slightly ironic smile. "And I expect you're eager to get your people started, considering the time limit we're operating under. I consider much of this a waste of time, but I would also admit to being biased."

One of the honor guard had left the bay and now returned with a thin man whose hair was as gray as the clothing he wore and whose most outstanding feature was his sad, heavy-lidded eyes.

"Let me introduce the foremost local authority on the chickens," Koban said. "Captain Picard, Dr. Crusher, Data, this is Josip Vossted. He can tell you much about our former masters. I add only one comment on his opinions: they're rejected on an order of seven hundred to one by this planet's population."

Still, Picard noted, Koban gave Vossted an affectionate smile as he said, "When we discussed your needs, Vossted suggested that he give you a tour of our facilities. I think that would make an excellent beginning."

Picard felt a shock of surprise from Riker and recalled what the first officer had said about the old overseer who seemed to occupy such an important position in Koban's mind. But hadn't Riker said the fellow was a prisoner?

Koban seemed to be waiting for him to comment. Seeing this, the captain schooled his features to imperturbability and said merely, "Ah. Thank you. Will you accompany us as well?"

"I'll join you later. I'm afraid I'm called away to a meeting now," Koban said. "We have so much to reorganize. Vossted is the best man for your needs. Despite our disagreements"—he shot the older man a piercing look from his bright blue eyes—"he will offer an excellent overview of our base and our people."

Vossted's smile was as ironic as Koban's when he watched the rebel leader go. Then he turned to Picard. "Well, Captain," he said, "welcome to the Koorn base."

Chu Edorlic frowned unhappily at Koban as they made their way through a warren of dingy tunnels. "It's bad enough letting more freaks and aliens down from that starship," he argued quietly. "But women—like that doctor?" His face was an odd mixture of concern and longing. "Is that wise? Even I feel—"

"I know. But they'll be establishing their own base up top, out of the way. We'll send a gang to help. That's your task. Select likable men, Chu—

careful men. And I want a watch kept on the paths from up top. Make sure the watchers are dependable men who will follow and protect any women who come down. Let it be known among the men that anyone who molests or even annoys the starship women goes out in the cold. Naked."

Edorlic stared at his leader. "They aren't going to like that order, you know."

"It doesn't matter. We need these people." Koban made the last turn before the meeting room. At least for now, he added silently.

They stepped inside to face a ring of men sitting or leaning against moldy sacks of grain. Tall or short, stocky or thin, they had certain things in common. They were all gray-haired, and their faces were seamed with age and hard work. Until Koban came along, gang leadership had come with experience and survival. But, although he was considerably younger, he had managed to unite them in his cause.

Until now. Another unifying factor was the angry looks the gang bosses directed at him.

Koban was glad he'd called the meeting in their old pre-revolution headquarters, a disused food storage room. The thick door, originally designed to keep out desperately hungry men, now kept in the shouts of dissent.

"How can you let them build their own base?" one man cried. "Especially when it overlooks ours?"

"No matter where they built their base, they'd still be overlooking us from orbit," Koban responded reasonably.

"From orbit they're a cause for concern. Among us they're a disturbance," another man said bluntly. "Before, the men depended on *us* for their needs. Now these starship people are giving them whatever they want."

"Except women," the first man put in sourly. "By the way, the men aren't very happy with that no-sex edict you proclaimed."

"Do the men want women more than they want freedom?" Koban snapped. "Oh, we've managed to seize Koorn. But we need the starship people if our war is to succeed." He gazed from face to face among his fellow leaders. Always before they had supported him loyally. Now their expressions were skeptical.

For years we planned together, he thought. Is that to end now that the first step of our rebellion is successful?

He decided to turn the conversation to more agreeable concerns. "What's the word from the search teams? Are all the overseers accounted for?"

"All but four," a lanky gang boss spoke up, leaning his hip against a grain bag. "Fritt's still on the loose, and we don't have a firm report on Haliger, though one of my squad saw him going for one of the ground cars."

"Hunh," Chu Edorlic grunted. "He won't get far. Not alone, without food or water. If the damned ice beasts don't get him, the planet will."

"I got that sadist Kemmel," a sullen-faced squad leader said. "Caught him right between the eyes with my ice chisel." His lips curled back from his teeth in a savage grimace of satisfaction.

"Haliger is probably outside, as I said," the lanky man continued. "Forns and Jevet definitely are. I saw them in one of the fliers yesterday, going through the east seal."

"The east seal?" Koban was puzzled. "What lies east of the base?"

"Nothing. Probably trying to fool us. They'll loop around and head for one of the Rift bases after a few kilometers."

"Wherever they go, they've had it," Chu said. "It isn't even winter yet, and already the snow's ten feet deep in some spots."

The lanky man cleared his throat. "There's one name no one's mentioned yet: Vossted."

No matter where we turn, we come to some controversy, Koban thought, frowning. Aloud he said, "What about him? He's in our custody."

"He's an overseer! And letting him act as tour guide for the strangers doesn't qualify as 'custody' in my eyes," a gray-stubbled man burst out.

"He's going nowhere. Besides, you know as well as I do that Vossted isn't *just* an overseer. Has he ever mistreated any of us?" Koban stared around at them. "Well?"

Chu scowled. "Personally I don't care whether or not he plays nice with us. He's still one of *them.*"

"He's different," Koban said flatly. "Besides, he has a lot of knowledge in that gray head of his, knowledge that might be very useful to us before long."

"I still don't like it," Chu muttered.

"You don't have to," Koban shot back. "Just live with it. But if it makes you any happier, Chu, I'll tell you this: if anyone brings me evidence that Vossted is hindering our cause in any way, I'll take care of him myself."

After a moment Chu lowered his eyes and ran a hand through his dark hair. "I know you will," he said. "I just hope it never comes to that."

So do I, Koban thought with a chill. Vossted had been almost like a father to him. All that Koban knew had been taught him by the old man: metallurgy, chemistry, computers, engineering, history . . .

But that was in time past. The present and the future belonged to the revolution, and if Vossted could not accept whatever the new times demanded, then he would have to go.

Koban glanced around at the other men, taking in their noncommittal expressions. They doubt me. They've never done that before, Koban thought. They doubt me.

"We know what Vossted means to you," the lanky man spoke up. "He saved your life after what happened to your face. But can you really trust him, Iarni? Especially with these starship people we don't even know?"

"You say they'll help us because they're humans, too," the gray-bearded man put in. "But some of them are freaks—monsters—aliens! I don't think we need that kind."

Koban saw the fear of the unknown on his lieutenants' faces as he looked around. Even Chu Edorlic refused to meet his eyes. "Iarni," Chu said uneasily, "you've led us farther than we ever dreamed. But these strangers . . . well, they're putting a wedge between us and the men. The medicine and the food they're giving out—it's nothing to them, with their technology. If they wanted to, they could snatch us out of this very room with that transporter device of theirs and beam us to God knows where. It's all very well to call them our friends, but we have to face the fact that they have huge advantages over us. Just how far can we trust them?"

Koban rose to his feet. "The important thing is to make sure that *they* continue to trust *us.*"

Chu's expression grew even more skeptical. But whatever he was about to say was interrupted by a pounding on the door. He leaped up to investigate. Then he grinned and threw the door open. "Another rathole heard from."

Two rebel guards frog-marched a squirming, pale-faced man through the entrance. "We found him in a secret tunnel," the tall black-skinned one said. "One of the passageways Lorens Ben showed us."

"Well, if it isn't Fritt, the flower of the overseer class," Edorlic said, gesturing for the men to haul their burden upright. "Why bother to bring him here?"

"Man wants a trial." The dark-skinned guard glanced over at his partner. "For some reason, Swagen thinks he owes him."

Color rose in the second guard's square, stubbled face. "He was pretty good, for an overseer," he said. "Didn't believe in marking people defective if they were only sick. He'd send them off to light jobs till they got better."

The men in the room nodded. As gang bosses, they'd done the same to protect their men. That an overseer would buck the control system was a surprise.

"When I got sick"—Swagen hesitated, embarrassed—"he brought me some of the overseers' medicine."

"So you think he should live?" Chu Edorlic's voice cut like a knife.

A mulish look crossed Swagen's face. "I thought he should have a chance to speak for himself."

"Maybe you've been listening to the starship people," Edorlic said disdainfully. "They're big believers in words."

Koban caught the looks between his lieutenants. How to handle this? "If you've got anything to say, Fritt, let's hear it," he ordered.

Fritt stood shivering in the grip of the two guards. Koban noticed that Yafeu was wearing a new overseer parka and Swagen had confiscated Fritt's jacket.

"I—I—" Fritt's teeth chattered from a mixture of cold and fear. "I always tried to do my best for the men who worked for me. Protect them. Help if they needed help—tried to go as far as I could."

"You mean as far as it didn't inconvenience you," the gray-bearded lieutenant sneered.

Fritt shook his head. "I listened to Vossted. I believed in what he said. I knew the way we lived wasn't right, and I tried to make it better. You can ask."

Koban faced Fritt, feeling the eyes of his lieutenants on him. First the argument over the starship people. Now this puling overseer was invoking Vossted's name.

"Ask who?" he inquired. "All the rest of your overseer friends are either dead or running for their lives."

"Vossted," Fritt said desperately. "I heard he was still alive. Or—or Shakra Ben's boy. *He'd* tell you."

Koban smiled grimly. "I'm afraid Lorens Ben's feelings about overseers wouldn't help you. And as for Vossted, well, I don't think this court needs to hear his testimony."

He drew himself up. "You want a trial? All right. I accuse you of half measures. Although you claim to follow Vossted, you did so on the sly, not acting in the light of day the way he did. That, I suppose, would have been too dangerous. So you left Vossted to face any danger alone, and you winked to the chickens while performing a few good deeds."

Koban glared into the overseer's shrinking face. "I don't believe those few deeds will save you, Fritt. Doing too little is a capital crime." He turned to his lieutenants. "What do you say, members of the jury?"

Chu Edorlic spoke up promptly. "Guilty."

"Guilty," the graybeard said.

The lanky gang boss nodded grimly. "Guilty."

The sullen-faced man glanced at Fritt. "Guilty."

Only Swagen hesitated for a moment. He licked his lips, then pronounced, "Guilty."

They're behind me again, Koban thought. Now I've got to seal the moment. . . .

His eyes fell on a laser drill lying untended on a pile of sacks. "You've been found guilty, and sentence will be executed immediately. Get him on his knees."

Fritt cried out, but his two captors were brutally efficient. Still pinioning his arms, they kicked him behind the knees. In a second he was kneeling, his arms thrust up behind him like an ungainly fowl with its neck sticking out.

Koban caught up the wand of the laser drill with one hand, the power pack with the other.

Twisting his head, Fritt could see the rebel leader's approach. "Koban! Please! No!"

Koban brought the wand down and flicked the fire button. A brief flare of ruby light lit the room for an instant. Fritt's head thumped to the floor, severed cleanly, the wound cauterized by the laser.

The guards released their hold, and the body sank into a boneless sprawl.

"That's the end of the overseer problem." Koban raised his hand, still clenched around the laser rod, feeling a strange mixture of triumph and fear. He'd led the gang to victory in a matter of hours. But as the events in this room had just proved, that fight might well have been the easiest part of his battle. The trick now was to keep the momentum going, to keep the men riding the crest.

"Where do we go from here?" Edorlic once again managed to home in on his leader's thoughts.

Koban leaned against a pile of grain sacks, stretching his long legs out in front of him as he debated what to say. Finally he decided to reveal a little of his plan to his men—the audacious, half-formed plan that even he wasn't sure of yet. The men needed a bone to chew on.

He swallowed hard, trying to look nonchalant. "We have to assume the chickens are on their way, ready to strike against us. So we've got to persuade the starship people to help us strike against them," he began.

"I don't think the strangers will fight a war for us," Chu said bluntly.

"What else can we do?" the gaunt gang boss asked. "Beg passage on their ship? Try to run away?"

"And what about the rest of our people?" The sullen chief's mouth was set in a grimace. "I've got twin sons on Foothold. There's no way I'd leave them to the chickens."

Chu's dark eyes were angry. "The starship people are soft. They don't understand what it is to be prisoners, as we are."

Koban smiled. Chu had hit on the problem once again. "But they can learn. Why do you think I allowed them to set up a base beside us?" He looked around his council, whose members now stared at him in puzzlement.

"As you say, we can't touch them in their starship," he continued, pitching his voice low for emphasis. The gang bosses unconsciously leaned forward, their faces intent.

"But the people on the ground," he said softly, "they *are* in our reach."

Chapter Seven

"WHERE TO FIRST?" Vossted asked brightly.

Captain Picard had just dispatched La Forge and Worf to oversee the construction of the research facilities. He, Riker, Crusher, and Data stood with Vossted just inside the doors of the Koorn base. They were ready to begin the tour.

Data spoke up. "The computer facilities would seem to be the logical place to begin."

"Right," Riker seconded the suggestion. "The faster we access your records, the easier it will be to fill in the blanks we're sure to find in all areas of our research."

"Logical indeed." Vossted chuckled briefly, his heavy-lidded eyes crinkling. "Well, then, follow me."

He beckoned, and the group moved through a small doorway into an ill-lit warren of hallways. As they walked, Picard quickened his pace and drew abreast of Vossted. "Tell me," he said. "Why is Koban allowing you to roam free? And why were you, presumably an opponent of the rebellion, chosen as an official spokesman?"

Vossted shrugged. "I could give you several reasons. First of all, under the Tseetsk, only the overseers had anything like free access to the computers and other sophisticated equipment. The gangs were taught just enough to enable them to operate the laser drills and machinery, set up the geothermal taps, things like that—and always under overseer supervision. Since the revolt, I am almost the only one left who can tell you about what you're seeing."

"'Almost'?"

"I believe in sharing knowledge. In secret, I taught a young man from the gangs what I could, both about the base systems and about other subjects that I deemed important."

"The young man was Koban?" Picard hazarded a guess.

Vossted nodded. "He was nearly a dead man when I first met him."

Picard raised an eyebrow. "His face?"

"He arrived here five years ago as 'fresh meat,' a new gang man only fifteen years old, on his first stint. His gang boss let him ride aboard an earthmover driven by an overseer while the rest of the gang walked. The overseer led them over an ice-covered crevasse and got them all killed except Koban. Through dumb luck, he was only knocked unconscious—a scalp wound."

"Then how—" Picard began.

"The cab of the machine was warm enough to keep his blood flowing," Vossted said neutrally. "But by the time he awoke, the metal had cooled. His blood—and half of his face—had frozen to the wall. The boy was young, but he already knew there would be no rescue parties coming. So he tore himself free and walked through a blizzard to return to base."

Picard shuddered at the mental picture.

"Needless to say, Koban was not expected to recover. But I—I persuaded the overseers' doctor to treat him." Vossted shook his head. "At least we saved his eye.

"While Koban recovered, he worked for me, and I found that he had a mind. Back then he was so bright, so eager." A note of ironic affection crept into his voice. "And as you can see, he's made use of my lessons.

"That old student-teacher bond between us is another reason Koban lets me roam free," Vossted continued. "He can't quite bring himself to confine me or to order my execution. And a third reason, I imagine, is that a part of him would actually be relieved if one of his men took a potshot at me. I'm a problem, you see. My presence undermines his authority."

Vossted's air of acceptance began to irritate Picard. "Forgive me, but I'm afraid I don't understand your position in all this," he said. "Your comments would seem to indicate that you sympathize with the rebels, and yet you're their prisoner. Are you for this revolution or against it?"

Unruffled, Vossted smiled. "Captain, I'm an overseer." He ran a bony finger along the side of his nose. "I also fancy myself a humanist. Puts me in rather an awkward position, wouldn't you agree?"

That wasn't an answer, Picard reflected.

Riker, who had been following the conversation with interest, now joined in. "Why did you become an overseer?"

"Runs in the family," Vossted said wryly. "When the Tseetsk discovered us two hundred odd years ago, the colony was in desperate technological shape, lurching from one crisis to another. The colonists' ship had nearly been destroyed on the journey from Earth. It was caught in some sort of space vortex that flung it into an area where the astrogators didn't even recognize the stars."

"A wormhole," Picard said. "The ship was caught in a wormhole and sent all the way out here." He was surprised those long-gone refugees even had a ship left after that experience.

"There was some such reference in the old books on physics," Vossted said with a shrug. "But theories of the universe were of little interest in the refugees' struggle for day-to-day survival. The ship crash-landed, and what technology the colonists enjoyed came from materials they'd scavenged from the wreck. But those machines were just about at the end of their useful lives. My ancestors were limping along on what crude systems they could cobble together, and they had no way of manufacturing more. They had the knowledge of microcircuits, but not a blacksmith technology. Their civilization was teetering on the edge of a Dark Age. The engineers among them were their only hope. And they knew it."

"You mean the engineers used their control of the systems to control the people as well?" Picard asked.

"Exactly. When the Tseetsk arrived, they saw that the engineers were in control, so they were chosen to supervise the rest of the human work force. Tseetsk society is caste-dominated, with membership based on heredity. So the children of the engineers have been overseers ever since, regardless of their qualifications."

"And regardless of their wishes?" Riker added.

Vossted shrugged. "I was never offered a choice. Anyway, it would be almost impossible for us to break out of the caste molds. Our people were already polarized, and the arrival of the Tseetsk only made it worse, with the overseers jealously guarding what privilege they had and the laboring slaves wallowing in class hatred. Anyone who tries to cross the lines is viewed with suspicion and dislike.

"But would I, in truth, have chosen the other way, if I could have? You could say I've actually taken the harder path. I've accepted dishonor and hatred in order to use whatever power I have to ease the suffering of my fellow men." His mouth twisted in a self-mocking grin. "Then again, you might note that the life of an overseer is rather more comfortable than the life of an ordinary slave."

They walked on, their footsteps echoing on the rock floor, until Vossted halted at a heavy steel door with rubber molding around the edges. Its padlock had been smashed and hung at a drunken angle.

"The door is insulated," Dr. Crusher observed, puzzled.

"The computers must be kept warm," Data pointed out.

"And the doings of the overseers kept secret," Vossted added. Opening the door, he gestured for the group to enter.

The air inside was much warmer than anywhere else Picard had been so far. He shrugged off his parka and laid it aside, gazing about him in frank astonishment.

"The computer looks a bit different from the rest of our equipment, doesn't it?" Vossted said.

One entire wall of the room was taken up by a smooth black surface. Colored light played across it in a coruscating pattern, but there were no knobs or buttons or microphone pads or any other visible indication that it was, in fact, a working machine.

Positioned at intervals in front of the black surface, in ludicrous contrast to its polished sleekness, were four old-fashioned satellite dishes. Wires trailed from them to clumsy monitors and keyboards that looked to Picard as though they had been lifted from the History of Technology display at Starfleet Academy.

"Satellite dishes and manual interfaces?" Riker said, unbelieving. "With a machine as advanced as that one looks to be? Strange setup."

"It's a hybrid. The computer is voice-controlled,

but it's programmed for the Tseetsk language."
Vossted warbled a low note, then followed it with a trilling whistle.

A holographic image of a laser drill appeared on the floor in front of the group. Glowing arrows pointed to pieces of it, with labels written in queer characters that looked for all the world like the tracks of a bird's feet.

Picard was surprised. "You speak Tseetsk."

"I do. Not many humans can get their tongues around it, though. So the Tseetsk had us patch in these keyboards and monitors, which we'd scavenged from the remains of our ship. The linkage is far from perfect, but it suffices for the work we do here."

Picard frowned. "Why doesn't someone write a translation program in English?"

"No one knows how," Vossted replied. "We may be descended from engineers, but none of us had much in the way of schooling, Captain." Again he cracked that wry smile. "We learned on the job, and only what we needed to know. And most of us don't have any particular aptitude for working with the machines."

"I see. I suppose the very inefficiency of your system is an effective safeguard. You certainly won't be able to manufacture any weapons to use against the Tseetsk."

Picard stretched out a hand and touched the glassy black surface of the computer. It was impossibly smooth, almost frictionless. When he took his fingers away, he noticed that they left no prints, though his hands were sweating from the gloves he'd just removed.

"Remarkable substance," he murmured.

"Isn't it?" Vossted agreed. "Koban was fascinated by it. Now *there's* someone with an intuitive understanding of computers. I made a copy of my key for him, and he would spend hours in here late at night when no one else was around. Just playing, exploring."

Riker touched the computer's black face. "What is this stuff? How is it made?"

"It's ancient Tseetsk manufacture. The culture is incredibly old, you know—thousands and thousands of years. And it seems at one time to have been technologically brilliant. This substance, the computer housing, is impervious to wear and tear, as far as I can tell. Sadly, I don't believe they know how to make it anymore."

Data spoke up. "The surface is not material, actually. It appears to be a forcefield, though I am unfamiliar with its composition." He stepped over to one of the keyboards, then looked up expectantly at Vossted. "Can you direct me to a lexicon of the Tseetsk language? Once I learn it, the pace of our work here will be enhanced."

"You think you can learn Tseetsk that quickly?" Vossted asked with a trace of disbelief.

"Oh, yes," Data replied obligingly. "My positronic circuits operate in excess of—"

"He can do it," Riker cut in, smiling. "Just take his word for it."

"You're a talented fellow, Mr. Data," Vossted

said admiringly. He crossed to Data's side and typed in a quick command. Then he pointed to the monitor. "There you are."

"I think Data and I can take it from here," Riker said. "I'm anxious to get started."

"Just what I was thinking, Number One," Picard said with an approving nod. "Time is of the essence."

"All right, then." Vossted glanced at Picard and Crusher. "Shall we three continue the tour?"

"I'd like to see the medical facilities," Crusher suggested. "To refine my idea of what you need."

"Doctor, our needs are great," Vossted said feelingly.

The moment they left the computer room the cold struck sharply once again. Shivering, Picard and Crusher pulled their coats closer around them.

As they strode on through the maze of tunnels a group of hard-faced men passed them going the other way. Two of them turned to look greedily at Crusher. She huddled into her parka, wishing it were even bulkier than it was.

"Tell me more about the Tseetsk culture," Picard was urging Vossted.

Vossted's mournful eyes seemed to gaze at something far away as he climbed up a short flight of steps.

"It's an odd mix—advanced in some ways, incredibly ignorant and superstitious in others. For example, Tseetsk medicine is extraordinary. They've eradicated every one of their major diseases, including those as trivial as their equivalent of the common cold. Yet some subjects, like genetics, are absolutely taboo. It's bad manners even to mention it, though how they get around it in the lab is absolutely beyond me. The same goes for cosmology and nuclear physics—they want no part of any science that deals with the fundamental structure of things." He paused, considering. "I think it frightens them."

"How do you know so much about them?" Crusher asked.

"When I was a boy," Vossted said, "I spent three years on the Tseetsk homeworld. I was taken there as a curiosity, I suppose—I sang, and they liked that. No human had ever before had such intimate contact with the Tseetsk.

"I went there hating them. To me, they were simply evil—a race who had made no attempt to understand mine and had merely enslaved us for their own convenience. But during my stay I was forced to look beyond that picture."

"And you saw . . . what?" Picard prompted.

"A planet of remarkable beauty and fertility. A benevolent social system that in many ways could serve as a model of good government. A rich, diverse artistic tradition. Oh, the music!" His voice was suddenly thick with yearning. "The music of the Tseetsk is so beautiful it would break your heart to hear it."

Picard studied Vossted. "I'd like to," he said softly.

"I also saw—people." Vossted sighed. "People like humans, in many ways. Decent, kindly, but not willing to look beyond their immediate concerns to the larger picture.

"It surprised me that most of the average Tseetsk were barely aware of our existence. And insofar as they do know of us, they believe us to be bestial beings of little intelligence and less domestic virtue."

"A classic rationalization," Picard pointed out. "Slavery was once accepted in many human societies, and one of the ways it was made palatable was by arguing that the enslaved races were somehow less than human."

"Interesting analogy. In fact, there are abolitionists among the Tseetsk, just as there were among humans toward the end of our own era of slavery."

"You mean the regent Drraagh?" Picard asked. Riker had said something of the kind to him. He raised a skeptical brow. "How much can she do out here on Koorn? Or is that the reason she was assigned here in the first place?"

Vossted's lips quirked. "Touché."

"Go on, tell me more about these people," Picard continued.

"The race is strictly hierarchical, and strongly matriarchal as well," Vossted said. "Males, in fact, have virtually no function other than to breed."

"Like drones in a beehive," suggested Picard.

"Exactly. They're large, docile, and stupid. The females do all the important work and make the decisions."

"Fascinating," Crusher murmured.

Picard looked sharply at her and caught a suspicious twinkle in her eye.

Vossted chuckled. "As I told you, the Tseetsk are

an ancient race. They once inhabited several solar systems." He steepled his fingers. "However, sometime in the distant past they suffered some kind of cataclysm that brought them to the brink of extinction."

Picard thought of the ruined planets the *Enterprise* had scanned in the past few weeks. "War?" he asked.

"I believe so. Exactly what happened is unclear; the subject is shrouded in strong taboos. But whatever it was, the Tseetsk emerged from it with a single objective: to keep the race from dying out. That, I believe, has shaped their consciousness ever since. I've never seen a people more caring toward their own. There's no poverty on Tseetsk-Home; no one goes hungry or homeless."

"That seems quite a contradiction. Commander Riker told me the Tseetsk were struggling with catastrophic overpopulation," Picard broke in. "How can they provide for all under such severe pressures?"

"It's getting more difficult every year," Vossted admitted. "But remember that they have come back from the brink of a violent extinction, Captain. Preserving the race for them means preserving every individual member of it. It is a moral imperative. They must obey it, no matter the cost.

"Medical science, as I said, is quite advanced. And the children are more prized than in any culture I've ever heard of. Having a child is the most sacred of rights *and* duties. Every Tseetsk life is a priceless gift."

"Admirable," Picard said dryly. The roots of the

present situation were becoming clearer and clearer. It was only a short step from every Tseetsk life being a priceless gift to every other kind of life being worthless—or worse, a threat, he mused.

And then he began to wonder how they would react to the news that some of their galactic neighbors had just turned up on their doorstep.

"Here we are," Vossted announced. With a slight bow, he indicated a doorway so low that Crusher and Picard had to duck their heads as they went through.

Inside, Crusher's eyes widened with shock. *"This* is your medical facility?"

The room was meanly proportioned, with harsh, glaring light from an unshaded overhead track. Three men lay on roughly fashioned pallets. A wall of shelves held grimy jars of unidentifiable viscous substances as well as row upon row of neatly rolled bandages.

"The Tseetsk are strong on their own medical science, but they haven't paid much attention to ours," Vossted said. "I believe our colony ship's only doctor died in the crash; at any rate, most medical knowledge died with the first generation of colonists. What texts there were left from the sickbay fell into the hands of the overseers, who used them as another means of controlling the population."

"That's criminal!" Crusher's nostrils flared angrily.

"We developed some herbal medicine." Vossted gestured, indicating the jars of goo. "And of course we can treat minor wounds. But those with serious illnesses or injuries are . . ." His voice trailed off.

Beverly Crusher didn't ask Vossted to finish the sentence. She didn't think she really wanted to know.

"All right, Dil, time to change your ban—" The light, youthful voice behind Crusher broke off suddenly.

She turned to see the boy from the rebels' unloading crew, the one who'd reminded her so strongly of Wesley. He gazed from Picard to her, and almost immediately his surprised look gave way to that cocky grin. "Star people!" he said in a tone of deep satisfaction.

"Well, hello there," Crusher said with a smile. "I'm Dr. Beverly Crusher. Who are you?"

The boy drew himself up, very much on his dignity. "Lorens Ben. *Doctor* Lorens Ben."

"Doctor?" Picard raised an eyebrow.

"That's right," Lorens asserted defiantly. He pointed toward the three pallets. "Those are my patients."

"Hello, Lorens," Vossted said gently.

The boy didn't reply to Vossted. "I change their bandages and clean their wounds and make poultices for when they have a fever," he told Picard.

Picard frowned. "Isn't anyone supervising this child?" he asked Vossted.

"I'm not a child!" Lorens cried hotly.

"How old are you?" Crusher asked him.

"I'm—I'll be thirteen soon."

"And you're here working as a slave already?"

A dark flush swept Lorens's young face, and he lowered his eyes without answering.

"He knows as much medicine as anyone here," Vossted spoke up. "He's doing a man's work, and doing it well."

Lorens's mouth set. Still, he didn't look at Vossted.

There was an awkward silence, which Crusher broke by clearing her throat. "Well, Dr. Lorens," she said gravely, "I'd like to examine your establishment. I believe you were about to change a bandage?"

For a moment Lorens looked unsure whether she was joking or not. Then his swift grin broke out again. "Okay, Dr. Beverly. Let me show you how we do it."

Crusher followed him to the shelves, where he selected a jar of salve and took down two bandage rolls. He carried them over to the nearest pallet, where a gaunt man lay with a bloodstained rag swathing his shoulder.

Lorens sat on a low stool and peeled the rag away with gentle fingers. "Pickax wound," he said briefly, when the long, jagged tear in the man's shoulder was revealed. He tore a piece off one of the clean bandages, dipped it in the salve jar, and began to swab the wound.

The man groaned. "Easy, Dil," Lorens advised. "I have to kill the germs. It won't sting for long."

Crusher was surprised and impressed by the authority in the young voice and by the unquestioning way the wounded man accepted it, simply nodding and closing his eyes.

When the wound was clean Lorens folded one of the bandages into a pad. This he laid over the injury and bound it in place with the other bandage. He put a hand on Dil's forehead, then looked up at Crusher. "No fever," he said. "I was afraid the wound would get infected."

"It might have, without your care," Crusher told him. She wanted to ruffle his dark hair, but she sensed he wouldn't like that. So instead she touched his shoulder approvingly. "You did a fine job, Lorens. From one doctor to another."

His eyes shone with pride. Then he cleared his throat. "Is it true that you're going to be working down here with us, Dr. Beverly?"

"Yes, it is," Crusher said. "I'm going to be helping with some research, and I'm also going to set up a clinic for anyone who needs medical attention."

"Maybe—maybe I could help you," he suggested with a hint of shyness.

Crusher was pleased and touched. "That's a great idea, Lorens! You certainly could, if you're willing."

In answer he simply smiled—a brilliant, child's smile, his guard down for the first time.

Picard, who'd been speaking quietly with Vossted, now addressed Crusher. "Time we were on our way, Doctor," he called. "Vossted suggests we speak to Koban about the possibility of an interview with the regent Drraagh."

"You're going to see Koban?" Lorens asked breathlessly.

Crusher saw the gleam of hero worship in his

eyes and took pity on him. "Why don't you walk with us?" she said. "You and I can talk about the clinic."

Lorens nodded eagerly and practically raced out of the room, pausing only to wait until Crusher caught up with him. Picard and Vossted followed at a slower pace.

"The lad does seem a bit young to be here," Picard commented in an undertone as they headed back toward the room where they'd arranged to meet Koban.

"Lorens isn't a gang member. Poor child, I think he'd be happier if he were. His father was Shakra Ben, the head overseer of Koorn. I believe you met him." Vossted glanced sideways at Picard. "Fat-faced fellow. Small eyes."

"Fat-faced . . . oh!" Picard suddenly realized Vossted was referring to the man they'd contacted from the ship. The one who'd been torn apart by a laser in front of their eyes.

"I see you've placed him." Vossted's face was full of pity. "Lorens is—was his only son. Shakra Ben pulled strings to have the boy brought here, but he shouldn't have bothered. Lorens is a romantic boy with a strong sense of honor. He despised the overseers—none more than his own father. And now he's Koban's most ardent follower."

"His father's death must have affected him somehow."

"Undoubtedly. And it doesn't make it any simpler that the man who pulled the trigger was Koban."

"Koban!" Picard's lips thinned. He didn't claim

any great insight into the minds of children, but it was easy enough to guess that this one must have troubles.

"I'm second on Lorens's list of bad people." Vossted sounded sad. "Right below Shakra. In some ways, I'm sure he thinks I'm even worse—an overseer with a conscience, which I've betrayed every day of my life."

Picard cocked an eyebrow at Vossted. "And do you intend to go on betraying your conscience?" he asked bluntly. "It seems to me that you, with your knowledge of the forces arrayed on both sides, could offer much-needed guidance in this affair. Yet you never answered my first question to you. Where *do* you stand, Vossted?"

"Nowhere." Vossted's voice was unexpectedly bitter. "I'm useless. I love both humans and Tseetsk, and therefore neither side trusts *me*. I had hoped for a bloodless revolution—an evolution, rather, of understanding between our peoples. But can you blame the poor men of Koorn for scorning me? What hope have the Tseetsk ever given them? And now they've taken matters into their own hands, and there's no hope for any of us. The Tseetsk will be here soon, you know. Their ships will come, they will discover the rebellion, and they'll crush it—and, with it, any chance of understanding.

"No, Captain." Vossted shook his head. "Perhaps another man could have shaped events differently. But I'm no leader. The best thing that could happen now is that some eager young rebel could make a martyr out of me." With a mirthless grin he added, "Maybe then people would finally pay me some heed."

Picard put a hand on the old overseer's arm. "I think you underestimate your importance," he said.

A din greeted them as they entered the room where they were to meet Koban. Brown-clad rebels gawked at the group of men and women in Starfleet uniforms who stood in the center of the room. The researchers had clearly arrived.

Picard left Vossted standing by the door and moved to join his people. Murmurs went through the crowd as Koban appeared beside the overseer in the doorway.

A figure in bloody brown burlap with a stained off-white bandage around most of his face suddenly pushed away from the chamber wall. Picard had assumed he was one of the walking wounded, but from the way he moved, the captain could tell that the blood on the suit and bandage wasn't his. The man raised his arm. In his hand was a disrupter, pointed right at Koban.

"Look out, Koban! He's an overseer!" One of the rebels shouted the warning.

"Haliger!" Vossted cried. "No!"

The man's finger flicked over the trigger of his weapon just as Vossted leaped forward.

A high-pitched whine filled the chamber. Then, with a terrible cry, Vossted crumpled to the floor.

Chapter Eight

EVEN AS VOSSTED FELL, a beefy young rebel hurled Koban to the floor behind him. The rebel unshipped and aimed his laser drill as if it weighed nothing. Other rebels whipped out nerve disrupters.

His advantage of surprise lost, the disguised overseer tried for one final shot at Koban. "You slag!" he yelled.

The tearing whine of disrupter fire cut his words off. There was no need, though. The glaring lance of the drill's laser beam had already bisected the overseer.

Beverly Crusher got up from the floor, where she'd thrown herself and Lorens when the shooting started. Her face was pale, but her hands were steady as she ran the medical scanner over

Vossted's still form. It was obvious at a glance that no aid was possible for the attacker.

"His status?" Picard asked.

"There's serious nerve damage in the upper chest and neck." Crusher paused for a second. "And in the head."

The captain's eyes flicked from Vossted's pale face to the overseer's disrupter, lying where it had clattered after the assassin was cut down. It looked so insignificant, lying there on the chilly plastic floor. But it seemed to have fried the brain of the lone voice for moderation in the Koorn rebellion. "Do what you can, Doctor," he said tightly.

The look on Beverly Crusher's face grew more and more strained. Abruptly she tapped her communicator. "Two to sickbay. Immediately!"

Koban was back on his feet. From the flush on that intense face, Picard imagined that he had not relished being knocked to a nice safe floor at the start of a fight. Koban stepped toward the wounded man, then recoiled at the glow of the transporter. "Vossted! He isn't—"

"Vossted is seriously wounded. Dr. Crusher has taken him up to our ship."

Koban nodded. "Certainly he'll have a better chance of treatment up there." He looked in disgust at the weapon holstered at his side. "These damned disrupters! On the low setting they create incredible pain without doing as much damage as a whip. At maximum they burn nerves into uselessness. A man with a dead arm or leg is an excellent example to others. He'll live just long enough for the lesson to penetrate the rest of the slave population."

He whipped out the disrupter and extended it in his open palm. Seeing it against a human hand, Picard realized that the grip on the weapon was slightly out of scale.

Koban saw the realization in the captain's eyes and gave him a crooked grin. "That's right, Captain, this weapon was designed for a chicken's hand. It is the only weapon given us by our masters —for use as a management tool."

Picard frowned as the young man reholstered the disrupter—a weapon without pity on a world scarred by genocidal war.

Koban bent to pick up the assassin's weapon. "We'll see how the chickens like it when we turn their management tools on them."

"Koban." Picard drew the rebel leader aside. "Hasn't enough damage been caused by hate already? Stop this talk of war. You would do far better to seek peace with the Tseetsk. We're willing to help you. You may never have a better opportunity than now."

"The opportunity I see isn't the one you see," Koban retorted. "The chickens will never let us live and be free if we give them the choice. Captain Picard, we have to take the offensive with them. Don't you understand?" He reached out with both hands as if to take Picard by the shoulders, then stopped, clenching his hands into fists. Muscles writhed in the scarred face. "The chickens are humankind's enemies. We cannot coexist with them. They will *never* accept another race as equals. It's us or them."

"I cannot accept your word on that."

"Then you have two choices. Stay here and die with us, or leave with our death on your conscience."

"There is a third choice," Picard said. "Arbitration by a Federation ambassador. My ship is large enough to hold every man on this planet, Koban. Let us take you to a Federation outpost. There your men will be safe and you can plead your case before a higher authority."

"What about the other people from Foothold?" Koban demanded acidly. "There are fifty thousand of us scattered on five or six planets in this region. Your ship may be big, but I doubt it can hold us all. If the chickens come here and find Koorn deserted, they won't wait around to find out what happened. They'll assume the worst and take steps to neutralize the rest of the human population." He shook his head. "My people are all hostages. I cannot leave them to be slaughtered."

"And I cannot assist in the slaughter of an entire race, when there might be another way. Koban, the cost of war is too high."

Koban laughed contemptuously. "When does the cost become affordable, I wonder? When it's your own people who are threatened, instead of a handful of ragged castaways in some deserted corner of the galaxy? Well, it may come to that, Captain Picard. It may come to that."

Before Picard could frame an answer, the rebel leader spun on his heel and walked away.

Frowning, Picard tapped his communicator. "Mr. Worf."

"Captain?" came Worf's basso rumble.

"Post two security guards on Drraagh. The situation here seems to be heating up. You and I have some things to discuss. I'm on my way."

He strode to the loading bay and out the small door at the left side, pausing only to seal his parka and lower his face mask against the frigid wind. Then he climbed the steep, icy footpath to the research compound site.

Worf was waiting for him at the top of the path, looking bigger than ever in his parka. Beside him Geordi La Forge stood stamping his feet and beating his gloved palms together. *Enterprise* crew members and a rebel work team hurried back and forth behind them, lugging curved sections of white carbon-fiber material to a site where a small dome stood half-constructed next to a ramshackle barracks.

Picard told his two officers about the assassination attempt. "Feelings are running high among the rebels right now. I don't know what might happen, but I'd like to be as well prepared as possible. If I send down more crew, do you think you can get these shelters erected by nightfall?"

"Tall order, sir." La Forge turned his face toward the sky, where Koorn's pale sun was already beginning its descent. "The days are very short here. And doing any kind of outdoor work in this climate is no picnic."

As if to punctuate his words, a gust of icy wind raked the plateau. A collective groan went up from the work crew as the half-built dome collapsed.

La Forge turned back to the captain and grimaced wryly. "See what I mean? But we'll do our best."

"I can't ask for more." Picard turned to Worf. "Lieutenant, I'm especially concerned for the regent's safety. We've seen enough bloodshed here; I don't want any symbolic killing."

The Klingon nodded, casting an appreciative gaze down the valley walls. "We have an excellent defensive position, sir, segregated from the rest of the base. I will set security personnel to watch the approaches as well as the entrances to the compound itself. Do you wish to restrict access to *Enterprise* personnel only?"

"That's not diplomatically feasible," Picard replied.

Worf gave him his usual Klingon scowl. "Then I would hesitate to describe our security as absolute," he said. "But it should be adequate to our needs."

"Good. I think I'll have a word with Drraagh now."

Picard headed for the run-down structure next to the dome. Before the uprising it had been a punishment barracks for recalcitrant slaves. Now it was a makeshift prison.

And "makeshift" was the right word, the captain thought, taking in the sagging prefab walls. With a high-pitched keening, icy blasts of wind penetrated ill-chinked seams.

The cold didn't seem to bother the avian alien inside, though Drraagh was clearly agitated. Picard bowed slightly. "I'm Jean-Luc Picard, captain of the USS *Enterprise.*"

"Iss strue?" the alien whistled in a fair approximation of the accented English of the human thralls. "Vossted iss shot?" In her trilling speech, the name sounded like "Oooo-ah-ssss(tick)ed"—a croon, a hiss, and a click.

Picard glanced at the guards, who were as shocked as he was to learn that the regent could speak English.

"I just explained why we were beefing up the guard," one security man said. "No one told me she spoke English." He pointed to a metal device that Drraagh wore on a collar around her neck. "We've been using a Universal Translator to talk to her in Tseetsk. It's more like singing than talking. I doubt if I could ever learn to speak it."

"Difficult for humans," Drraagh admitted in Tseetsk. "It requires a voice and a musical ear of the highest order." She ducked her head. "Vossted has both. In other circumstances, he might have had a career in—what is the art form?" She spoke in English again. "The o'era?"

Picard's eyebrows rose. "Opera? It would seem, Drraagh, that you have knowledge not only of our language but of our culture as well."

Again, Drraagh responded with that abrupt ducking of her head. "What I know, I learned from Vossted. He devoted much of his time to studying us as well. He sings my language far better than I speak his."

She looked at Picard fixedly. "What happened to him? Your people did not say."

"Apparently one of the escaped overseers attempted to head off the revolt at the top. A gunman —an overseer disguised as a rebel—tried to assassinate Koban. Vossted intervened and was struck in the head by a blast from a nerve disrupter."

A hiss of indrawn breath came through Drraagh's beak. She looked down at her hands, smaller than the human norm, with four taloned fingers. "You may have noticed that those weapons were built for my people to handle. I always believed we were wrong to arm the overseers with disrupters. My people salved their conscience with hope that the threat was much more effective than any physical punishment.

"The nerve disrupter has a limited range, but it is most dangerous within those limits," she went on. "We were not so foolish as to arm slaves—even favored slaves—with weapons that were *too* dangerous. I'm sure that by now you have heard of what the humans call 'the stink.'"

"A repellent pheromone," Picard said.

"Exactly. Its effects are felt well beyond the range of the disrupters."

The security team in the old barracks exchanged alarmed glances at their supposed prisoner's bland announcement that her own body provided a potential weapon against them.

Paying no attention, Drraagh gazed at Picard. "You have people examining the base computers?" she asked. At his nod she said, "I can supply passwords for the medical sections. There may be some information on treating damage caused by disrupters."

"Good." Picard touched his communicator. "Mr. Data?"

"Data here."

Picard explained once again about Vossted. "Take note of these passwords," he ordered. "See what you can find in the computer about treating disrupter damage."

He nodded to Drraagh, and she warbled several phrases in Tseetsk.

"I will attempt to access the files immediately," the android said calmly. "Data out."

"You have a high regard for Vossted's well-being," Picard remarked to Drraagh, looking around the chilly, drab interior of the barracks.

"More than for most humans, you mean." Drraagh followed the captain's eyes around the squalid accommodations. "But then, I know Vossted better than I do the other thralls. I also believe he is more important than most."

Picard opened his mouth to speak, but Drraagh went on. "Captain, my name developed from the word *drraagh!*"

The vocable was similar to the regent's name, but it had more of an edge, like a rising squawk.

"It was the ancient warning cry of my phratry," Drraagh explained. "No, I am not being irrelevant. The tone and note of that cry, modulated downward, denotes 'warder.' To me, my name is more than a personal symbol; it means I am a guardian of my people. Although Vossted's name has no such meaning he, too, strives to be a guardian of his people."

She fixed Picard with an unwinking eye. "As I

said, Vossted taught me his language. He also discussed human culture with me. I was struck by a figure from your history, Benjamin Franklin. He lived centuries before Vossted's people fled your planet, but Vossted had a particular fascination with him. Do you know of Franklin, Captain?"

"An inventor and writer of our eighteenth century," Picard said. "He also discovered electricity, I believe?"

"Yes. He was also a diplomat for a very young nation trying to break away from an older, more sophisticated culture," Drraagh said. "The courts of Europe considered Americans little better than barbarians. Franklin charmed the ruling classes, teaching them the worth of his country and his countrymen."

Picard nodded. "As Vossted tried to do for humans on the Tseetsk home planet."

Drraagh looked hard at the captain. "That is no easy undertaking, and it is not often that a Franklin or a Vossted appears to meet the challenge. The humans need Vossted. And I believe my people need him, too."

"You face a serious challenge as well," Picard said. He stood, towering over the alien in her gaily hued plumage.

"You mean my personal safety?" Drraagh asked.

"I had hoped that Koban could bring order," Picard said shortly. "But if the overseers are now organizing—"

"Believe me, Captain, I have no desire to be rescued by the overseers." Drraagh made an abrupt gesture. "As a class, they are motivated by fear and greed. Their elimination is one of the things I fought for on the homeworld." Her downy hackles rose. "Though I sought only an end to their powers of cruelty, not their extermination."

"Still, you remain a symbol to them and to the rebels. I can't guarantee your safety here." He paused. "But I can offer you sanctuary aboard my ship."

Drraagh made a small gesture of negation. "We all must live with political realities. Koban put me in your custody as a gesture of good faith. However, I am sure he views me as a prime element in his long-range strategy. I am a hostage, Captain. And I believe relations between you humans would become strained if you were to make me disappear."

Picard nodded. "Much as I regret it, I believe you're right. But I do ask that you move into our research compound as soon as it's completed. It will be more comfortable than this place, at the least."

"As you wish."

Picard tapped his communicator. "Picard to *Enterprise*. One to beam up."

The small chamber housing the Tseetsk computer center was a hive of activity, with three instrument-wielding technicians in Starfleet uniforms crawling around the edges of the forcefield screen and four others pounding diligently on the keyboards of the patched-in terminals.

Commander Riker stepped into the room, shedding his parka gratefully. He'd just come from checking the progress of the construction team.

Things seemed to be going well enough up there, but they still had several hours of work ahead of them—as, obviously, did the team in this room.

Sighing tiredly, Riker rubbed the back of his neck. "Data, give me a progress report." He glanced at the android, who stood motionless before the blank black wall.

"I have been examining Tseetsk-language files. The human-made equipment interfaces with very little of the system," Data said, turning. "The slaves could access only a tiny percentage of the available processing space—just enough for simple calculations and record-keeping. This system has far greater capacity. Curiously it has gone unused not only by the humans but also by the Tseetsk."

"How do you know?" Riker demanded.

The android gave him a guileless look. "I asked."

"And it just . . . told you?"

"I take your meaning," Data said gravely. "Though this equipment is technically extremely advanced, the security programs appear to have been written by operators who were not fully conversant with the machines."

"You mean the work is shoddy," Riker said.

"It is haphazard. I believe this is true because, although it looks like a single unit, in fact the computer represents several systems salvaged from different locations, each with a separate plasma memory core."

Riker was startled. "You mean there's plasma contained behind that forcefield?"

Nodding, Data turned to the vast blank space

and began warbling Tseetsk phonemes. The wall went from blackness to an eye-tearingly quick montage of images and graphics, along with a high-pitched narration.

"Whew!" Riker exclaimed. "That was a dazzling light show. What does it mean?"

"As far as I can understand, what you just saw was an astrogation subroutine from a ship's computer, which was incorporated into this system."

"These people are way ahead of us in cybernetics."

"In shipbuilding as well," Data added. "The constants for the size and strength of the warp field indicate that the ship this computer navigated was five to seven times the size of the *Enterprise*."

"Five to seven—" Riker whistled. "Data, the more I hear about these people, the more they worry me. Tachyon missiles, giant starships, supercomputers. They should dominate this area of space, and we should have heard about them long ago."

"I suspect—" Data began.

Riker interrupted him, thinking aloud. "There are so many anomalies," he mused. "If they have all this high technology, why do they need slaves? Why patch an astrogation computer into a ground operation? It doesn't make sense."

"I think I have an explanation." Data's gentle voice seemed to get even softer. "It begins with what is apparently an unpurged memory file from the captain's log of the shipboard computer."

"Unpurged?" Riker echoed.

"Large sections of memory were deleted throughout the system. I discovered it while attempting to create a memory map. Most of the deletions occur in sections dealing with biology and science, but some history disappeared as well. We see the development of a group called the Sree-Tseetsk, the forebears of the present aliens. But there are also censored references to factions called the Joost, the Loor, and the Kraaxaa-Tseetsk. And there is this surviving history file."

Again he warbled a complicated command to the Tseetsk computer. His sallow unlined face showed no trace of effort as he created the liquid melody.

"You'd win the galactic bird-call competition hands down," the first officer remarked.

Riker's smile faded as a large Tseetsk face appeared on the wall, trilling in the warbled language.

"I have slowed down the speed on the file," Data said. "Apparently Tseetsk eyes have an extremely rapid optical-processing capacity."

While the voice-over went on, the scene changed to show a planet in space. Superimposed arrows suddenly appeared, pinpointing a bright flash. "Energy-weapon discharge!" Riker exclaimed. He could identify that much, even without knowing what weapons were being fired. "Ships must be intercepting something out there."

The scene unfolded, showing that the interception was futile. The computer eye zoomed in on three spaceships slashing at an angular, crater-pocked chunk of rock, which was moving with horrific speed toward the planet.

"That thing must be going at eighty percent of light-speed," Riker muttered.

The scene disappeared in haze as a spread of missiles was fired at the oncoming asteroid. Ghostly images appeared through a thin film of ionic haze on the screen. One missile struck the asteroid, but even that wasn't enough to stop it. The huge mass simply broke into several pieces, each still moving at that unnaturally high speed.

The on-screen ionic haze dissipated as the space debris spiraled around, glowing with hellish intensity. Even from space, effects could be seen on the ground below. Vegetation was seared away; the oceans roiled. The burning fragments made a full orbit while still in the planet's atmosphere, then traversed another three-quarters of the way around the globe. Their final collisions were catastrophic. Huge segments of the planet's temperate zone disappeared in enormous dust clouds as the asteroids plowed into the ground. The ship's scanners followed the trail of destruction around the planet, to its nightside.

Then Riker noticed the points of light, some spread out, some concentrated, all disappearing in haze or destruction. "Cities," he said hoarsely. "That planet was inhabited. *Heavily* inhabited."

"It might be less distressing to you if I increased the speed of the recording here," Data said. He sang more instructions to the computer, and the images on view accelerated, a high-speed view of planetary cataclysm. Riker made out one round of continental convulsions—oceans boiling out of their beds, flaming pinpoints, then sheets of volcanic action—before the whole planetary surface disappeared under roiling dust clouds.

A secondary explosion took place before the cloud cover cleared, as one of the orbiting starships plunged toward the planet's surface. The flare of matter-antimatter reactors cut even through the murk that surrounded the world.

"The commentary refers to that as an act of self-immolation," Data said. "It seems the crew of the ship came from that planet."

At least one of the remaining ships stayed in station over the ruined world, probing other wavelengths besides visible light.

"Please note this," Data said. "The captain of that one remaining ship recorded several schematics of the world's surface."

Appearing as ghostly images beneath the clouds of debris, pictures of the devastated world appeared. The oceans were gone, continents had changed shape, and a long trail of craters snaked across the face of the planet. Data sang a command, and the image halted on the screen.

Riker stared. "Wait a minute. That's the world we charted right before we came to Koorn."

"Correct. It was called Loor-sskaawra," Data said.

"Loor-sskaawra." Riker tried out the unfamiliar name.

"Yes. The prefix 'Loor' indicates that the planet was occupied by the Loor-Tseetsk clan. Apparently, the Loor and the Kraaxaa were allied against the Sree and the Joost. Between them, they succeeded in destroying a culture that had spread to fourteen worlds in nine solar systems."

Riker opened his mouth but could find nothing to say.

"Though four distinct dialects are referred to in these records," Data went on, "the only one used at any date after the cataclysm is Sree-Tseetsk, leading us to surmise that the Sree were the lone survivors."

"It's hard to believe any of them survived," Riker murmured. "When did all this happen?"

"Judging by the position of background stars in these images, Loor-sskaawra was destroyed 10,432 years ago," Data replied promptly. "From what I understood of the captain's narrative, the Joost-Tseetsk used something called a warp sling to send the asteroid into a collision trajectory."

"Let me be sure I understand: you're saying this salvaged computer has a memory file in it that's more than ten thousand years old," Riker said. "And according to that file, the Tseetsk are the ones who wrecked all the planets in this region."

"That seems to be what happened," Data said. "The evidence is admittedly sketchy, as this is the only record of its kind to be found in the entire computer system. There are a few references to war, though, and much about rebuilding."

"Vossted mentioned that their history is shrouded in taboos. Sounds as though the Tseetsk would be just as happy to forget this war," Riker remarked. "Does that make them peace-loving, or warlike?"

Riker thought for a moment. "Maybe this also

explains the odd gaps in their technology. The truly advanced components have actually been cannibalized from older machines, with the necessary interfaces just cobbled together by Tseetsk or human technicians." He frowned. "What does—"

"Sir," a technician called from one of the keyboards. Riker and Data went over.

"I don't know if this means anything," the young woman said eagerly. "I undeleted a file and found a map of the base that doesn't agree with the official one in the overseers' directory. Here it is, with the official map superimposed over it."

She tapped four keys. A tracery of red and green lines leaped into position on the screen. Riker scrutinized the map.

He recognized the green lines as belonging to the map he'd already seen. Most of the red lines followed the green exactly, but extra branches appeared in a few places, presumably to mark tunnels.

"Hmm. There's supposed to be a tunnel that goes from the flier bay up to the plain." With his finger, Riker traced the red route from the bay, past the punishment barracks and out onto the open tundra. "And another one here, from this storeroom to way out behind the base."

"The precise distance is seven hundred twenty-four meters," Data said equably.

"That's a long way to plow through frozen ground, even with a laser rig," Riker commented.

"Perhaps the tunnels in red were never dug," Data said. "When the map was updated, the old version was deleted."

Riker nodded. "Probably so." Seeing the disappointed look on the young technician's face, he patted her shoulder. "Nice work anyway."

"Sir!" another technician called. "Over here!"

As he crossed the room, Riker discreetly massaged a blossoming ache in his back. It had been a long day, and it looked as if it wasn't going to be over soon.

A day later, in a tunnel that didn't appear on any of the official maps from the overseers' files, Chu Edorlic ran a final inspection of his five handpicked warriors. The lithe man gave the squad a habitual frown, his eyes flicking over their equipment.

Two men—the best rock cutters in Koban's old gang—held out their laser drills. The fiber-optic lines were in perfect condition. Next Edorlic tested the rungs on the two assault ladders.

"Stay out of the way while the drillers cut the ceiling down," he growled at the ladder-bearers. "But I want those ladders up the second after the rock stops falling."

Chu turned to the final man in the group, and together they checked their nerve disrupters. "Remember, keep your weapon on the lowest setting, and use it only if you have to. We don't want to kill people. We're going for hostages."

"What about those disrupters of theirs?" a shaggy-haired driller asked.

"Phasers," Chu corrected him. "They don't pack half the punch of a disrupter. And besides, how will they see where to aim them after the kid releases the stink?"

"The stink." Every squad member's face tightened.

Edorlic clicked his tongue in disgust. "Come on, you've all been trained to beat it."

"To slow it down, maybe," the shaggy-haired laser driller muttered. "It still gets to you."

"We'll be in and out before the stink has a chance to get to us," Chu said impatiently. "If you're going to worry, worry about the starship people. They'll be getting the full force, without any protection." He glanced at the chronometer on his wrist. "Time to get ready. Grease up."

The men pulled out small jars, unsealed them, and started rubbing a greasy salve over all their exposed flesh. Edorlic smiled at the pungent smell. Redgrass oil. It came from a plant the Tseetsk called thweetra. It had been found on Foothold by the first human colonists, and on all the planets the chickens had sent them to terraform. Chewing redgrass was an antidote for Tseetsk pheromone.

Six months ago one of Koban's followers had discovered that redgrass, when reduced to an oily paste, provided limited protection from the spray. Since that discovery, the rebels had built up a supply of it in anticipation of action. Although, Edorlic thought ironically, this wasn't exactly the action they'd had in mind.

He worked the goo into his scalp, face, neck, and even his nostrils. Then he tied a mask impregnated with the oil over his lower face and pulled on a pair of gloves.

"Any minute now," he warned after another glance at his chronometer. "Get ready."

Chapter Nine

"QUITE A DIFFERENCE from the last time I was down here." Picard looked around in satisfaction. Gone was the ill-built punishment barracks whose walls had let in the icy wind the day before. In its place stood a secure prefab dome.

"Geordi, you did a terrific job," Riker agreed. The three men stood in the doorway of Geordi's on-site "office," a small domed hut made of the same material as the larger dome.

Geordi La Forge smiled. "Thanks. But my crew deserves the credit—my crew, and the rebels who helped us out. We couldn't have gotten this far without them. They're the ones who suggested the low dome construction, to keep the wind from getting a purchase. From what I hear, windstorms here can be unbelievable."

"Is the facility complete?" Picard asked.

"Not yet, but this dome is fully operational. We were supposed to be surrounded by four smaller outlying domes—sort of like interconnected igloos —again, for protection against the wind."

"And to restrict access." Picard nodded.

"Right. At this point, however, we've only gotten the main dome done. Luckily, this is where the labs and crew quarters are, so we were able to move the personnel in. Dr. Crusher has also set up a small clinic and dispensary in one area, though so far Koban's men haven't exactly been pouring in for treatment. They're a pretty macho group. I get the impression that they think going to the doctor is somehow unmanly, unless they're at death's door."

"I see." Picard shook his head slightly. The foibles of human pride. "Well, Number One, shall we have a look around?"

"Yes, sir."

Struck by a gloomy note in Riker's voice, Picard shot his first officer a sideways glance. Riker's expression had suddenly become clouded.

La Forge headed back to his work. "Something wrong?" Picard asked Riker quietly.

Riker started. "What? Oh, no, sir. I was just . . . thinking." His hand went to his beard in an automatic stroking gesture.

"About our macho group of rebels, perhaps?" Picard ventured. Taking Riker's lack of response for an affirmative, he went on, "I don't much like their general attitude, either. They're so steeped in hatred and bitterness that they may be very hard to deal with."

"Koban can handle his men," Riker said firmly.

"If he chooses to, Number One. If he chooses to. Don't let your understandable admiration for the man cloud your judgment. Koban hates as much as the others—more, perhaps." Picard touched his own cheek, thinking of Koban's scars. "I'm afraid his intransigence could seriously compromise our peace efforts."

"Assuming we get that far with the Tseetsk."

Picard frowned. Riker had a point, but it wasn't one that made the captain happy. In silence they went inside.

The dome was warm and well lit, with skylights to catch as much of the weak sunlight as possible. Riker led the way to a transparent partition behind which a team of biologists were running a battery of tests on Drraagh. The Tseetsk regent's attention, however, was focused on another corner of the room. Picard followed her gaze to where Beverly Crusher was talking with a boy.

"Aha, the young overseer-turned-rebel. He seems to have made an impression on Dr. Crusher," Picard said, watching her auburn head leaning close to the boy's dark one. "I wonder if it has anything to do with his rather marked resemblance to a certain young Starfleet cadet."

Riker's expression relaxed into a slight smile. "She has taken quite a shine to Lorens, hasn't she?"

Picard walked over to the pair, pushing back the hood of his parka as he did so. Catching the movement, Lorens Ben turned around. He stared at Picard with such lively curiosity that Picard finally asked, "Is there something unusual about me?"

"I thought maybe it was just the light when I saw you yesterday. I wasn't going to say anything." Lorens looked a little embarrassed. "But aren't you kind of . . . well, *old?*"

Picard stared down at the boy, momentarily speechless.

Crusher frowned at her young protégé. "Lorens! What kind of thing is that to say?" But she didn't, to Picard's mind, sound particularly outraged.

"I knew I should have kept my mouth shut," Lorens said, crestfallen. "But he looks older than Vossted, even, and he's *forty.*"

"Forty?" Riker whistled, eyes twinkling. "That's *old.*"

"I would have put Vossted at nearer sixty," Crusher muttered. "This environment ages people very quickly."

"Do you teach?" Lorens asked Picard.

"Teach?" Picard echoed, nonplussed.

"We do things a little differently, Lorens." Crusher turned to Picard. "The human children on Foothold are brought up communally," she explained, "by the older people—retirees, I suppose we would say."

"Indeed?" Picard finally managed. He cleared his throat. "Ah . . . if you have a moment, Doctor, I'd like you to attend while I get a report on the progress with Drraagh."

He went over to the alien while Crusher attempted to shoo Lorens Ben out of the lab. "You seem fascinated by the interaction between Dr. Crusher and the boy," Picard said to the regent.

"I have never before seen human young," the alien admitted. "They are raised on the colony planet—Foothold, the humans call it—in brood groups."

"A difficult upbringing, I should imagine," Picard said. "Being groomed for slavery by bitter old slaves."

"I am told it is the method that was used by the humans our explorer ship found long ago."

"From what I gather, the human colony was in a period of transition when your ship arrived. The measures in force then should not have been mistaken for normal practices," Picard said. "In most human societies, neither the young nor the aged are treated that way."

"I begin to believe so." Drraagh watched Crusher zip Lorens Ben into his new *Enterprise*-issue parka and then affectionately ruffle his hair as she sent him off. "Never had I expected a human to act so"—she searched for a word for a moment—"motherly."

"Dr. Crusher *is* a mother, which may have some effect on her relationship with the boy."

"Ah," Drraagh said, as Crusher came toward them, her face set in a studiously businesslike frown.

Riker had been speaking with the xenologist in charge of the biological research team, Dr. Iovino, a middle-aged woman with sharp features and a perpetual faint smirk on her lips. She nodded to the captain.

"It's been difficult to work under these conditions, but I believe we've made some progress," she said, punching up some data on a small computer.

"What conditions?" Riker queried.

"I don't mean to criticize, but you must understand that the *Enterprise* is not well staffed for a study of this sort." She waved a hand around the lab. "I mean, these people are not experts in xenobiology—though they're quite competent, I'm sure." Her tone suggested that she wasn't sure at all.

"Ah." Riker nodded gravely.

Iovino spun the monitor so that it was facing Picard. "Would you care to have a look at the data, Captain?"

Gazing at the columns of figures and notations on the screen, Picard was torn between irritation and amusement. Iovino was surely aware that no layman could know what they all referred to. "Summarize for me, Doctor, would you?" he asked coolly.

"Certainly." Picard thought he detected a slight, superior twist to her thin lips. "In terms of anatomy, the Tseetsk appear remarkably similar to certain of Earth's flightless birds. The strong, thick leg bones recall some smaller moas of New Zealand, whereas the body and wings—or, I should say, flippers—are almost sphenisciform."

"Sphenisciform?" Picard murmured.

"Like penguins," she explained with a half smile. "I would guess that the Tseetsk started out as shore-dwelling, swimming birds, probably in a climate somewhere between this"—she waved a hand toward the outside—"and what we consider temperate."

"Fascinating." Picard nodded.

She scrolled down to a new set of data. "Of course, on the molecular level everything changes. But as far as gross anatomy goes, there are only a few surprises, such as the presence of hands."

"And the brain's relative size, surely," Picard added. "Those two surprises are vital to Tseetsk cultural evolution."

"Quite so, Captain," she agreed with a touch of irritation. "Of course we haven't delved much into Tseetsk sociology yet. We're waiting for Commander Data to give us a report on what he's found in the computers. With luck, his material will help us develop a rounded picture of the Tseetsk. From what Drraagh has told us so far, they seem to have a fascinating culture, quite unlike that of the Aurelians."

"The Aurelians are also avian, aren't they, Dr. Iovino?" Riker asked.

The xenologist drew back as if Riker had just made a rude noise. After a moment she sniffed. "That's correct. The first avian race ever encountered by the Federation. I assumed you'd be familiar with Aurelian culture; a landmark study of it was completed four years ago."

A study in which Iovino had participated, Picard guessed. He and Crusher hid smiles as the xenologist raked Riker with a frosty gaze.

The outer door of the dome suddenly banged

open, admitting Counselor Troi along with a gust of blowing snow.

"Ah, Counselor," Picard called. "Good. Now we can begin our roundtable." He bowed slightly to Drraagh. "If you'd care to join us, we'd like to learn something about your people, and perhaps teach you something about ours."

"Captain." Dr. Iovino sounded piqued. "Surely the sociological cross-check is a matter for the experts—"

"Surely, Doctor," Picard agreed blandly. "And we look forward to your report on it, when it's ready. Now, if you'll excuse us, we're going to enjoy an informal exchange of cultures and let you get back to work."

Enjoying the flustered look that came over Iovino's face, he turned to go.

An hour later Riker was still marveling at Picard's finesse, not only in handling the prickly Dr. Iovino but also in moderating the roundtable discussion between the humans and the Tseetsk. It was having its own tense moments.

Drraagh was fascinated to learn about the lives of "free humans," as she called them. "I hope you do not find this personally offensive, but our exploration team initially believed they were dealing with a kind of hive mentality," she explained.

"What's a hive mentality?" piped up Lorens. The boy had just come in with a small notepad and a stylus, which he held out to Beverly Crusher. "Here. Neela wants you to okay this requisition."

Crusher gave him a smile as she initialed the form. "There. Now scoot. We're trying to have a meeting."

"Can I come back and listen?" Lorens asked. "I want to know what a hive mentality is."

"It's sort of a collective consciousness. Individual people are expendable, so long as the community as a whole is safe," Crusher explained, and Riker wondered at the warmth and indulgence in her voice.

Picard cleared his throat meaningfully. Crusher flushed. "All right, you've had your one question. Now go *on*, Lorens. Get going. Neela's waiting for you."

The beginnings of a rebellious frown appeared on the boy's face. "Can't I come back? I'll be quiet."

Crusher seemed to be trying to summon up the will to be stern.

Riker took pity on her. "Why not?" he said good-naturedly. "I tell you what, Lorens, we could use a few cups of coffee here. Would you bring us some?"

Lorens broke into a wide grin. "Sure, Commander Riker." He hurried away.

A good kid. Riker smiled after him.

Picard coughed. "If we could get back to the subject," he said pointedly. "You were saying, Drraagh, that your early explorers thought humans might have a hive mentality."

"Yes," the alien agreed. "The communal activities, especially child-rearing, the disregard for personal safety, and the apparent subordination of individuality to achieve common objectives all contributed to the notion."

"Selfless actions don't necessarily mean that people have no sense of self," Troi said gently.

"How could your scientists come to that conclusion?" Beverly Crusher asked. "An examination of the evidence—"

"You fail to understand," Drraagh said. "Our team expected to find nothing on Joost-klaara— the planet your people call Foothold. Not intelligent life, at any rate. Our people had never found non-Tseetsk sapient forms in our entire sphere of exploration.

"Thus, though no Tseetsk had been on Foothold for"—she suddenly ruffled her feathers—"for many years, our explorers were amazed and frightened to find the human colony. And they had no specialists on alien cultures to guide them."

Drraagh's orange eyes shifted from Crusher to the other humans. "Study of your people only alarmed our explorers further. First of all, males seemed to be dominant, and many of them were quite aggressive. Second, we learned that the humans had fled a catastrophic . . . war on their home planet. There was speculation in the humans' records that the rest of the race was . . . extinct."

"And this gave the Tseetsk the right to enslave the survivors?" Riker demanded.

"At first the explorers seriously considered . . . extirpating the colony," Drraagh said. "Several feared the humans were a mad, warlike race."

Picard nodded in thought. "Imagine if Earth's

first contact had been with the Romulans or the Borg."

"One of Earth's first contacts *was* with the Klingons," Riker pointed out heatedly. "Surely they qualified as a mad, warlike race at that time. Yet we never had any thoughts of 'extirpating' them."

"How was the dilemma resolved?" Picard asked Drraagh.

"The captain of the ship suggested that the humans might be a mad race, but that this shattered fragment could perhaps be integrated into Tseetsk society. Utilized."

"Some of the more dangerous human cultures tried such experiments," Picard said with some irony. "There was one that preached 'freedom through work' to imagined enemies while working to exterminate them."

Drraagh ruffled her feathers again. "When I hear that a human culture could consider extermination of its own sisters as an option, I begin to think my culture's response was understandable."

Riker bridled. "I begin to understand Koban's fear of genocide."

"Remember, then, that Koban speaks of genocide for *my* people," Drraagh retorted.

"Take it easy, Will," Beverly Crusher put in. "Drraagh isn't trying to defend Tseetsk policy. She's just explaining how it came about."

"Understood." Riker battled his growing frustration. "But let's not forget that one voice is not represented in this discussion. The rebels have a point of view as well, and it must be taken into account if we hope to succeed with our strategies for peace. Someone has to speak for them."

"I can understand how a team of explorers might make the cultural generalizations that you describe, Drraagh," Picard said, steering the conversation back to a less personal track. "But what about the rest of your people? How could they simply have used the humans for dangerous work without challenging those first impressions?"

"I imagine there was limited contact between humans and Tseetsk," Crusher said.

"That's true," Drraagh admitted. "By the second human generation there was only a single Tseetsk regent with each working group, and, as I've already indicated, it was not a position of honor."

"But you had contact with humans. With Vossted," Riker argued. "Why didn't—"

He was interrupted as Beverly Crusher turned. "Lorens!"

Glancing over, Riker saw Lorens Ben framed in the compartment entrance. The boy was wearing his parka, but his hands were empty. "Hey, where's our coffee?" Riker asked him, smiling.

"Oh, I forgot!" Lorens reached the table, his eyes bright. He thrust his hands into his coat pockets.

Then madness attacked.

Riker caught a whiff of acrid, musky odor, and the room suddenly went out of focus. The stink! He whirled toward Drraagh, who seemed very close, then abruptly receded. The alien seemed as disoriented as Riker himself felt.

Riker tried to slap his communicator, missed on

his first try, and shouted for Security, warning of Drraagh's attempted escape. He hoped his words were coherent. In the background he heard running footsteps, then cries of distress.

Reeling, he stumbled after Drraagh, trying to catch hold of her. She was huddled on the floor, much as she had been when he'd first seen her. However, the effects of the Tseetsk pheromone did not intensify when he came closer, as they had the first time.

An elbow caught him in the side, upsetting his perilous balance and sending him to the floor. Riker turned to see the captain moving drunkenly toward Drraagh as well. His hand also clutched at his communicator and his lips moved, but Riker couldn't make out his words.

Something stumbled across him, and Riker realized it was Lorens Ben. White foam bubbled on the child's lips. Dead weight struck Riker, and something heavy and hard hit him in the chest. A new wave of giddiness passed over him.

Other forms writhed on the floor. He recognized Troi on hands and knees, crouched as if resisting a terrible weight. Beverly Crusher was in a fetal ball. The biologists from the science stations were equally helpless.

Then a roar drowned everything out. A lambent spear of light rose from the floor. To Riker's distorted senses it seemed to flicker and twist. Is that how noise looks? he asked himself. Or is that roar the sound of light?

He tried to groan. Instead, his brain's command

seemed to be misdirected to his left hand, which flopped and clenched like a fish on dry land. He stared at it in consternation until his beleaguered mind decided that it had had enough, thank you— and efficiently shut itself down.

Chapter Ten

"Ooннн . . ." Riker struggled to raise his head, but someone seemed to have weighted it down with about a hundred kilos of feathers. Rank-smelling feathers that stung where they touched his skin.

"Coh'ander. Coh'ander!" A soft, trilling voice with a strange accent kept insinuating itself in his ear. He wished it would leave him alone. All he wanted to do was sleep—sleep for a hundred years. . . .

"Coh'ander Rah-ker, ooake!"

Ooake? He forced his eyes open.

A drifting haze obscured his vision. Riker frowned and squinted. Was there a fire somewhere?

Something dark loomed over him. Two enormous orange eyes peered down into his face, and a small hand waved a vial of something sweetly pungent under his nostrils. A few droplets fell on his cheeks.

Riker twitched irritably. He was about to push whoever it was away, but then he noticed that wherever the drops touched his skin, they made the stinging subside. He relaxed and drew in a deep breath. As he did so, the world came back into focus.

The dark blur overhead resolved into the soft, round face of the regent Drraagh. She was disheveled, with a patch of bare, yellow skin where some feathers had apparently been torn from her neck ruff. "Coh'ander Rah-ker," she fluted urgently. "Are you ah-ooake?"

Her translator was missing, Riker realized suddenly. That was why she sounded so odd. He hiked himself up onto his elbows, wincing at the throbbing ache in his temples. "Yes, I'm awake," he said. He gazed around the dome. Bodies in *Enterprise* uniforms were sprawled on the floor. "My God, what happened?"

"They are unconsciousss, not . . . dead. It ooas the ssstink," Drraagh informed him.

"The stink? You mean your pheromone?" Riker stared at Drraagh, aghast. "I don't understand."

She bobbed her head several times in dismay. "It ooas not I, no. The sla'he did it. Ko'an's lieutenant, the one whoo hates I sso. I do not know how."

"Koban's lieutenant. Chu Edorlic?"

"Yess."

"But how? Why?" Riker scowled. If only his

head would stop buzzing! "And why wouldn't it affect Edorlic just as much as it did the rest of us?"

Drraagh held up the vial she had waved under his nose a moment ago. Now that his vision had cleared, Riker saw that it was filled with a reddish jelly. "Thiss wass 'orgotten. In Tseetsk, it iss called thweetra. Iss a—what iss the word? It holds the stink ah-ooay. Edorlic and hiss hel'ers wore it on their sskin."

"An antidote," Riker guessed. "What were they doing?" He glanced at her again, taking in the bare patch on her neck. "Are you all right?"

"I am ooell. He tore ah-ooay the transslator, iss all. Rah-ker." Drraagh's unwinking eyes caught and held his own. "They took your ca'tain and Troi."

"*What?* Where?" Suddenly Riker forgot the pain in his head. He grasped Drraagh's wing, feeling slender bird-bones under the feathers. "Tell me!"

Agitated, she twisted away. "They oocnt through there," she twittered, pointing at the floor next to the left wall. "I know nothing else."

Riker saw a dark, gaping hole in the plastic flooring under one of the worktables. A tunnel! He slapped at his communicator pin.

It wasn't there.

"Damn!" He struggled to his feet, cursing the sick weakness that made his knees shake, and stumbled over to the nearest body.

It was Dr. Crusher. She lay facedown, arms flung out as if she were embracing the earth. When he rolled her over, she moaned. A small, ragged hole at the breast of her uniform showed where her communicator had been ripped away.

"Oh, hell." Riker held out his hand to Drraagh. "Give me that antidote," he commanded.

Drraagh scooped a little of the viscous stuff into his palm. "I ooill attend to otherss," she suggested.

"Fine." Riker dabbed a drop of the salve under Crusher's nose. "Come on, Doctor," he muttered. "I need your help."

After a moment her eyes fluttered open. "Wha—"

He gripped her shoulders. "Beverly, it's Will Riker. I need to contact the ship, but our communicators have been taken. Is there any other communications equipment in this dome?"

"Huh?" she said in a syrupy whisper. "Quipment?"

"Communications equipment!" He resisted the urge to shake her. "I need to contact the *Enterprise.*"

Crusher's brow furrowed. "Use y' communicator."

"Physician, heal thyself," Riker muttered. "It's clear you won't be healing anyone else in the near future."

He stood up again, noting gratefully that strength was returning to his legs. His head still throbbed damnably, though. The salve seemed to have its limits.

Around him, men and women moaned as they began to revive. "Let's see." Riker's eyes flicked over the lab. All communicators gone. His eyes went to the computers, all data-linked to the *Enterprise*'s systems in orbit above.

"Computer!" He cleared his throat. "This is Riker, William T."

"Identity acknowledged," the machine's melodious voice responded.

"Message to main computers, security station. Koorn compound attacked. Communications out. Send security team, medical aid."

"Acknowledged."

Drraagh looked up from Lorens Ben's still form. "You are signaling your ooessel?"

"And I hope we get a quick response." He strode over to Drraagh. "Are they reviving?"

"Thiss one iss not ooaking yet," she chirped, fluttering one of her tiny wings over Lorens. "The others iss all ooell."

Riker knelt by the boy's side. Lorens's face was pasty, and his breath came in shallow gasps. Dried foam flecked the corners of his lips. "He looks bad," the first officer said worriedly. Poor Lorens, so eager to be included. Already Riker was regretting the impulse to let the boy stay.

"Commander! Wha—what's going on?"

He looked up into the dazed eyes of Beverly Crusher. "Why is the lab a shambles? These people need help!" She managed a few wobbly steps, then stopped, her face pale. Taking in Lorens Ben's ominous stillness, she dropped to her knees. "What happened to him?" she cried.

Riker put a gentle hand on her shoulder. "Take it easy, Doctor," he began.

She shuddered away from his touch. "Take it easy?" she said shrilly. "This child is clearly near death, and you want me to take it easy? I've got to get him to sickbay." She fumbled for her communicator, then noticed that it wasn't in place. "Medkit!" She swayed to her feet, gripping the work station to remain erect.

"Doctor," Riker said. "I'm sure he's all right. The pheromone isn't fatal." He turned to Draagh for confirmation.

The regent hunched her head into her shoulders. After a pause, she said softly, "It hass caused . . . ill things in others. He iss slight of stature."

Crusher's face went dead white. "Exactly what happened to him?"

"We were attacked, Doctor," Riker explained in as neutral a voice as he could muster. "A gang of rebels broke in here. They had apparently managed to bottle the Tseetsk repellent pheromone somehow, and they dosed us all with it." He felt the tension knot tighten in his stomach as he added, "Captain Picard and Counselor Troi have been kidnapped. The rebels also took our communicators, so we all seem to be stranded down here, at least for the moment."

A murmur of shock from behind told him that the rest of the lab crew had regained full consciousness.

"Sir!" Someone tugged at his elbow. Riker stood up and turned around.

A shaft of shimmering blue arced down in the middle of the domed room. Dancing motes coa-

lesced into the huge, decidedly solid figure of
Lieutenant Worf. He crouched in the full alert
position, phaser drawn, mouth twisted into a scowl
of concentration.

"Worf!" Riker strode toward him. "You got my
message."

"Yes, sir. I decided it would be best to reconnoi-
ter in person."

"Thank God for your suspicious mind," Riker
said with heartfelt warmth. "Contact the ship. Tell
them to beam everyone in this room directly to
sickbay. I'll explain when we get there."

Worf nodded once, tapped his communicator,
and issued the order. An instant later Riker found
himself in the *Enterprise*'s sickbay. Beverly Crusher
hurried over to grab a medical tricorder in her
trembling hands.

"Drraagh, do what you can to help him." Riker
gestured to Lorens.

He beckoned to Worf. The two of them left
sickbay at a near-run. "The rebels have turned
against us," Riker explained as they went. "They've
kidnapped the captain and Troi; their present location is unknown. I suspect their communicators
have been removed, so there'll be nothing for our
sensors to lock on to, but check anyway."

Worf growled low in his throat. "Those animals!
Sir, I recommend I lead a security party down. We
can search the base for the hostages."

"Agreed. We have to try it," Riker said. "Though
I doubt Koban will have hidden them anywhere so
accessible. He's no fool. I'm sure he's the one who

figured out the link between the communicators and the transporter." He ground a fist into his palm. "I should never have been so open with him."

Worf didn't comment. He said merely, "Permission to leave immediately, sir."

"Go. And—good hunting." Riker stepped into a turbolift and said, "Bridge."

Moments later the lift doors swished open on the bridge. Riker strode forward. "Open a channel to the rebel base," he said to the security officer on duty. "I want a word with our friend Koban."

"Hey, what's going on?" Geordi La Forge asked from the engineering console.

Riker explained in a terse voice, ignoring the gasps from the bridge crew. "I want you to scan for the captain and Deanna in any way you can think of," he ordered Geordi. He looked at the science console officer. "You, too. And you, Data." He aimed a finger at the android, who had relinquished the captain's chair for Ops when Riker entered.

"Sir, I can't establish contact with Koorn," the security officer reported.

Riker frowned. "I thought we'd set up a two-way relay with the rebels."

"We did," the woman concurred. "Complete with visuals. But it doesn't work when they don't answer our signal."

"I see." Riker tugged worriedly at his beard. Why weren't the rebels standing by, waiting for the *Enterprise* to begin negotiations for the hostages?

Was Koban simply playing hard to get? Or had Worf's search party been discovered?

"Contact Lieutenant Worf," he rapped out.

Below the surface of Koorn, a security team made its way along the tunnel the kidnappers had taken. Worf took the lead, his Klingon eyes piercing the dimness. Unwilling to provide a target for possible ambushers, he'd ordered that no lights be used.

A moment later his decision was shown to be justified. At the point where he'd estimated the tunnel would rejoin the mapped part of the complex, six brown-clad figures milled around. "A rear guard," Worf said quietly to his people. "We'll have to go through them. Phasers out."

The security team caught most of the rebel guards standing silhouetted against the light of the occupied tunnels. Four men dropped, stunned. A fifth dove to the floor of the tunnel, firing one of the Tseetsk nerve disrupters. For an instant the dark tunnel filled with the garish blue glare of disrupter bolts. Caught without cover, the *Enterprise* team threw themselves against the walls. Worf hurled himself forward firing blast after phaser blast until a cry ahead told him he'd hit the sniper.

When they reached the lighted tunnel, however, the sixth man was gone.

"Sounding the alarm, most likely," Worf said, calling up a map of the complex on his tricorder. "This tunnel leads to the western gate of the base, which is also the flier bay." He started down the tunnel. "That will be our objective."

The security team moved fast in the wider, lit tunnels of the base proper. They traveled in the diamond-shaped pattern they adopted when traversing hostile terrain: point, flankers, and a rear guard.

Except for one abortive attack from an intersecting passage, though, the Koorn rebels didn't try to stop them. Just beyond the last turn before the flier bay, Worf saw why. Crates, old machinery, even canisters of supplies donated by the *Enterprise* had been erected into a barricade. Behind the makeshift wall was a body of men armed with everything from disrupters to ice chisels. Ironically, most of them wore parkas from the *Enterprise*'s replicators.

Worf growled. "A frontal assault will make us vulnerable, but we must get through." He divided his people into a covering-fire party and an attack group.

It was right after their first attempt had failed that Worf's communicator twittered to life.

"Worf here," he responded instantly. "Sir, we have engaged a party of rebels near the western exit. No sign yet of the captain or the counselor."

"Proceed with extreme caution, Lieutenant," Riker said. "Remember, their lives are in the hands of the people you're fighting."

"Acknowledged. Worf out."

So it had come to out-and-out fighting. Riker could only hope the rebels would be pragmatic enough not to retaliate by harming the captain or Deanna.

He twisted around in the chair and addressed the

officer at the science console, a meek-faced ensign named Tho. "Any trace of them?"

Tho seemed to sink a little deeper into his seat. "Negative, sir," he quavered. "The captain and Counselor Troi appear not to be inside the rebel base. I fed their medical profiles into my search program and tried scanning for their unique characteristics." His mouth twitched nervously. "But I've come up blank."

"Good thinking, Tho."

The ensign's wan face brightened a bit at the praise. Riker turned to Data.

"Anything?"

"No, sir. I am running circular sweeps in an expanding radius around the base, but I have detected nothing unusual so far." The android cocked his sleek head. "I fear the turbulent weather conditions on Koorn's surface may be obscuring any clues to our colleagues' whereabouts."

"I'm coming up dry, too," Geordi piped up.

There was a soft hiss as the bridge turbolift doors slid open again. To Riker's surprise, Drraagh stepped onto the aft platform.

Every head on the bridge turned, and a dozen pairs of eyes stared. The avian alien bobbed her head in a repetitive pattern. She was clearly ill at ease, but Riker wasn't sure whether her new surroundings unnerved her or something specific had happened to upset her.

Suppressing a sigh at this added distraction, Riker rose from his seat. "Regent! What can I do for you?"

"I-I was in the way among the sick ones. I came to see if I could be of any service to you, Commander." Drraagh's speech was smooth and unaccented; she had been fitted with a new translator.

Riker's blue eyes narrowed as an idea occurred to him. "Perhaps you can," he said thoughtfully. "You know Koorn as well as anyone. Tell me: if you were a kidnapper on Koorn and you wanted to take your hostages somewhere where they wouldn't be found, but where both they and you could hide out in tolerable safety, where would you go?"

"To the Rift," the alien replied promptly. "That huge asteroid-impact scar. You must have seen it on your scans of the planet. It runs from southeast to northwest, and it is nearly three thousand of your kilometers long."

"On screen," Riker commanded. The forward viewscreen was suddenly filled with white. Angling across the center of the picture was a jagged, sharply shadowed mountain range of lunar starkness.

Drraagh's voice was reflective. "Yes, I think that would be the best place to hide. The Rift valleys offer some protection from the worst of the weather. Also, the whole area is riddled with underground caves—Koorn used to be a mining planet. The workers had barely begun to explore them all."

"Get on to it, people," Riker ordered. "Sweep the area for life forms of the proper mass." He looked at Drraagh. "I take it Koorn does not support any large native fauna?"

She hesitated.

"Regent?" Riker prompted with a sinking feeling.

"I believe not," Drraagh replied at length. "There were some reports, but . . ." She trailed off.

"But what?"

Drraagh preened her breast plumage with stubby-fingered hands. "I am certain there was no truth in them," she said. "Every so often men would disappear from the job site. Some of their fellows claimed to have seen large white animals near the places where the men had disappeared. A few overseers even claimed to have . . . shot these creatures, but bodies were never found. I am sure it was only a trick of the senses. The blizzards on Koorn are horrific. When one is cold and frightened, it is easy to imagine all sorts of monsters."

"Mmm. Well, let's hope that's all it was," Riker said. He strode over to Ops. "How about it, Data?"

The android looked up at him. "Curious, sir," he said. "My sensors detect no life forms at all. They show only what appears to be an extremely turbulent river." He glanced down at the panel. "It corresponds to the dimensions of the Rift."

"What?"

"Skip it," Geordi advised from behind them. "Data's readings are all screwed up; so are mine. Something's playing tricks on our scanners. I think it's some sort of weird mineral deposit. Could be a remnant of the asteroid that hit, or something plowed up by the impact."

"Can you filter it out?" Riker asked impatiently.

"I'm working on it." Geordi spread his hands in a frustrated gesture. "So far it's no go."

The first officer sucked in a long breath. "Launch shuttlecraft. Data, estimate how far a Tseetsk flier could have gone. That will give us a search zone to work in."

The crew got busy, and Riker sat back in silence, trying to plan the next move. If the kidnappers had caves to disappear into, the search might have to proceed on foot.

He stared at the desolation that filled the screen, and the chill seemed to seep from it into his very marrow. Picard and Deanna were there somewhere, in ten thousand square kilometers of hell.

And it was up to him to figure out a way to find them.

Chapter Eleven

BEVERLY CRUSHER pushed a lock of red hair out of her face. Her deep blue eyes under the arched brows were weary as she looked around the sickbay ward. The room was unusually full. "This mission has been far too good for business," she muttered.

In addition to the young Jeremy in post-op, there was an ever-popular appendectomy, the security man with the minor head wound, and Martinez, the man recovering from a nerve disrupter blast. Now three more beds were filled by lab personnel still suffering from the effects of the Tseetsk pheromone.

In the bed by the far wall lay Vossted. He was a constant source of worry to Crusher. She had repaired the overseer's blasted neurons, and he should have been on the road to recovery by now.

But instead he lay in the grip of a deep depression. He was awake at the moment, staring at the ceiling with dull eyes. But most of the time he drifted in a dark hinterland of nightmares.

Not even Vossted worried her so much as the patient who lay before her now, though. Dr. Selar joined her at the foot of the bed to look at the diagnostic boards.

"The outlook is poor," Selar admitted.

Crusher bit her lip and smoothed the pale brow of the child who lay on the recovery table.

"Among other things," Selar went on, "the pheromone seems to cause neurons in the brain to misfire. The boy's were firing at random for several minutes, until Drraagh administered the antidote."

Crusher jammed her hands into the pockets of her blue smock, nodding.

"There was extensive damage. Many of his neural pathways were altered, the cells themselves were damaged, and several crucial minutes elapsed before he was brought here."

Tears welled up and threatened to spill down Crusher's cheeks. "He's young," she murmured. "Maybe his resiliency—"

"In terms of brain development, twelve is not young. His neural pathways are largely established. Doctor, you know it will take more than youthful resiliency to bring him through successfully." Selar's dark eyes looked steadily at her superior.

Crusher sighed. Through all her years as a doctor, she'd never managed to develop fully the armor of detachment that would allow her to view her patients more as problems than as people. Selar encountered medical disasters and attacked them logically. Beverly was always stricken by the pain of the victims and the grief of those who loved them.

She felt it even more keenly with this boy, who had in a short time, inexplicably, become dear to her. As he lay unconscious, his dark hair and pale, fine-boned face once again reminded her strongly of her own son at a younger age. But now he was more to her than just a shade of Wesley Crusher. Now he was Lorens Ben.

Selar pointed to the monitors above the boy's head. "We already performed emergency surgery to remove several blood clots."

"I know." Three hours of surgery, Crusher added silently. Three muscle-kinking, fatigue-building hours of ceaseless concentration and tedious manipulation of the molecular scalpel. In the aftermath of the pheromone attack, Crusher had not been up to surgery. She could only hover like some ghost on the periphery of action as the other doctors worked.

"His systems have stabilized," Selar pointed out.

"Yes. I don't think he'll die," Crusher agreed. "The question is, how far can he recover?"

Selar's calm eyes met hers again with almost a hint of surprise. "We cannot even theorize until the child regains consciousness."

"Why him?" Crusher suddenly burst out. "Why is he the one to suffer so badly? It doesn't make sense."

Selar called up a file. "Our tests show that, for

some reason, Lorens received a more concentrated dose of the pheromone than anyone else, perhaps because of his position in the room or his relatively low body weight."

Crusher put a hand over her eyes, mentally reliving the attack for a moment. If only it could have been averted. But how? Who was there to blame? Certainly we had no reason to suspect the rebels would turn on us after we'd established friendly relations with them. Will Riker is agonizing over that problem right now. Poor Will. What we both need is the services of a good counselor, someone like . . .

Her throat constricted as she thought of Deanna Troi, somewhere on Koorn in the hands of those brutal, brutalized men. And Jean-Luc, too. Where were they now? Were they all right?

Taking a deep breath, Crusher picked up the diagnostic wand and ran it lightly down Lorens's body. "I think it's safe to begin neural scanning now," she said, amazing herself with the steadiness of her own voice. She swung the bridgelike device into position over the boy's head and clamped it down. "We'll begin with medullar traces, at the lowest setting."

A dry, strong hand—Dr. Selar's hand—took hold of her wrist. "Doctor, you sound as if you intend to undertake the scan yourself."

"Why not?" Crusher wanted to know. The probe was a noninvasive procedure, sending a low-energy pulse through the neuron strings of the brain to detect anomalous connections, connections harmed by the pheromone. It would give them a clear picture of Lorens Ben's neural damage—and she was perfectly capable of running it.

"You worked down on the planet for hours, and then you were exposed to a psychoactive pheromone," Selar pointed out. "In spite of your evident fatigue and illness, you refuse to rest. Now you wish to start working again, on a patient who is, by your own admission, special to you." Selar raised an arched Vulcan eyebrow. "Is this logical? Would you allow any other doctor to operate in those circumstances?"

Crusher stared, her lips quivering with a retort. Then she sighed. Selar was blunt, but she was also correct. "Will you take over the procedure?" she asked evenly.

Just then the door to sickbay slid open and Drraagh came in. "Hello, Dr. Crusher. I hope I am not disturbing you." She paused. "I wanted—I wanted to see Vossted."

"Of course. You're welcome, Regent," Crusher replied, glad for the interruption. As she led Drraagh to Vossted's bed, she glanced curiously down at the avian alien.

Drraagh's green ruff was bristling, and she kept uttering soft, cooing noises, which the translator did not seem to recognize as language. Though Crusher knew nothing about the alien's psychology, it struck her that Drraagh was rattled. "Is something wrong?" she ventured.

Drraagh turned huge orange eyes on her. "Vossted is dear to me," she said. "He is like

Tseetsk. Precious. I am afraid to see what has become of him."

Crusher halted, puzzled. "He hasn't been disfigured in any way, if that's what you mean," she said.

"You misunderstand. I am not speaking of the injuries to his body. I mean the ones to his spirit. He has seen the face of . . ."

"Of death," Crusher finished for her.

"Yes. Death." Drraagh said the word in fluting English. Then she went back to Tseetsk. "Your word for it is so brief, so inconsequential. But what happened to Vossted is obscene! And at the hands of a fellow human!"

Having begun to speak, Drraagh seemed unable to stop. "We Tseetsk have much stronger societal proscriptions against violence than you humans do. We dislike even to think about it. It is all bound up in our ancient racial preservation imperative. Any Tseetsk who knowingly harms another Tseetsk is . . ." She hesitated, searching for the word. "I cannot really describe it."

Crusher nodded. "I remember Vossted telling us that the homicide rate on Tseetsk-Home is vanishingly small." She smiled crookedly. "Seems to me we could take some lessons from your people."

"Indeed we could," another voice broke in.

Crusher and Drraagh turned toward the source. It was Vossted. He turned his head on the pillow and gazed at the alien.

"Drraagh," he said. For a moment a smile of pure pleasure chased the melancholy from his eyes.

With a trilling sound, Drraagh hurried to his bedside, pushing the translator away with stubby fingers. She warbled something in Tseetsk, and he responded with a series of chirps.

Crusher smiled. Drraagh seemed to have forgotten her fears. And Vossted was speaking more than a monosyllable for the first time since he'd regained consciousness.

Suddenly there was a peculiar choking noise from across the room. It came from Dr. Akihiko, who'd been quietly absorbed in analyzing the rebels' version of the Tseetsk pheromone. He was doubled over at the chem station, coughing and clutching at his wounded shoulder.

"Akihiko, are you all right?" Crusher started toward him.

Slowly he straightened up. "I think you'd better have a look at what I just found," he said hoarsely. "And maybe Security should see, too."

Intrigued, Crusher strode over. "Show me."

Akihiko's round, pleasant face was troubled. He held up a child's-size gray parka with a fur-lined hood. "Do you recognize this coat, Doctor?"

"It's Lorens's," Crusher said, surprised. "Why?"

"I just wanted to be sure. Look at this." He held open the coat's left pocket.

Nestled into the lining were two squat canisters with tapering nozzles. Crusher leaned down for a closer look, and was rewarded with a whiff of something acrid that made her lungs burn and her eyes sting. "It smells like the pheromone—" Suddenly shocked comprehension flashed through her. As if against her will, her head turned slowly toward the bed where Lorens lay. There was a grim silence.

At last Selar said, "Now we know how he received the heaviest dose."

"My God," Vossted exclaimed softly.

Crusher's lips felt curiously stiff as she forced the words out. "This means Lorens was working with the kidnappers. He carried the synthetic pheromone on him, in those canisters. That's how it got into the lab."

"And that's why he was so severely affected," Akihiko put in. "He was standing in the middle of a cloud of the stuff." An uncharacteristic scowl darkened his face. "Those bastards could have given him the antidote before they sent him in."

"Perhaps he *was* given the antidote," Drraagh spoke up. "I found the vial of thweetra salve not far from the child's outstretched hand. It could be that he had it in his hand, but in his excitement he neglected to put it on. He is young."

"He looked so excited when he came in," Crusher said hollowly. "I thought it was because he liked being around—"

She broke off, squeezing her eyes shut. "I can understand," she whispered. "He *is* only a child, after all, caught up in the greatness of the moment. The rebels are romantic, inspiring figures. Perhaps he didn't fully understand what he was doing, what was at stake."

She fell silent, her thoughts going once again to Wesley. If he'd been in this boy's shoes, would he have done what Lorens did?

Vossted abruptly sat up in bed. "Whether or not Lorens Ben understood what he was doing, you may rest assured that at least one person did understand—full well. One person knew the boy worshiped him and used that admiration to make him commit a crime, placing the child's life in deadly peril." His large eyes were full of a new hardness as he swung his legs down to the floor.

"I'm going to see Commander Riker," he said. "It's time I took a stand."

First Officer's Log: Supplemental. Our lab reports that the substance used in the kidnapping was actually a close synthetic approximation of the Tseetsk repellent pheromone. Apparently the rebels have chemical production capabilities of which we were not made aware.

The whereabouts of Captain Picard and Counselor Troi are still unknown. Lieutenant Worf's team was unable to complete a search of the Koorn base, as they encountered rebel fire while engaged in the mission. Crewman First Class Olivier Previn was wounded in the exchange of fire; our team subsequently withdrew, on my orders.

I am increasingly certain that the regent Drraagh is correct; they have been taken to the asteroid track known as the Rift. All attempts to contact the rebels and open negotiations have thus far met with failure.

Commander Riker paused, massaging the bridge of his nose with his thumb and forefinger. *Failure.* The word was beginning to loom depressingly large in his personal vocabulary. But he couldn't allow himself the luxury of self-pity at the moment. There was too much at stake.

"Sir, I'm getting a response from Koorn," the officer at the security station reported suddenly.

Riker closed out his log entry and sat up straighter in the captain's chair. He wanted to appear as assured as possible for the confrontation with Koban; he knew instinctively that the rebel leader would sense and despise any uncertainty in an adversary.

Next to him, Vossted sat in the chair that was normally Riker's. The first officer stole a glance at the overseer's stony profile. Since he'd heard the news about Lorens, Vossted had seemed to become a new man. Gone was the air of melancholy irony; grim purpose now radiated from that slight figure. For all his shaggy gray hair and hollow cheeks, at this moment Vossted looked every inch the leader he'd always claimed he wasn't.

"Hailing channel open, sir," the security officer said.

"Put it on visual."

In an instant the screen filled with Koban's ravaged visage, larger than life. Riker gazed at those piercing blue eyes, the expanse of scarred flesh. How strange, Riker thought. He had a hero's face yesterday. Now it's the face of a dangerous fanatic.

Irrelevant. Riker pressed his fingers against the arms of his chair and spoke. "Koban. You have violated our trust by the forcible abduction of two members of this ship's crew. Return Captain Picard and Counselor Troi to us immediately and unconditionally. If you fail to comply with this demand, be sure that we will take swift measures."

What measures? he asked himself in disgust. He's got us and he knows it.

Koban's voice rang into the bridge. I'm sorry that I cannot comply with your request, Commander Riker," he said courteously.

Riker clenched his fists. Damn it, the bastard actually sounded sincere!

"The hostages are at present unharmed," Koban went on, "despite the fact that members of your security force attacked and wounded several of my men. Please take note that I will not tolerate another such attack." He paused, and his gaze moved slightly to Riker's right. "Vossted! I'm pleased to see you well," he said with what seemed like genuine pleasure.

"I wish I could say the same." Though Vossted's voice was soft, it carried the sting of a lash.

Koban recoiled visibly.

"Are you aware," Vossted continued, "that Lorens Ben is at this moment lying in a hospital bed, poisoned with a massive overdose of the stink, and that he may never recover? And that you have done this to him?"

"Lorens?" Koban's jaw dropped. "But how is that possible? He had the redgrass oil."

"No one bothered to make sure he used it," Vossted shot back. "Koban, what have you become? What kind of monster sends a child to his death?"

A flush colored the undamaged side of Koban's face and mottled the scar tissue. "I did not send the boy to his death! You know I like Lorens. He volunteered for this mission. And—and we gave him the oil."

"Tell that to his mother and father. Oh, I forgot —his father is dead," Vossted mocked. "You killed him, didn't you?"

Koban's blue eyes flamed. "We are fighting for the greatest of all causes! I thought the boy faced little enough danger. But when sacrifices must be made, then some whom we love will die. We can't let *anything* sway us from our goal." He leaned forward, speaking rapidly at the monitor. "This is war, Vossted. Realize that."

"You don't use children to wage war," Vossted said with flat certainty. "Koban, I thought you had great potential. But if you believe that your holy cause justifies the death of a child, then there is truly no hope for you, and I will do everything in my power to stop you." In silence he stood up, turned his back on the broad screen, and left the bridge.

Koban's larger-than-life jaw worked with strong emotion as he directed his gaze back at Riker. "The boy," he said. "Is he really as bad as Vossted says?"

Riker was silent.

Koban leaned toward the screen, realized what he was doing, and pulled himself back. "Perhaps we should continue with business." His voice shook ever so slightly.

Riker jerked his head toward the door through which Vossted had just exited. "He's right, you know. Koban, can't you see that what you're doing has become wrong?"

"Enough!" the rebel leader suddenly shouted. "I'm not here to justify my actions to you. The chance for that is gone. Now all I require is that you listen to my terms."

"What do you want of us?" Riker asked, though he already knew the answer.

"That question is disingenuous, but I'll answer anyway." Koban sounded more in control now. "As you well know, we believe that the ch—the Tseetsk race is an abomination and a menace to humanity. As yet, the menace is contained on a single planet, but this will not be so for much longer. With the power of your starship, though, we could eradicate the evil before it spreads."

"You're talking about genocide," Riker replied. "The death of an entire race. Think carefully, Koban. Are you really ready to take on that responsibility?"

"The choice is made." Koban said it with stark simplicity. "The Tseetsk must die.

"I said that the hostages are as yet unharmed," he went on after a moment. "I hope they will remain so, as I would hate to have to hurt them, especially the woman. However, rest assured that I shall take whatever measures I deem necessary to secure your cooperation." He glanced at his chronometer. "You have twenty hours to surrender command of your ship."

"What happens after that?" Riker demanded.

Koban just smiled. "Twenty hours," he repeated. "Don't be late."

Chapter Twelve

JEAN-LUC PICARD sucked in a deep breath, trying desperately to find something real, something to hold on to amid the awful welter of distorted information threatening to overpower his mind. He found his sensory anchor in a low, droning hum, a mantra of reality among the strange gibbering he seemed to hear, the disturbing sights he seemed to see.

He didn't know how much time passed before the phantasms began to clear. I wonder what Dr. Crusher will make of that Tseetsk pheromone, he thought, finally opening his eyes.

He found himself face down on a worn metal deck. At first he didn't take that fact in; he merely felt happy that the plating didn't bubble, twist, or spiral as other objects had in his pheromone-inspired hallucinations. Finally, however, he realized that worn metal had no place in the *Enterprise*'s new base camp. And that droning hum remained in his ears.

Only when he tried to push himself up did he discover that his hands were somehow trapped at his sides. Hunching on the floor, he looked down to find a strip of roughly woven material around his thighs—a leg cuff, with a smaller cuff for his wrist attached on the outside. The inside seams of the leg cuffs were also joined. *Even if I got to my feet, I could barely walk,* Picard thought. *Elegant.*

Somewhere nearby he heard a woman moan. Picard twisted around, trying to locate the source, and found himself looking into Deanna Troi's eyes—eyes that were open and large with fright. "C-Captain," she whispered.

"So, you're back with us, are you?" Chu Edorlic's voice sounded almost cheerful as he came over to join them. "I can imagine that you have lots of questions. Even a brief brush with chicken stink leaves things a bit fuzzy."

"Chicken stink," Picard repeated. "Tseetsk pheromone. Why would Drraagh—"

"This was our own home brew," Chu assured him. "Effective enough, I'm sure you'll agree. Now for the 'Where am I?' that is bound to crop up. You're aboard a flier, heading for . . . well, let's just call it a safe place."

Chu knelt to check Picard's bonds. "As for the 'Why?' Well, let's just say you've been called to the service of the revolution, like it or not."

"You mean we're hostages?" Troi asked.

"Koban would rather think of you as guests who'll help bring your starship in line with our goals."

"Do all of Koban's guests wear fetters?" Picard inquired tartly.

"I just gave you Koban's words." Chu Edorlic stared down at them, his dark eyes glittering slits. "We could perhaps spin some pleasant fantasy that your bonds are in place to keep you from being hurt." He tested Troi's bindings, as professional as a doctor examining a wound.

"But we should face facts, I think. You are prisoners; hostages for the action of your ship—you, Captain, for obvious reasons, and the counselor because Koban thought a female hostage might have greater effect, considering the way you hid your women away from us. Not that you should worry about that," he said hurriedly. "Counselor Troi will be treated with respect. Better than you, Captain."

Edorlic pointed to Picard's chest. The captain looked down and saw that his communicator was missing—obviously torn off, along with a shred of cloth from his uniform. He glanced at Troi. Her communicator was gone, too, but her clothes were unharmed.

Picard wormed himself around for a better look at his surroundings. The flier had obviously been built to accommodate Tseetsk. Its low ceiling left Chu Edorlic slightly crouched. Five more men sat in the main compartment, in seats too low to be comfortable, their knees up too high. A sixth man sat in a small cockpit at the far end of the compartment, his eyes on a control panel. The eyes of the others were on Deanna Troi.

She shuddered.

Chu Edorlic's gaze went from Troi to the other men, who abruptly found other sights to interest them. He glanced back at the prisoners. "You're hostages, yes. Important hostages. My orders are to let no harm come to you. And I assure you, as long as you give us no problems, nothing will happen." His eyes went again to the rest of his team, and he raised his voice. *"Nothing."*

As Edorlic went forward to glare at his men, Picard turned to Troi. "Are you all right, Counselor?"

She managed a shaky nod. "Physically, I'm fine. But mentally—you can't conceive it, Captain. It's like—" She twitched, and Picard saw another rebel's eyes on her. "You can't conceive it," Troi repeated, her voice low.

"And Chu Edorlic?" Picard whispered.

"His words are sincere, as far as they go."

Picard tried to force himself up. "You see him as a . . . personal threat?"

"Not in the way you mean, Captain," Troi said. "His initial reaction is to a female, but that is damped down by his realization that I'm somehow alien. A fr-freak." She stumbled over the last word, then looked Picard in the eyes. "The problem is not his reaction to me but his response to this situation. Chu Edorlic is a fanatic, Captain. He'll follow Koban's orders. But if a choice arises between Koban and what Edorlic conceives as the Cause—"

"The divergence could be fatal for us," Picard murmured. "Understood, Counselor."

All the more reason to escape, he thought. But we can't even begin to plan until we know where we are.

"Mr. Edorlic," he called. "Where do you think you can go without being traced by the *Enterprise?* Do you think your flier can outrun our tracking beams?"

"You must excuse the clumsiness of our technology, Captain Picard," Edorlic said. "We can't pop ourselves neatly from place to place." He glanced at his chronometer. "But we'll be leaving this machine behind soon in favor of a healthful walking tour of the Great Rift."

At Picard's reaction, Chu Edorlic smiled. "I expect your scanners will have as much trouble down there as our instruments have. It's impossible to get a comprehensible reading in the Rift. The late lamented Vossted theorized that there may have been some strange heavy metals in the asteroid that crashed here. Or maybe they welled up from the planet's core in the shake-ups after the crash. Or maybe it's just the lovely Koorn weather . . ." He pulled a pair of ragged parkas out from under the seats. "Speaking of which, we'd better get you prepared for the outside."

"You could at least have brought the new warm gear we gave you," Picard said.

"Ah, but we don't know what kind of communicators or other gadgets you might have sewn into those garments, do we? These old coats may not be the best quality, but at least we know what we're getting."

Soon Picard had even more reason for his grim appreciation of his slave restraints. While one man covered Picard with a nerve disrupter, Edorlic undid the right-hand cuff and told Picard to shrug halfway into his parka. Even while changing clothing, the rebels could keep their captives virtually helpless.

Another rebel picked up a parka for Troi and approached her. Chu Edorlic drove the man back with a single glare.

Then he gave the captain a long look. "Of course there is an easier way. Easier for you, without your hands and legs tied. Less dangerous, too. If you'll promise no nonsense on the trip."

Picard and Troi exchanged a long look. "You have our word," Picard said. For the duration of the trip, he added silently.

"Camp One ahead," the flicr pilot called out.

Edorlic freed Picard and Troi from the restraint devices. "Our first stop," he said, "is a geothermal tap, the first of six that were sunk to start warming the climate on this ice ball." He gave them a crooked smile. "They're easier to dig in the Rift, since its surface is that much closer to the planet's core. Still, we've lost thirty men on the work down here."

He led the prisoners toward the cockpit, where they could see their destination. The weather was moderate by Koorn standards—just snow scud blowing off drifts, and a leaden sky overhead. To the right was a towering wall of rock. Glancing up, Picard couldn't even tell where it ended. Its upper reaches were hidden in the blowing mist, like a mountaintop obscured by cloud.

But it was no mountaintop, he guessed. It was merely one side of the enormous scar that had been torn across the face of the planet millennia ago. How wide was the canyon? he wondered. He couldn't see the far wall.

Once, perhaps, heat and compression had left sheer cliffs of rock. Ten thousand years, however, had weathered the walls. Cracks had appeared, sections dropped off, ledges formed.

The drone inside the flier went up a note as the pilot veered toward a wide ledge jutting out from the rock wall. Picard could see that the rough stone had been planed smooth and freed of ice to create a landing zone. Against the cliff wall, shelters rose, clinging to the rock. What looked like a mine adit had also been cut into the wall—the opening for the thermal tap, Picard imagined.

As the flier came in for a landing, the rebels shrugged into their parkas, sealed them, and began shouldering bags of supplies. Picard noticed one of the men slinging a heavy boxlike carrier over one shoulder. Communications gear, he realized. Perhaps if he could get ahold of that, they could end this foolishness.

He also noticed that Edorlic and another man were checking their nerve disrupters while the others hefted pick handles and other makeshift weapons.

"Don't worry, Captain," Chu Edorlic said as he

caught Picard's expression. "These aren't meant for you or the counselor. I think I mentioned that we've lost thirty men in the Rift. Those deaths were not all due to accidents. Some of the men were found mangled. There's animal life on Koorn, although we don't know much about it; the chickens didn't come here to explore, just to change things. Judging from the way we've found some of our people jammed into clefts of rock, though, we think we may be dealing with a large carnivore, one that stores its food."

The pilot set the flier down with a perceptible thump, and the omnipresent background hum died away. "This is our first night's shelter," Chu Edorlic announced. "We've been building up supplies here since before the rebellion, intending to use this place as a bolt-hole if necessary."

"I should think base camps would be the first place the overseers would look," Picard said.

Edorlic gave him a tight smile. "This camp isn't our final destination. You'll see."

One of the rebels threw open the flier's hatch, letting in a blast of frigid air.

"I don't know why they needed our parole," Troi muttered as she huddled into her parka. "We'd have to be more than idiotic to run off without knowing where we were going in a place like this."

"Indeed." Picard felt as if tiny icicles were attacking each pore on his face as he pulled up his parka hood. He lowered the face mask, squinting. "The question is, where *are* we going out there?"

Edorlic took the point position, his disrupter out as he emerged from the flier. "Tarbin!" he barked, glancing back at the pilot. "You were the last one to visit here?"

"That's right," Tarbin answered.

"Did you leave the door open on the central shelter?"

Tarbin's eyes widened in shock. "Not me!"

The rebels suddenly jerked into action, charging out of the flier in a rough skirmish line. Edorlic and the other man with the disrupter took the ends, covering the whole area. Three others came forward, their improvised weapons at the ready. The pilot, Tarbin, stayed behind to guard the cockpit from the prisoners. He held a pick handle angled across his chest and glared at them suspiciously.

Through the cockpit behind the guard, Picard saw the rebels burst through the doorway of the largest shelter. A moment later they came back out and began searching the other structures.

Finally Edorlic returned to the flier. "It appears your logic was correct, Captain Picard," he said grimly. "Not only would this camp be the first place overseers would check for fleeing rebels, but it would also be the first spot they'd run to *escape* rebels."

"I don't sense any human presence," Troi said.

"No, I don't think you'd detect dead men." Edorlic gave the crags above them a careful scrutiny. "The door was smashed in, the men killed, equipment battered to pieces, supplies stolen or destroyed, and the shelters . . . fouled."

His lips twisted as he turned back to them. "I don't suppose you wish to see the work of the local life-forms? You couldn't get a psychic spoor off them or something?"

Silently Deanna Troi shook her head.

The rebels gathered outside the flier, their hands gripping their weapons fiercely.

This excursion had suddenly become much more a matter of life and death, Picard realized, observing the tense, pale faces.

"This place is useless to us now," Edorlic told his followers. "But we can still stick to our plan, with a little modification. If we push on, we should be able to make it to the caves before dark." He looked at the supply bags the rebels had retrieved from the shelters. They made a depressingly small pile on the deck. "We'll certainly be carrying less than we'd expected. Tarbin!"

The pilot stepped forward.

"There should be some more emergency rations aboard the flier. Add them to our stores, along with anything else you think might be useful. Then we'll push the flier over . . . Let's see . . ." He trailed off, gazing around him.

"We know where to push it, Chu. Those—those whatever-they-ares did the same with the overseers' flier."

Chu Edorlic was very quiet as he stared at the rebel who'd spoken. "What do you mean?" he finally said.

"The overseers must have landed their flier about where ours is. But now it's down in the gorge below, half covered with snow."

"I see." Edorlic's lids came down to hood his

deep-set eyes as he nodded. "Yes. You'll know exactly where to push it, then. Get going."

Soon Troi and Picard stood shivering as the group gathered by the cliff face. "We'll set off in single file along this ledge," Chu Edorlic said. "You two will be in the center of the line. You won't be carrying anything." He gave them an ironic smile. "Not because we fear you'd try to run off with valuable supplies, but just so you won't be burdened. We'll be moving fast. I hope that transporter of yours hasn't withered your legs away."

"She has good enough legs," one of the men muttered.

Edorlic rounded on his men. "We don't have enough trouble, do we? The next man I hear talking like that goes out as advance scout. He can look for female companionship from the ice creatures—a nice ice bitch, maybe?"

He started off, setting a demanding pace as they negotiated the icy, winding cliff ledge. Sometimes it was wide enough to accommodate them all walking abreast. At other points the ledge narrowed so that they had to pass singly, their backs to the cliff wall.

Even when we stop, there's no rest, Picard thought as he waited his turn to negotiate one of the trickier passages. In these damned rags, as soon as we stop moving, the cold begins to freeze us numb.

Finally Edorlic reached a metal spike set in the rock. "Rope!" he called. "This is where we climb down to the ledge below."

"Where are we going?" Troi asked the man behind her.

His bony cheeks turned almost as red as his sharp

nose. "The hot caves. There's a volcano or something down there, so it always stays warm."

"Fendager!" Chu's voice came sharply from the head of the line. "Did someone appoint you information officer?"

Fendager nervously shifted his pack and stepped back.

They skidded down the rock face, then marched along another ledge, this one with a perceptible downward incline. By following a series of barely noticeable signs, Chu Edorlic led them to the floor of the Rift. A sparse forest of stunted needle trees showed dark green against the white ground.

Life has the most amazing capacity to weather even the unfriendliest of environs, Picard thought with a momentary lift of spirits.

But the rigor of their pace soon made him forget his pleasure in the trees. After marching along the boulder-studded base of the cliffs, Edorlic led them up again.

"A good brisk climb, a little more ledge-crawling, then we'll cross the crevasse and we're almost home." He glanced back at Picard. "I hope you can handle a rope bridge, Captain. It's the only way across."

The struggle upward wasn't merely a battle against gravity. The wind picked up, as if determined to dash them to the rocks below. And the task of testing hand- and footholds with nearly numb extremities was a daunting challenge. To add to their difficulties, the light began to fade even earlier than usual, since they were in the shadow of the Rift walls.

Dimness turned an already arduous climb into a nightmare. The uncertain light played tricks on even the experienced climbers in the party. Did that dark smudge above signify a toehold that would bear the weight of a human body? Or was it merely a shadow?

Picard reached for one such hold and found an insufficient grip for his tired fingers. His hand slipped away, and for a terrifying moment, he swung, scrabbling, supported by a barely adequate pair of finger- and toeholds. For what felt like forever he slid downward until his free foot found purchase. He clung to the rock, gasping, the cold air feeling like razors in his lungs.

"Captain!" Troi called from her place below him. "Are you all right?"

Jean-Luc Picard forced the icy cold grip of fear from his throat. "For the present, Counselor. For the present."

Moments later they reached a ledge. It was not their destination, Chu Edorlic explained, but a resting point before they continued the climb.

"I saw your balancing performance on our last ascent, Captain Picard. You and Counselor Troi are too valuable to us to allow any more such cliff-hanging."

He turned to the rebel who'd spoken to Troi earlier on the march. "Fendager! You're a good climber. Rope yourself to the captain."

As the two connected themselves, the other men all glanced at Troi.

"Dream on, brothers," Edorlic told them, tying a

length of rope around his waist. "The counselor climbs with me."

He glanced at Picard as he handed the other end of the rope to Troi. "It's not a case of rank's privileges, Captain, if that's what you think. I've got no taste for aliens. I just want to make sure none of these idiots forget themselves."

Troi's pinched face grew a shade paler.

Chu Edorlic checked the lines. "If you fall now, you'll have someone to belay you. And if *we* fall, well . . ." He simply shrugged his shoulders.

The next leg of the trip went more easily, partly because they had climbed out of the shadow, and partly because each of them had the confidence that came from being attached to a fellow climber. Chu Edorlic led the way along another twisting, undulating ledge. By the time he called the next halt, it was nearly dark.

Picard could not have cared less. He suspected he'd used his last reserves of energy a good mile or so back. A stumbling body fell against his back, nearly sending him into a sprawl. Picard fought for balance as he turned, his numb hands clumsily striving to keep Deanna Troi upright. Behind her mask, the counselor's dark eyes, usually so expressive, were glazed with fatigue.

As he helped her along, Picard had to marvel at how the rebels could have discovered the caves they were heading for. As he and Deanna seemed to prove, the gang-issue parkas he and the others wore were woefully inadequate for long-distance travel.

What courage must it have taken to explore for

escape routes when the very attempt could have proved fatal? he wondered. The rebels had no dearth of bravery, despite their other shortcomings.

"I'd like you and the counselor to rope up again." Edorlic handed them lengths of line. "The going gets a little difficult from here on, and I want to be ready."

Picard could see what Edorlic meant as he peered into the deepening dusk. The ledge broke away from the cliff wall, inclining downward in a sequence of broken rock slabs, culminating in a crazily tilting rock pinnacle that leaned toward another, more solid rock shelf. In between was thin air, a gorge whose bottom was already lost in darkness.

Taking a deep breath at the sight of the proposed route, Picard tied the rope around his bruised, tired body.

"Cheer up, Captain." Edorlic had an ironic smile for Picard's expression. "After we're past this, it's a short stroll to the caves." He glanced at the two of them. "I expect you'll be too tired to try to escape tonight."

Somehow Picard and Troi kept up as they set off on the last leg of the journey. The captain didn't know if Edorlic had slowed his pace because of them or because his attack on the rock face was made cautious by the lack of light.

At last they reached the pinnacle, where more metal spikes had been driven into the ground.

"All right, Fendager, you've swung over before," Chu said.

Picard's climbing partner disengaged the rope from around his waist and took a new length of line. After winding one end of it around one of the spikes, he swung out across the gorge and landed on the farther shelf of rock. There he tied his end of the rope to another spike.

Picard stared through a haze of fatigue. Did they expect him and Deanna to do a tightrope act? Certainly they couldn't cross that drop hand over hand. Then he saw Edorlic kneel and attach one end of a new length of line to yet another spike. Chu threw the free end of the second rope over to Fendager, who attached it to a belaying pin on the other side. Two ropes now stretched across the chasm, one about a meter and a half above the other.

"We now have a bridge," Chu announced to the team. "The bottom rope's for your feet; the top one is for you to hold on to. Tarbin, tie yourself to the captain. Welken, you'll go first. Then Tarbin with Picard, Troi with me, then Gord, and last Kalik." He clapped the last man on the shoulder. "Be careful with that communicator. We all want to know when to come home."

Picard had crossed similar bridges in his training days at the Academy. Of course that was more years ago than he liked to think, and never after so punishing a cross-country climb and hike. He could barely feel the rope, although he was sure he was clinging to it as he tiredly shuffled his feet along.

"You're doing fine, Captain," Tarbin muttered, a tone of admiration in his voice. "I never thought you'd make it halfway up the first cliff at your age."

Praise or not, Picard all but collapsed once they were on solid rock again. He huddled on the ground, watching Troi's nerve-gnawing progress. Finally she and Edorlic were across. That left the last two of the team, both young rebels. Gord made his way quickly, and finally Kalik, the communications man, started across.

He made it halfway before he suddenly stiffened, a hand going to his chest. Then he tumbled down in the darkness.

"Kalik!" Tarbin shouted.

Could it be? Picard asked himself. Or was it a trick of the light? In the instant before Kalik fell, Jean-Luc Picard could have sworn he saw a two-foot shaft suddenly appear in the man's chest.

Chapter Thirteen

SELAR'S LEAN FACE was as impassive as ever. Only a slight squint in the eyes and a tightness of the lips conveyed the tiredness Beverly Crusher knew the Vulcan must feel. For the last two hours Selar and a medical team had been trying to create a map of Lorens Ben's brain, following barely detectable charges down neuron paths.

It would have been a hopeless job without the sickbay's medical scanners and computer equipment. But this was not a task that could be left to machines alone. It required judgment to identify the anomalous pathways, the mental circuits that had been switched around by exposure to the Tseetsk pheromone—judgment that Beverly Crusher had to admit was beyond her right now.

She'd been right to allow Selar to take over while she merely observed from a quiet corner of sickbay.

The procedure hadn't been all exploratory. Crusher had watched as Selar repaired various parts of the boy's autonomic nervous system to restore the original pathways for his breathing and heartbeat. It was brain surgery of the most demanding order. No wonder Selar looked tired.

Even so, Crusher knew that only the most basic functions had been repaired. Lorens would be kept unconscious under a stasis field—better for him, and the medical staff, not to experience the effects of the scrambled circuits of his conscious mind.

Selar turned the med console over to another doctor to continue the neural charting process and headed for her office. Crusher joined her.

"Doctor," Selar said resignedly, "I thought you had gone to get some rest, as I advised you to, hours ago."

"I had to see how the procedure would go," Crusher replied.

Selar sank into her seat, as much of an admission of fatigue as she would ever make. "The prognosis remains uncertain. The boy is no longer on life support, and I do not expect a fatal result. How well he recovers . . ."

Crusher shook her head. "I know. We're dealing with a brain. It's not like troubleshooting computer circuits. It's more like tracing a single strand of spaghetti through a bowl, without disturbing either the bowl or its contents."

"You knew that hours ago, Doctor," Selar said

with unexpected gentleness. "You do the boy no good in your present state, and you do only harm to yourself." She paused for a second. "Besides, we may have need of your skills soon."

Selar was as logical as ever, Beverly thought. And worse, she was right.

"All right, Doctor," she said. "But let me know when the team finishes—and get some rest yourself."

All too soon Beverly was awakened by a computer page: "Doctor, we've finished tracing Lorens Ben's neural paths."

Getting groggily to her feet, she said, "Thank you, Akihiko. What percentage of pathways were defective?"

"Not counting the ones already repaired, about thirty percent."

Crusher sighed. "We face a long job yet," she said.

Even with computer assistance, the work was tedious and exacting. Crusher knew she was still unready to take over, so she opted to play a supervisory role while Selar and Akihiko did the hands-on work.

Four hours later she blinked back pain from a pounding headache, unwilling to distract herself from the monitoring boards long enough to get some relief. It's worse for the others, she thought, watching Akihiko and Selar finish the ticklish surgery. I don't have a microscalpel in my hand.

"I think that concludes the procedure," Dr. Akihiko finally said, releasing a puff of breath. He straightened up, rubbing his lower back. He had subtly worked himself into a cramped position as he worked the microprobe console.

"We have rerouted every anomalous pathway that we discovered," Selar agreed. "There are likely to be more, but locating them would require the patient's conscious assistance."

"I agree," Crusher said. "Terminate the stasis field, and we'll wait for Lorens to come around naturally. Med-tech, inform me when he regains consciousness." Crusher headed for her office. She wanted to be alone.

Updating medical records was desultory work, a welcome way to fill the time before Lorens Ben rejoined the land of the aware. She hoped the hours of painstaking treatment would pay off, and the transition would not be as awful as the boy's last conscious moments. The microneural surgery should at least have reduced his terrifying sensory synesthesia. Perhaps now . . .

When Beverly Crusher realized that an entire report had crawled down the screen of her computer without her even reading it, she knew that her mind was going to stay with the action in the main part of sickbay. After closing out the file, she headed back outside.

"Doctor! I was just about to call you!" the med-tech said. "The readings say he's coming around."

On the bed Lorens Ben began stirring, a moan bubbling from his throat.

Crusher moved to monitor his progress. The boy's eyes fluttered open; then he stared at the medical equipment surrounding him with incomprehension. When he saw Crusher, his eyes went wide. "Wh-where am I?" A slight tic tugged at his cheek, and his arms and legs quivered in apparently uncontrollable spasms as he looked around. "This . . . I— I—" His voice dissolved into a gurgle.

At Crusher's call, four med-techs rushed over. Together they worked frantically to stabilize the boy's condition. "Neural scanner!" Crusher snapped.

By now Selar and Akihiko were well practiced in scanning the boy's nerve pathways and restoring them. For Lorens, however, it was a new and terrifying experience. It was up to Beverly Crusher to calm him.

"Lorens, listen to me. It's Dr. Beverly. Everything will be all right. Just try to keep calm. We can fix this." As the staff cleared more and more misfiring circuits, the shuddering grew less pronounced, Lorens's face less terrified. He stared at Crusher as if she were the only anchor in a mad world.

She remembered the onset of the pheromone attack. To awaken and still find everything so twisted . . . Fear made Lorens seem even younger. Perversely, it heightened his resemblance to Wesley.

"What . . . happened?" His speech was slurred, but his voice no longer sounded as if it had come from the bottom of a bubbling pit. With the increase in clarity, his voice also conveyed more emotion.

Crusher detected the edge of raw fear. What could she tell him about what had happened to him? "You were exposed to a . . . chemical . . . in the air. It had some unexpected side effects."

Lorens's face suddenly became a rictus mask as muscles pulled in opposite directions. His control was so fragile that anything could upset it.

At last, pale, he regained enough control to look around the sickbay. "S-so bad," he managed. "Wh-why . . . alone?"

"Why are you alone here?" Crusher guessed his meaning. She glanced at the empty beds. "The other people who were exposed have gotten over it. You were too close, and got a concentrated dose." She hesitated, then went on. "We know why, too. We found the canisters in your parka." Better to get the story out of the boy. Letting Worf attempt the interrogation would be a complete disaster.

Lorens's lips went into an involuntary snarl as his arms and legs jerked spastically again. "F-f-found—"

"Yes. We also found a vial of something that might have been a protective antidote."

Agitation shook the boy so violently that Beverly considered restoring stasis. "Forgot!" His eyes jerked to his quivering limbs. "No wonder . . . so bad! Told me . . ."

"Who told you?" Crusher stared into the boy's eyes.

Lorens Ben turned his head away.

"You should have been protected, Lorens," Crusher went on. "You're only a boy. Who made you do this?"

For a brief second she saw the ghost of the cocky grin he'd worn when she first met him.

"Volunteered!" he said. Then the tremors reinvaded his facial muscles. "Koban. Secret weapon . . . beat your science." Lorens sucked in a deep gasping breath. "Needed . . . get into base." Painfully he raised a shaky hand to his chest. "Needed *me!*"

"But what about us?" Beverly Crusher tamped down her shock to pose the question in a quiet voice.

"Needed," he repeated. But he couldn't meet her eyes.

"Ah, the brave hero." Vossted joined them. "I hope I'm not intruding, Dr. Crusher, but I asked one of your people to inform me when this boy awoke."

"Traitor!" Lorens shouted at him, his face distorted.

"But you, I suppose, have struck a great blow for our people." Vossted shook his head. "Koban deserves to lead such fools."

"Volunteered!" Lorens raged.

"You mean the great Koban asked you, and you fell all over yourself in your eagerness to take on the duty. Tell me, did your fine and caring leader bother to tell you just how dangerous the contents of those canisters were? Were you strongly warned to put on that protective salve? Did he insist on that?" Vossted leaned over the bed, bringing his face closer to the boy. "Because Koban surely knew what would happen to someone who was exposed to too much of the stink. It ruins nerves—turns people defective. That's what the great and glorious Koban sent you off to."

Lorens sank back. "D-defective?" he whispered.

"Defective? What does that mean to you?" Crusher had inferred that the word had special significance here.

"Unlike your culture, ours does not tolerate long-term medical problems," Vossted said.

"It's over now! Koban—"

"Koban let you volunteer to carry and release a container of chemicals that attack people's nerves," Vossted cut in coldly. "What kind of medicine does he have to treat that kind of damage?"

"Th-they gave me cream," Lorens continued doggedly.

"The redgrass salve." Vossted turned to Crusher. "Doctor, did you look into that?"

"We analyzed it, as a possible treatment for Lorens's condition," Crusher admitted. She took a deep breath. "In my opinion, it wouldn't have protected him adequately against the dose he got."

"So, my young friend, Koban sent you off on a mission that he knew would leave you mad or crippled. Not exactly the clean death a hero expects, hmm? You're lying there able to understand what I'm saying only because of the efforts of the people you attacked."

Lorens Ben's form seemed to shrink on the bed as he mulled over Vossted's words.

"War needs s-sacrifices," the boy finally said.

"Koban had no right to sacrifice your life!" Vossted thundered. "At the very least he should have warned you. But he was more interested in getting the canisters inside our friends' base."

Lorens didn't answer. His eyes blinked closed, but not before Crusher saw in them the shine of anguished tears.

"I'm sorry I had to do that," Vossted said to Crusher, stepping back. "But I needed to put it to him in terms that he could grasp."

"I understand," Crusher said in an undertone. "The problem is, you've left him with nothing to believe in."

Lorens's face was as tight as a clenched fist. A tic appeared at the corner of his mouth, leading up his cheek.

Selar stepped forward. "Scanning cannot go forward if the patient remains disturbed." She motioned both Crusher and Vossted away from the bed.

As they left sickbay, Crusher stared back at the small, still figure. There were wounds here that she couldn't treat with a molecular scalpel. Would they ever heal?

Huddled on the surface of Koorn, Jean-Luc Picard watched the man with the communicator topple from the rope bridge into the dark gorge below. There goes our only link with Koban, he realized. Whatever the plan was, it's well and truly wrecked now.

It was a measure of his weariness that in spite of these thoughts he did nothing.

"Captain!" Troi scuttled over to him on her hands and knees. "You're not safe there."

She knocked him sprawling as something whistled through the spot where his head had been an instant before. The missile shattered on the rock beyond. Picard stared. It was a crude wooden arrow.

"They're armed," Fendager gasped. "The ice creatures have weapons!"

"That much is obvious, idiot. Get down!" snapped Chu.

"Come on, Captain!" Troi half tugged, half guided him into the shelter of some fallen rocks.

The snarling whine of disrupter discharges rang out, as Edorlic and one of his men returned fire. They were at a severe disadvantage, though; only two out of the six rebels had weapons with any range, and even that range was severely limited.

As Picard peered out through a cleft in the rocks, he saw a silvery gray shape, amorphous against the background of dusk and rock, dash forward. Chu Edorlic must have seen it, too. His disrupter snarled, and the creature fell back with a weird, fluting cry.

"I winged one, I think," he said. "Tarbin, do you want to finish him off?"

The pilot, slapping his pick handle eagerly into his palm, stepped forward to join the battle. A moment later he was on his back screaming, impaled by two arrows. More hidden archers seemed to zero in on the noise, and a flight of shafts whistled through the air. Abruptly Tarbin stopped screaming.

"I guess he wised up and shut up," one of the trapped rebels muttered.

"He's no wiser," Edorlic said. "He's dead."

"We have to make sure!" another man cried. "If he needs saving—"

"We're too late for that!" Edorlic cut him off. He looked over to Troi. "Are you getting anything from him, Counselor?"

Deanna knelt behind a boulder, her forehead resting against the rock. "At first I felt fear, pain. Now there's nothing. I think you're right," she told Chu.

"I'd rather be out of here than right," Edorlic growled. "If we hang around, we'll all end up like skewered beef."

"We should head back for the shelters," one of the men said.

Ah, the problem with rebel movements, Picard thought, is that when trouble begins, people think they're in a democracy.

But Chu Edorlic wasn't about to call for a vote. "Right," he said, his voice dripping with sarcasm. "All we have to do is cross the rope bridge again, right under the ice creatures' fire. Or maybe you forgot what happened to Kalik?"

"But we can't stay here," another voice called out of the darkness.

"So we go in the one direction they might not expect us to take. Straight ahead," Edorlic rapped. "The warm caves are our only hope for shelter, not only from the night and the cold but also from these . . . whatevers. But we've got to do it right, in staggered rushes while Welken and I cover. Understood?"

After a moment the men grunted their assent.

"All right. Pick your cover, and when I call your name, dash for it, head down. And don't try anything fancy. You saw what happened to Tarbin when he tried to play hero."

Edorlic glanced toward Picard and Troi. "The prisoners will move together, with Fendager shepherding them." He gave Picard a hard look. "Don't think about running off, Captain. We know that whatever is shooting at us doesn't like humans. I wouldn't risk my life in the belief that the creature can distinguish between human factions."

He called to his fellow shooter. "Ready now, Welken. All right. Rekking!"

The man who'd suggested retreating broke from cover and dashed for the protection of another boulder.

"Prisoners!" called Edorlic.

Picard pulled his legs up under him. "That leaning outcrop should hide us all," he said. Then, his compact frame bent almost double, he leaped into the open. An arrow shattered on the boulder he'd just left, followed by the snarl of a nerve disrupter. He paid little attention, running a zigzag course for the cover he'd chosen. Behind him he heard a wordless cry as Troi followed his example, pursued by the pounding feet of Fendager. They reached the outcrop and threw themselves behind it as a rain of arrows spattered on rock. The disrupters firing in reply sounded pitifully inadequate.

Gord, the next rebel to run, was out of luck. He'd almost reached cover when he fell, an arrow in his eye. Chu made it to safety, but disaster struck again when Welken made his run. A storm of arrows hit him before he'd taken three steps from concealment. He dropped, mortally wounded.

Rekking, the nearest to him, tried to backtrack and pick up the fallen rebel's disrupter. He joined Welken in death as the unknown enemy concentrated its fire again.

"Got to keep moving." Edorlic snapped off a shot, but the invisibility of the archers prevented him from taking serious aim. "Judging by where the arrows came from, I'd say most of them are on the slope above us. There's another group blocking the path down the ledge.

"I'm going ahead to clear the way," he went on, grimly checking his disrupter. "The rest of you follow in ten seconds. All I can say is keep your head down, and if you have a patron deity, pray to it."

He set off, disappearing into the darkness. Soon, ahead, they heard the snarling discharge of his weapon and surprised piping cries.

"Come on," Fendager said. He shooed the prisoners ahead of him with one hand, his other wrapped around the pick handle in a white-knuckled grip.

They dashed along the ledge path, crouched to present the smallest target, hoping that the darkness would hinder pursuit as well as it slowed their escape.

Picard was wobbling when they reached the first hairpin curve. Once around that bend, we'll be out of sight, he told himself, even if the ice creatures can see in the dark.

He certainly couldn't. A projecting piece of rock caught his foot, tripping him. He staggered into the rock face, hands out to keep from falling.

"Captain!" Troi cried from behind him.

"Keep going!" Picard told her. She passed behind him as he pushed himself off the wall with nothing worse than scraped palms. Shambling into a run again, he heard Fendager close behind.

Ahead he heard a cry from Troi. "Look, Captain! One of the creatures!"

Picard caught up and grabbed Troi's elbow to propel her forward. He cast a quick glance at the shape sprawled across the ledge, a curious combination of dun and silver. There was no time for a long look.

Troi kept staring over her shoulder at the creature, nearly sending them to the ground in an ungraceful tangle. "Captain, I think it's—"

The shape suddenly bounded up off the ground and stood erect on two legs. One side of its body seemed ungainly, probably the result of a hit from the nerve disrupter. But the stubby arm that held a club looked whole and strong.

A wild cry came from behind the creature, and Fendager charged in, his pick handle high. He brought it down on the creature's head, crushing it to the ground. He kept hitting it, again and again.

"Stop! Stop! You've killed it!" Troi yelled.

"Like it would have killed us." Fendager raised his handle for another blow, then froze with a gurgling cry, the head of an arrow protruding from his chest.

Together Troi and Picard turned and ran. The track zigzagged madly along the cliff wall, then opened into a wider, pebble-covered sloping expanse. The cliff receded into darkness, from which a voice called, "There you are! Where's Fendager?"

"Dead," Picard reported bleakly.

Chu Edorlic sighed. "At least we've reached the caves. Come up the slope. Follow my voice."

The two struggled up against tricky footing. As Picard strove to pierce the darkness, he realized that the deeper shadow behind Edorlic was real. It represented an opening that went deep into the cliff face.

"Almost there . . . now!" A hand shot out to pull Picard onto a rock shelf, a sort of natural porch in front of the cave entrance. Edorlic did the same for Troi.

"We've survived, and we still have a chance," the rebel leader said. "In this warren we can hide from any pursuit."

He rounded on Troi. "Can you tell where the ice creatures are?"

Troi shook her head. "My abilities don't work that—"

The clatter of pebbles below not only interrupted her but made Edorlic's question moot. Obviously the pursuers had reached the large open space.

Chu Edorlic grabbed one of Picard's arms and one of Troi's. "Well, come on, then," he whispered hoarsely.

But Deanna Troi didn't move, just stood there, stiff. "There are more of them waiting inside an enclosed space."

Picard stared hard into the cave entrance. "Enclosed?" he said. "Inside the cave?"

"Can't tell. But I sense hatred." Troi's voice cracked. "And the desire for death—*our* death."

Chapter Fourteen

"DOCTOR, I REALLY don't have time for this right now." Riker was trying hard to keep his voice to an irritated undertone. "I've got a crisis on my hands. I can't leave the bridge!"

Beverly Crusher folded her arms and nailed him with an implacable blue gaze. "The crisis will be a lot worse if the commanding officer suddenly starts hallucinating on duty," she informed him. "Commander, we still don't know the full extent of the Tseetsk pheromone's powers, but a couple of other people who were exposed to it are experiencing flashbacks. Please come with me to sickbay for an examination. It'll only take a few minutes."

"But—" Riker winced as pain lanced through his temples. The headache he'd developed in the aftermath of the kidnapping didn't seem to be getting any better.

"That's it. I insist," Crusher said firmly. "It's obvious you're still feeling some effects. At the very least, let me take care of that headache. You'll need to be in peak condition when things start to happen."

"Oh, all right," Riker agreed. Crusher had a point.

He cast a glance around the bridge, where Data, Geordi, and Tho were bent industriously over their various sensor arrays, searching for signs of Picard and Troi in the frozen wilderness of Koorn. The fact was, there really wasn't anything for Riker to do right now, anyway.

"Mr. Data, you have the conn. If anything happens while I'm gone, contact me immediately."

He followed Crusher into the turbolift. As it whizzed them toward sickbay, he asked, "How's our young rebel?"

"Lorens Ben?" Crusher's brow crinkled anxiously. "I think he'll recover. Physically, at least." She was silent for a moment. Then she said slowly, "I hope you don't hold him too much to blame for what happened to Jean-Lu . . . to the captain and Counselor Troi. The boy worshiped Koban. He did whatever that man said without hesitating. And now that he realizes how Koban used him, he's utterly broken up. He feels betrayed. I'm—I'm very worried about him."

The lift doors slid open. "Too bad Deanna isn't around to talk to him," Riker commented ironically as they walked the short distance to sickbay.

Then, seeing Crusher's stricken expression, he patted her arm. "Sorry, Doctor. I've got bigger problems on my mind right now than how to deal with a juvenile offender. But I did mean what I said about counseling. I suspect Lorens would benefit more from that than from any punishment we might set him."

"I'm glad we agree."

Dr. Crusher led Riker over to one of the diagnostic beds and made him lie down. Then she swung the neural scanner into place. "This won't hurt a bit," she promised.

"Famous last words." Riker closed his eyes and waited for the probing to begin.

"Okay, you can sit up now," Crusher announced a few seconds later.

His eyes popped open. "Aren't you going to scan me?"

She laughed. "I just did. You're fine. No permanent damage."

She pressed a hypospray against the hard muscles of his upper arm. There was a soft hiss as the drug insinuated itself into his blood. "There. That should take care of the headache. Commander, I pronounce you fit for duty."

"You weren't kidding when you said it'd only take a few minutes," Riker said, standing up. "Since I'm ahead of schedule, mind if I look in on Lorens?"

Again the worried frown marred Crusher's brow. "Be my guest. But don't take it badly if he doesn't respond."

She led Riker through a low, rounded doorway

into the smaller recovery ward. "Every bed was occupied earlier today," she commented. "I'm glad to say the place has emptied out a bit since then. Vossted is up and around now, though I suspect that's more thanks to Drraagh's presence than to my medical skills. The two of them are hunched over a computer console right now, catching up on a few hundred years of galactic history."

"Vossted also seems to have benefited from a healthy dose of outrage. What he had was mainly an illness of the spirit." Riker smiled down at her. "But don't worry, Doc, your status as a miracle worker is untarnished in my eyes. There isn't a disease or injury you can't lick."

Her return smile was decidedly halfhearted. "Except, as you say, illnesses of the spirit." She pointed. "He's over there."

Lorens lay in the last bed, his face to the wall, his eyes closed, and his breathing deep and regular. "Lorens?" Riker called softly.

There was no response.

"I think he's sleeping," Riker whispered. He tiptoed back to Crusher.

She shook her head. "I doubt it. He's been lying like that since we brought him in here. I think he just doesn't want to talk to anybody."

They went back into the outer room. "Even you?" Riker said. "I thought the two of you had a good rapport."

Crusher shook her head again. "Not good enough, I'm afraid."

She followed Riker into the corridor. "Well, here's one less thing to worry about," she said as they walked toward the turbolift. "You're not going to go insane on the bridge. At least, not from the effects of the Tseetsk pheromone."

Riker gave her a mirthless smile. "I'm afraid there are more than enough alternative causes to choose from."

"Data to Commander Riker." The android's summons rang in the corridor. "The rebels are asking to speak to you, sir. Request your presence on the bridge."

"Here's a prime cause now." Scowling, Riker tapped the comm panel on the wall with his closed fist. "On my way."

"Sir, rebel commander Koban is standing by," Data advised Riker as he strode onto the bridge.

"Let him cool his heels a minute," Riker ordered. "Any progress on the scans?"

"No. Nor has either of the shuttlecraft reported success in locating the captain and Counselor Troi. The aberrant magnetic effects in the vicinity of the Rift have, fortunately, not impeded their communications capability, but they have rendered all the on-board tracking equipment virtually inoperative."

"Speed it up, Data." Riker made an impatient circling motion with his hand. Then, as he saw the android pause and cock his head, he added hastily, "Wait! Forget I said that."

"What Data is trying to say is that the shuttle crews have been reduced to searching the Rift by eye only," Geordi spoke up. The chief engineer's face was lined with tension and frustration. "And given that the nutty topography of the place makes it impossible to fly lower than seven hundred meters in most spots, that the wind has been blowing snow into the scanners ever since the craft got down there, and that it's now the middle of the night—"

"I get the picture," Riker said wearily. "Thank you, Mr. La Forge."

He sat down. "All right, Mr. Worf, put Koban on visual. Let's see what he wants now."

When Koban's face appeared on the viewscreen, Riker's first impression was that the young rebel was extremely nervous. But except for his eyes, Koban's scarred face gave so little away that Riker wondered if he had imagined the preoccupied frown and the tense set of the shoulders.

Deanna would have been able to tell me, he thought, and felt the knot in his gut twist tight once again.

"You kept me waiting, Riker," Koban said. "Why?"

It was a childish, manipulative question, and a surprising one, coming from Koban. Riker was annoyed by it. "I had things to take care of," he replied shortly. "What can I do for you, now that you've got me?"

Koban scowled. "I want your answer. Are you prepared to surrender your ship to us?"

"Wait a minute! What is this?" Riker demanded, astonished and angry. "Less than ten hours ago you told me I had twenty hours."

Something flashed for a moment in Koban's eyes. Almost imperceptibly he relaxed. "I've

changed my mind," he said coolly. "I see no reason
to give you so much time, when the conditions will
not change between now and then. Come, Commander, you're a man of action, able to make
decisions quickly. What will it be? The use of your
ship, or the lives of your friends?"

"Stand by," Riker said through gritted teeth.
Turning to Worf, he made a slashing gesture with
his finger across his throat. Worf nodded his understanding, and the big viewscreen went blank.

"All right, people." Riker stood up and paced to
stand in front of the forward consoles. He wheeled
around, facing the bridge crew. "You all saw that
exchange. *Something* just transpired between
Koban and me, but I don't know what it was. I
want any ideas."

"Koban was definitely hiding something," Worf
asserted.

"Yeah. It was like he was trying to get the answer
to a question from you, but without asking you the
question," Geordi put in.

Riker nodded. He'd gotten the same impression.
"From the way he acted, I'd say he got his answer,
and it was the one he wanted. So what I need to
know is: what's the question he was afraid to ask?"

Silence. He glanced at the android. "Data? Any
ideas?"

"I am afraid this speculation is beyond my
capacity," Data replied sorrowfully.

"He has had some news that affects his strategy,
presumably with regard to us. Otherwise he would
not need to sound us out." Worf spoke slowly, his
deep voice almost hesitant.

"News that affects his strategy . . ." Something in what Worf had said made Riker's mind start to tick over. His eyes narrowed to sapphire slits, shutting out his surroundings as he tried to focus on the elusive idea. News that affected his strategy, presumably with regard to—

"Sir, Koban is hailing us again," Worf reported.

Riker winced. Gone. Whatever the thought had been, it had now retreated to the back of his mind, and he knew it was useless to try to pursue it. He'd just have to wing this interview and hope that he could out-stoneface the rebel commander.

"Put him through," he ordered.

"Commander, I don't like this waiting game," Koban said as soon as the link was established. "I require your decision."

"These things take time, Koban," Riker said smoothly. "I assure you, I'm considering every—"

"Commander!" Worf's voice was an urgent shout. Suddenly the screen went blank again.

Riker slewed around to stare at the Klingon. "What happened?"

"Sir, I cut the link. Two large ships of unfamiliar configuration have just entered this solar system, traveling at warp speed." Worf checked his panel again. "They are on course for the planet Koorn."

Riker's heart jumped. "How large are they, Mr. Worf?"

"Each is"—Worf consulted his panel, did a double take, and consulted it again—"roughly seven times the mass of the *Enterprise.*"

"The Tseetsk," Geordi breathed. "They got the tachyonic signal sent by the overseers."

Riker nodded. "It looks that way." He turned back to the blank viewscreen, stroking his beard. "I wonder what they'll make of us."

As it turned out, they didn't have to wait long for the answer to that question. Within the hour the two ships were in viewing range and Riker ordered them put on screen.

Two monstrous gleaming black arrowheads shimmered into place, blotting out nearly half of the stars in the sky behind them. A translucent image of the *Enterprise,* which the computer had superimposed between the alien ships for scale, looked pitifully tiny. "Look at the size of those mothers," Geordi breathed.

"They appear to be shielded by forcefields similar to the one shielding the Koorn computer," Data reported. "These have an efficiency quotient roughly twice that of Federation shielding technology."

"Incredible," Riker murmured in frank awe.

"All our shields are up," Worf announced. "Recommend we go to yellow alert, sir."

Riker gnawed on his thumb, pondering for a moment. "All right, as a precaution. But I don't think it's really necessary," he said at last. "If what Drraagh and Vossted have told us about the Tseetsk is accurate, they'll be reluctant to exchange fire with us. The risk of severe casualties is too high.

"Hail them, Worf."

"Aye, sir. Response coming through." Worf sounded disgruntled. "On screen."

A moment later the panorama on the screen was replaced by a closeup of a round feathered face with enormous, solemn orange eyes and a snubbed beak. There the resemblance to Drraagh ended, though. This Tseetsk's face was crimson, with bold green lines radiating out from the eyes like the strands of a spiderweb. A crest of long, curling plumes, rakishly swept forward, added a touch of the ridiculous.

The Tseetsk gazed at the bridge crew for a moment, then said without preamble, "Humans, how did you acquire that vessel?"

Riker blinked. The translator tended to blur inflections, but he'd caught a definite peremptoriness in the Tseetsk commander's query. They're used to thinking of all humans as slaves, he reminded himself. Don't take it personally.

"I'm Commander William Riker," he said. "This is the Federation starship *Enterprise—*"

"Commander?" the Tseetsk cut in, a note of outrage in her voice. "You are a human."

"Well, yes," Riker admitted. "But—"

"Humans are slaves," the Tseetsk stated.

Riker folded his arms, wondering if she planned to let him finish any of his sentences.

It appeared she didn't. "Slaves may not possess starships," the Tseetsk said coldly. "It is an unacceptable risk. Humans, you are directed to abandon the vessel immediately and return to Koorn."

Riker was getting more and more disturbed by the tenor of the conversation. "I'm afraid we can't comply," he said. "You see—"

But the Tseetsk commander wasn't listening. In a disconcertingly alien movement, her head swiveled almost all the way around on her shoulders. She made an indecipherable gesture to someone behind her. Then the screen abruptly snapped back to an exterior view of the alien ships.

Riker's scalp prickled. "What's going on?" he asked softly.

"Sir, two ports just opened on the nose of the nearer ship," Worf called.

On the screen Riker could now clearly see two small yellow squares on the belly of the ship closer to the *Enterprise.* "Gunports," he said.

"Sensors indicate conical objects moving into position inside them," Data reported. He looked up at Riker. "Sir, their configuration is identical to that of the tachyonic missile we encountered two days ago."

"Red alert!" Riker barked. A cold hand closed around his heart.

Suddenly the Tseetsk commander reappeared on the big viewscreen. "Humans, you were foolish to think you could menace us this way," she said. "Now it is necessary to destroy you."

Chapter Fifteen

"WHAT DO WE DO NOW, Mr. Edorlic?" Picard asked.

"Do?" snarled Chu Edorlic. The weak light of Koorn's combined moons gleamed on the barrel of his disrupter as he checked its charge. "We fight, of course."

"With what?" Troi asked quietly.

Picard eased his back against a rock, feeling the cold strike through the cheap material of his parka. Beneath his mask, the perspiration that had beaded on his forehead after that last sprint was rapidly freezing solid.

He drew a rattling breath and knew he couldn't go on. Between the lingering effects of the pheromone and the grueling chase through Koorn's hostile landscape that he'd just endured, he was at the limit of his strength.

"The counselor and I are unarmed," he reminded Edorlic. "And if you think I'm up to any
hand-to-hand nonsense at the moment, you're sadly mistaken."

Behind them, about fifteen meters down the
slope, snow crunched softly under a stealthy foot.
Somewhere an arrow rattled out of its quiver.

"Hear that?" Edorlic said. "That's the sound of
death on the approach. Now, you can go down
fighting or not, as you choose. But I intend to take a
few of these creatures with me when I go."

"Your disrupter must be nearly drained," Picard
remarked. "You can get off two or three more shots
at the most, and who knows if you'll hit anything in
the dark? After that you're defenseless."

Edorlic growled. "Your point, Captain?"

"My point is this. We don't need the considerable talents of Counsclor Troi to tell us that these
creatures are intelligent. They fight in an organized
fashion, and they have relatively sophisticated
weapons."

"So?"

"Since they are intelligent, they may well be
susceptible to reason. Mr. Edorlic, I suggest we try
to communicate with them."

"What?" The rebel captain's voice rose to an
enraged bellow, then quickly modulated to a whisper. "Surrender? Has the cold addled your brain,
old man? You heard what Troi said. Those creatures are lusting for our corpses. You think if we put
down our weapons and go peacefully, they'll just
forget all about that feast they were planning?"

"I never said they were planning to eat us," Troi

objected. "In fact, I don't sense any desire for food coming from them at all. I just sense hatred."

"Well, that's enough for me." Edorlic jumped as a pebble rattled. He swung his disrupter around to the source of the noise.

"Kindly stop aiming that at me. I'm sorry if I startled you when I shifted position," Picard said wearily.

"Where are those damned creatures?" Edorlic muttered. Hunching his shoulders, he peered uneasily into the frigid gloom. "Why are they taking so long? Why don't they just get it over with?"

"They're—they're waiting to see what we do next, I think," Troi's voice was hesitant. "I sense puzzlement. They're wondering what we're up to."

"And there's our opportunity." Picard leaned forward and seized Chu Edorlic's arm in a forceful grip. "Let's not waste it. Lay down your weapon now, while their curiosity is stronger than their hatred."

Edorlic wrenched himself free. "What happens if the balance changes again?" he demanded. "Then they'll kill us at their leisure."

"At least there's an 'if,'" Picard pointed out. "In your plan, our death is only a question of when."

"The captain is right. Chu, listen to him," Troi pleaded. "It's our only chance."

Picard peered anxiously at the other man.

Edorlic's scowl was blacker than the shadows that clumped behind them. After a long, tense moment he laid his disrupter on the ground. His fingers hovered over it briefly, caressingly. Then he snatched his hand away. "All right." His voice was thick with indecision. "What do we do now?"

In answer, Picard climbed carefully to his feet and pushed back his hood. Hands held high over his head, he began to move forward out of the shadows.

"Captain!" Troi gasped.

"Since it was my idea, it's only right that I should be the one to test it," he said quietly. "If I am attacked, Mr. Edorlic, I leave it to you to decide your next move."

Picard took another step forward. At that moment the moon broke through the clouds, illuminating his face and throwing the silhouette of his bundled-up figure over the two humans crouched behind him.

Silence. The wind had momentarily dropped, and all Picard could hear was the pounding of his own heart, like a muffled drumbeat in his head. The clearest, simplest sort of communication—hands open and empty. What message would the other return? He resisted the urge to close his eyes and wait for the arrow. With great deliberation, he lifted his foot and took one more step.

Then he waited.

Time passed. He had no idea whether he'd stood there for a second or an hour. He was in that rather uncomfortable position long enough for the blood to drain out of his arms, at any rate; his hands were completely numb.

Were the ice creatures still out there? he wondered fleetingly. Wouldn't it be ridiculous if they'd simply gone away, leaving him standing there like some idiotic scarecrow for half the night?

A burst of soft, staccato vocables interspersed with complex clicks drove that idea out of Picard's mind. It was answered by another, slightly longer burst. Evidently the ice creatures were discussing him.

"Captain," Troi's voice came from behind him. "I don't think they're going to shoot. When you first appeared there was a flare of aggression, but that's mostly subsided now."

"Mostly?" Picard repeated—or at least began to repeat. His throat was bone dry, and all that came out was a rasping croak. He swallowed twice and tried again. "Mostly, Counselor?"

"A few of the creatures still feel nothing but belligerence toward you," Troi admitted. "But more of them are giving off caution. And curiosity."

"Let's hope the curious ones are the commanders," he said. "What do you think they'll do now?"

"I'm not getting anything decisive from them."

"So once again the ball is in our court," Picard murmured. "Mr. Edorlic, why don't you come out and join me?"

"Me? Why me?" Edorlic muttered. "Why not your precious Counselor Troi?"

Troi began to get to her feet. "All right, I'll go."

He grasped her arm and pulled her roughly back down. "Never mind," he hissed. "I don't need to be outfaced by some female—"

Freak. Troi flinched as she caught the word Edorlic hadn't spoken.

"If you hope to live through the night, Mr. Edorlic," Picard said in an even, unemphatic voice that Troi and Edorlic both recognized as furious, "you had better broaden your horizons. Now stand up slowly and put your hands over your head."

Sullenly Edorlic did as directed. It seemed to cost him some effort to stand; he rose slowly, hunched over, with his hands clutched tightly to his body.

He moved out to stand by the captain. Again Troi felt a flare of belligerence from the ice creatures, but it was less intense than the previous one. When it subsided, the curiosity was markedly stronger.

She copied Edorlic's movements and went to stand beside the captain, hands raised.

There was a prolonged burst of staccato conversation. The clicks and pops of the creatures' language made it sound like the snapping of hundreds of dry twigs.

Edorlic's brooding eyes were the first to discern movement in the darkness. "Something's coming toward us."

"Just keep calm and still," Picard advised.

A tall, silvery form, roughly man-high, loomed out of the shadows. Others followed, stepping silently from behind boulders. A rustling behind the three humans suggested that they were being ringed by the creatures. All appeared to be armed; most with long bows and quivers of arrows, but two or three carried wicked-looking spears and clubs.

Slowly the creatures converged, weapons at the ready. When they were three or so meters away, they halted. Picard was able to see that they were lean and wiry, with coarse, shaggy, dun-mottled silver pelts. Or were they wearing the furs of some other animal? In the fitful moonlight, he couldn't be sure. They had small, smooth wedge-shaped heads with a bushy crest at the crown. He squinted, trying to see more clearly. The shape of those heads . . .

At the same moment Troi gave a muted cry. "Captain, they're avian!"

That was it! That was what had struck him as so familiar. Those triangular snouts were beaks! And the odd shagginess of their bodies was actually due to the fur garments they wore over their feathers.

"By God, you're right," he said, keeping the excitement out of his voice with an effort. "Another intelligent avian race! What are the odds of finding two such in the same sector of space, I wonder?"

One of the bird people suddenly darted up to Picard and shook a spear threateningly in his face. Picard jerked back, alarmed. The creature glared at him out of one wide-set eye for a second and said something that sounded like "Ki-ni-ka-la."

"I'm sorry, I don't understand." Without lowering his arms, Picard spread his hands in a questioning gesture.

"Ki-ni-ka-la-k-k-k!" the creature said. Then, apparently in response to a command from one of the other bird people, it darted back to its place in the circle.

"Maybe it wants you to shut up," Edorlic whispered.

Perhaps. In any case, Picard considered it wise to

remain silent for now. Clamping his lips shut, he gazed wonderingly at the ring of avians.

Birdlike they might be, but they couldn't have looked less like Drraagh. Apart from their coloration—or lack of it—and the fact that they were nearly twice the size of Drraagh, their bodies were much leaner, with longer, stronger legs and, as far as he could see, longer arm-wings. In addition, the shape of their heads was altogether different. Where Drraagh's was essentially round, with a tiny, dainty beak and large eyes, these creatures' heads came to a predatory-looking point in the front. Their beaks were large and curving—quite lethal, he judged. And their black eyes were smaller and set so far apart that Picard doubted their vision was stereoscopic.

Fascinating. Simply fascinating.

The leader seemed to be the largest one, a battered veteran with only one eye. He—she? it?—clicked another command, and three of the strange beings sidled cautiously forward. Reaching out with arrows, they jabbed lightly at the humans.

"What the—" Chu Edorlic sounded frightened.

"Don't be alarmed," Troi whispered. "I don't think they mean to hurt us. Maybe they're checking for weapons."

It seemed she was correct. After a few moments, the scruffy leader called out again, and the three searchers tucked their arrows away.

Slowly, cautiously, Picard lowered his aching arms. Edorlic and Troi followed suit. This seemed to agitate some of the bird beings, but the leader simply gestured again. One of the searchers un-slung a coil of nubby rope from around his neck and cut three lengths from it with a bone knife. They're going to bind our hands, Picard guessed.

And so they did, though with what seemed like the utmost trepidation. As the blood flowed back into his hands, Picard flexed his tingling fingers—and the creature who was binding him fell back with a squawk of alarm. Picard froze.

After a second, during which the other creatures made noises of unmistakable derision, Picard's captor returned and finished his task.

When the three humans' hands were bound securely behind them, the leader of the bird people gestured with his spear. Their captors nudged them, and the party began to move toward the yawning cave entrance.

Inside the entrance, the leader stopped and drew a small object from a pouch that hung around his neck. Sparks flared as he made a striking motion with his hands. Picard's surprise grew. A tinderbox!

Several of the creatures now drew torches out of their quivers and lit them from the leader's flame. Whatever the torches were made of, they burned with a clear, relatively smokeless flame and a faintly aromatic scent. Picard looked around and saw that they were in a long, low-ceilinged cave.

The walk resumed, the creatures moving silently along on splayed, three-toed feet with thick pads.

In the flickering light Picard sought Troi's eye. He was pleased to see that, though her teeth were chattering from the cold, she looked reasonably composed.

"Where do you suppose they're taking us?" he asked in a quiet voice.

"I don't know. I'm not getting anything useful from them," she replied.

From the captain's other side, Edorlic spoke up. "This is the entrance to the hot caves. Somewhere in here we figure there's a vent or a shaft that links up with a subterranean volcano, but we've never found it. It heats the caves pretty efficiently, so we'll be comfortably warm soon. Unless, of course, the creatures intend to roast us over a nice magma pit." He gave a snort of humorless laughter.

At the explosive sound, one of his captors prodded him none too gently with an arrow. Scowling, Chu fell silent.

They walked for some time through an incredible series of natural caverns and tunnels formed from the featureless gray bedrock. Icicles and stalactites dripped from the ceiling in glittering profusion.

Though they'd left the keening wind behind after the first few caves, Picard didn't yet detect any appreciable warming in the air. He did, however, take note of the fact that their path sloped gradually but definitely downward.

"When do we get to the hot part?" he whispered to Chu Edorlic. Now that the initial shock of meeting up with their strange captors had abated, his abused muscles were beginning to protest even more strenuously than before.

"I'm not sure," the rebel leader admitted. "I've never gone this far before. Back in the fourth cavern we went through, there's a tunnel that leads due east and much more sharply downward. That's where the hot caves are."

"Due east." Picard pondered that for a moment. "Do you know which way we're heading now?"

Edorlic's black brows drew together. "Roughly southeast, I'd say—following the line of the Rift."

"Impressive," Picard murmured.

"Maybe we backward slaves aren't as dumb as you think," Edorlic said with a sneer.

Sighing, Picard let the remark go. It was unfortunate, he reflected, that even in their present presumably dire plight, Chu Edorlic couldn't let go of his private hatred for long enough to pull together with his companions.

By this time they were marching along a fairly narrow winding corridor. Suddenly the column in front of him came to a halt. Picard sagged, grateful for the rest, but he soon realized that it was to be short. One by one the strange bird beings were disappearing into a narrow crevice in the wall.

The crevice was concealed from the view of anyone coming down the passageway by an overlapping lip of rock. As soon as he saw it, Picard wondered if it could possibly be a natural formation. Though it looked as ragged and weathered as the rest of the tunnel, its placement was so artful that it seemed to point to deliberate intent.

Again Picard exchanged glances with Troi. "The creatures get more interesting every minute, don't they, sir?" she murmured.

"Indeed they do," he agreed.

Then it was his turn to slide through the narrow

crevice. It appeared to extend some distance back, presumably turning at least a couple of times en route, for Picard could see no sign of the torches of the creatures who'd gone before him.

He eyed the crack with distaste. He'd never been particularly fond of small, dark spaces. But now, he supposed, was no time to be finicky.

Taking a deep breath, he plunged ahead. Almost immediately, the crevice narrowed so that, with his bulky coat and leggings, he found it quite a tight fit. Having his hands bound behind him didn't help, either. Once he got caught on a projecting spur of rock, and for a moment the beginnings of panic stirred within him. But with a wriggle and a tug, he was able to free himself.

The crevice—or tunnel, as he supposed he ought to call it—made a hairpin turn after about ten meters. Feeling more confident by now, Picard eeled his way around the turn and was rewarded by the friendly flickering glow of torchlight on rock walls once again.

He strode forward—and his foot slid out from under him on a smooth, worn surface. His other leg windmilled briefly, and then he was flat on his backside, bumping ungracefully down a strangely angular slope.

"Ooof," he grunted as he finally came to a halt at the bottom. Fortunately the padding in his garments, such a hindrance only moments before, had served to break the worst of his fall. He felt battered and bruised, but essentially undamaged.

A ring of wedge-shaped silvery heads gathered

around him, and shiny black eyes gazed impassively down at him. Groaning, Picard tried to get to his feet, but with his bound hands it was impossible. Finally one of the ice creatures reached down and hauled him upright with one hand. Strong, Picard thought. Very strong. Must remember that.

He turned to see what had caused him to fall, and an involuntary exclamation fell from his lips. "Stairs!"

There was no mistaking the artifice this time. Picard had tumbled down a short flight of wide steps carved into the rock. They were just a bit too shallow for the average human stride, but they looked as if they'd be perfect for a giant bird with stumpy, muscular legs.

He saw immediately why he had slipped, too. The steps were incredibly worn, with gleaming bowl-shaped depressions down the middle where, presumably, bird feet had trod over hundreds, maybe even thousands, of years.

Troi was picking her way carefully down the steps now, Edorlic behind her. When she joined Picard at the bottom, she raised her eyebrows. "Our captors are definitely not as primitive as they appear at first glance. They must have metal to have carved these stairs, don't you think?"

"It seems likely. Also, judging from the condition of the stairs, I'd conjecture that they've been here quite some time," Picard said softly. "Perhaps the creatures look on the Koorn humans as interlopers, threats to their way of life. It would certainly explain their initial hostility."

The leader of the bird beings seemed to feel that the humans had talked enough for the present. He gave a harsh-sounding order to one of the other creatures, whereupon it clicked and made threatening gestures at Troi and the captain until they moved apart.

They resumed the trek, making a series of twists and turns that Picard suspected were leaving even the resourceful Chu Edorlic without an idea of which way they were going.

The only thing that wasn't in doubt any longer was that they were heading deeper into the bowels of the planet. The air grew rapidly warmer. After fifteen minutes or so Picard was sweating freely inside his coat. It was pleasant at first to be warm again, but soon he began to feel distinctly uncomfortable. And still the temperature rose.

If anything, the heat was more exhausting than the cold had been, he decided. He was flagging badly, his head down, his legs aching with every step. How much farther are we going? he wondered dizzily. To the liquid core?

Suddenly he collided with a soft, furry back. The troop had stopped again. Shambling to a halt, Picard looked up wearily.

They stood at the entrance to a lofty cavern. It was natural, Picard decided, gazing around, but in places it looked as if the contours had been smoothed artificially.

Perhaps a dozen more bird people were lounging around the cavern, mending arrows or spears. When they caught sight of the captive humans, they sprang to their feet with clicking cries, brandishing their weapons.

The one-eyed leader engaged in a rapid-fire discussion with the agitated ones. At length one of them hurried off through a doorway in the far wall. Its stumpy, rocking stride looked a bit clumsy, Picard mused, but it moved with quite respectable speed.

After a few moments the messenger returned and beckoned. The one-eyed leader said something, and nine of his band closed into a boxlike formation around the humans. They were marched through the far door, into another cavern. They were then herded to a stone dais, where a powerfully built creature in a cloak of white and dun fur sat in a kind of cushioned nest lined with more furs. Through the feathers on the creature's breast, a foot-long puckered scar was clearly visible. The bird creature regarded them in silence.

"The boss," Troi murmured.

Picard's eyes narrowed. "Have you noticed that both the leaders we've encountered thus far bear rather horrific scars?" he whispered. "It suggests this culture places a premium on valor in battle."

"Well, that's something, anyway. At least they aren't cowards, like the chickens," Chu muttered.

"Ki-ni-ka-la!" One-Eye said, then shut his formidable beak with a snap.

The creature on the dais leaned forward and said something to Picard. One-Eye spoke again, presumably telling his chief that the humans didn't speak their language.

The chief sat back for a moment. Then he leaned

forward again, pointing with a taloned finger at his own breast. "Kraax-koorn-aka," he said slowly.

His meaning was unmistakable. Picard nodded. Since his hands were bound, he couldn't point to himself, but he said, "Picard." He inclined his head toward Troi. "Troi." Then he indicated the rebel captain. "Edorlic."

"Ik-kard. Troi. E-dor-lik-k." The chief repeated the names. He gazed at the humans for another long moment, then said something to One-Eye.

Nodding, One-Eye gestured to the guards, and once again the humans were prodded into motion.

They went through a door into an even larger cavern. This was a square roughly thirty meters by thirty meters, with an impressive expanse of polished stone floor.

"It feels like a museum in here. Or a church," Troi whispered.

Picard was too exhausted to be awed by the scale of the room, but his eyes widened at the sight of the object in its center. It was a gleaming metal mushroom a full fifteen meters high.

Beside him Edorlic drew in a sharp breath. "That's one of our geothermal taps!" he exclaimed.

So that was the source of heat for the caves. As they neared it, Picard could see that the device was maintained to an almost painful degree. Every plate of its metal surface shone mirror-bright, reflecting the glow of torches set in wall brackets. But the joins between the plates were black with age, and the fittings and bolts were worn away to nothing. "It looks older than anything you might have worked on," he commented, puzzled.

"But it must be one of ours," Edorlic insisted. "The housing is identical. I should know—I've set three of the damn things up for the chickens!"

"Yes, you should know," Picard said slowly. An incredible idea was forming in his mind.

They moved past the tap, and Picard saw that their guards dipped their heads and ruffled their neck feathers in a ritualistic manner.

Suddenly Troi gasped. "Captain, look!"

He followed her eyes to a shining, featureless black cube set into the wall behind the ancient thermal tap. "My God," he said. Then they were going through another doorway into a small room. Their guards halted and moved into sentry positions around the walls.

"That looked just like our base computer." Chu sounded bewildered. "How'd the ice creatures get one of those?"

Picard hardly heard him. His thoughts were too busy with the incredible clues he'd just been handed: the avian race, the thermal tap, the computer, and above all, the indisputable signs of antiquity. . . . Looking up, he caught Troi's inky gaze. "Are you thinking what I'm thinking?" he asked her.

She nodded. "I am."

"What?" Edorlic growled. His eyes swung back and forth between Picard and Troi. "What are you talking about?"

"It seems these ice creatures, as you call them, are not an indigenous group of primitives," Picard explained.

"No?" The rebel perched on a stone bench.

"Enlighten me, then, O man from the stars. What *are* they?"

"What we've seen should tell us," Picard said. "There's even a linguistic clue—the 'Kraax' prefix in the chief's name. Commander Data found references to 'Kraaxaa' in your base computers."

He stared at the rangy avian beings. "These are descendants of the survivors of a war of annihilation that ravaged this planet and many others ten thousand years ago—a war that reduced them to a primitive, marginal existence in underground caves and brought the rest of their race to the brink of extinction." Picard raised one eyebrow. "In fact, Mr. Edorlic, they're Tseetsk!"

Chapter Sixteen

THE TSEETSK COMMANDER'S FACE vanished from the screen, and Riker took in the image of the huge arrowhead-shaped vessels with open missile ports. "Mr. La Forge," he said, "what can we expect, and what can we do about it?"

"Looks like a salvo of twelve missiles," Geordi said from his station. "We *might* be able to take out a first wave with a spread of photon torpedoes." He sighed.

"I think I hear a 'but' coming," Riker said.

"You do, Commander. The problem is that the wake from the first Tseetsk salvo will still do a number on our systems. I can boost power to the shields to give us more protection, but they won't be able to hold all of the ionization out. Our detectors and scanners are going to be blown out, just like before."

Riker frowned. "So just when we'll need them most—"

"We'll be blind," Geordi confirmed. "If you'll pardon the expression."

"Geordi, this is not good news."

"What can I say? These guys used to toss asteroids at planets that they didn't like. They're pretty tough."

Riker stared at those missile ports, muttering, "If only we had something to toss back."

Then an idea struck him. "Computer," he said. "Locate Vossted and Drraagh and ask them to come to the bridge." We can't outshoot the Tseetsk, he thought. But maybe, with some knowledgeable advice, we can outthink them.

"Commander!" Worf's voice rumbled from behind him. "We're being hailed from the planet."

"On screen," Riker responded.

The warships disappeared, to be replaced by an image of Iarni Koban. The rebel leader looked amazingly confident. "Our instruments have detected the approach of the chickens' ships," Koban said. "I've just spoken to their admiral and informed her of the Koorn revolution." He raised his eyebrows. "Like it or not, you'll have to join us now."

Riker managed an ironic smile for the rebel leader. "Well, since we're all on the same side now, perhaps you can return the captain and Counselor Troi. They'd certainly be helpful in handling this crisis."

Koban gave him a smile in return—an odd one, Riker thought. "Ah, but we know that Picard and Troi are the only reason you've remained here, Commander. Certainly you don't feel great solidarity with our cause."

Riker's smile fell away. "I'm sure your cause is enough justification for you to put your life on the line—maybe all your people's lives. But don't expect my sympathy when you endanger *my* people as well—after trying to extort our help."

Koban bridled a little. "I only meant—"

"It doesn't matter what you meant," Riker cut in. "Here's what it means now. My ship is facing two hostile craft that outmass us by a combined factor of more than ten to one, besides which they possess a totally unknown technology. You wanted the Federation joined in a war with the Tseetsk. Well, you may have succeeded—posthumously."

Koban's frozen visage disappeared from the screen.

Behind his back, Riker heard a sigh. "Ah, Koban."

He swiveled to see Vossted and Drraagh. "I had hopes for him," the overseer said, his eyes still on the blank viewscreen. "I thought he might grow to be the leader who would change our world. But he's gone so far wrong. . . . I wonder if there's any hope for him at all."

"Yes, well, that's an interesting question. But our immediate problem isn't so much with Koban as with those." Riker pointed to the vessels that were again on the screen. "Armed Tseetsk ships. They're threatening to destroy us unless we can come up with a way to defer their attack."

"So we heard," Vossted said briefly. "Drraagh and I will do everything we can to help you. Those ships can precipitate a disastrous war if we don't stop them."

Riker had to smile at the irony of it. *I started with my heart on the side of the rebels, who wound up putting the ship in danger. And now, to avoid disaster, I'm relying on the last two slave masters of Koorn.*

"We aren't exactly dealing from a position of strength," he said.

"Then we shall need our best words to convince them," Drraagh said, and gave a brief squawk.

Riker blinked. Had the alien just laughed?

"Mr. Worf," he said, "hail the Tseetsk vessels."

The enormous starships disappeared from the screen and were replaced by a huge Tseetsk head. Although the red-plumed face was similar to that of the first caller, Riker noticed that the designs— marks of rank?—were much simpler.

"A junior officer," Drraagh whispered.

"Are you ready to submit, human?" the Tseetsk asked.

"I am ready to teach you some courtesy," Drraagh snapped at the young officer. "I will speak to Hweeksk."

The junior officer squawked in surprise. Then she disappeared, and the captain of the lead vessel swelled onto the screen. "Drraagh! We thought the humans had—had murdered you. Instead, I see they hold you hostage." The feathers of Hweeksk's neck ruff rose in agitation.

Riker thought he understood. Killing a shipful of humans—even a planetful of them—wouldn't have troubled Hweeksk unduly. But the notion of killing Drraagh, another Tseetsk, was a major taboo in her culture.

He was not surprised when Hweeksk immediately focused on a target to blame. "Vossted. Of course, we need look no further for the father of this revolution."

Even through the translation functions, Riker could detect the emphasis on the word "father." Hweeksk seemed to hesitate, as if referring to something distasteful, obscene.

"I've fathered no revolution here," Vossted responded. "But your culture has mothered one."

"Whatever you think is being born here can be . . . aborted."

Riker got the distinct feeling that Hweeksk was being offensive. In a culture dedicated to unceasing increase, such a reference had to be in the worst taste.

"Perhaps you have found a starship here," Hweeksk went on, "but it will do you no good. You humans lack the necessary skills—"

"Hweeksk, take a good look at this vessel," Drraagh broke in. "Does it look like anything you've ever seen in our shipbuilding annals?"

"It seems primitive," Hweeksk said disdainfully.

"Could our people build it today?" Drraagh asked.

The captain only stared in silence.

"Hweeksk, be careful. The crew of this ship has not lived under Tseeksk protection. They are representatives of the government of the humans' homeworld."

"Government?" Hweeksk shrilled.

"We made a serious mistake in our first contact with this race, setting a dangerous pattern. But we are no longer dealing with a small planet-bound group of supposed survivors of racial suicide. The humans are a star-faring race. They've formed a great confederation with other races." She gestured to Worf, standing at the security station. "Their United Federation of Planets takes in more worlds than the greatest extent our Sphere of Clans ever achieved."

Riker glanced at the small figure beside him. Drraagh had certainly spent her time well in the history banks of the *Enterprise* computers.

"Young, barbaric, expansionistic races," Hweeksk said. "All the better to drive them back now, before they use our incorporated humans against us."

"So you're willing to fight to keep your—what did you call them?—incorporated humans?" Riker demanded. "You cannot maintain a stable society based on slavery."

Drraagh's question was more to the point. "Hweeksk," she asked, "when was the last time your missile ports were opened in earnest? How many battles have you seen?"

Hweeksk stood again in silence.

"Ah," Drraagh said. "I certainly don't wish to reveal military secrets, but . . ."

"So you would join with these outsiders? Unstable creatures who have already nearly destroyed themselves?" the Tseetsk captain demanded. "Remember why the humans first came to our space!"

"I do remember," Drraagh said quietly, "but *you* must remember why the humans found an uninhabited planet to colonize. They aren't the only race that has flirted with self-immolation."

"But they are barbarians!" Hweeksk cried.

"They're not so different from us. I've been among them. Human mothers cherish their young as we do ours."

"But . . ." This time Hweeksk trailed off.

Drraagh stretched out her stubby arms. "Please, Hweeksk! We have a chance to start again with this race. Don't make war. There must be a better way."

The captain ruffled her feathers in extreme agitation. "I—I do not see any alternatives, Drraagh."

"Give me just a little time. I'll construct a case."

"Very well." Hweeksk bobbed her head. "You have one orbit."

The screen went blank.

Late that night Beverly Crusher sat in her small office, poring over the back issues of the *Federation Physician's Quarterly* that she had never found time to read before. Not that there was much news in them; still, the reading helped push the awful strain of suspense at the *Enterprise*'s predicament to the back of her mind.

At least Wesley is safely away at the Academy, she thought. Then she smiled. After all her worrying about him, there was something grimly amusing about the fact that she, not her son, was the one in imminent danger. She supposed it just went to show there was no predicting what fate had in store. . . .

She just wished she could see him one more time. There was so much she'd never said to him. Crusher lowered her head onto her folded arms, longing for her son.

But as she sat, half dreaming, the picture of Wesley in her mind's eye gradually transformed itself into another, younger face: one with brown eyes instead of hazel, and a closed, desolate expression. She straightened up slowly. Then, with a sigh, she rose to her feet.

"There's still time to say some important things to *that* child," she said aloud.

Outside, the sickbay ward was bathed in a warm, gentle blue light. Crusher tiptoed toward the bed by the far wall, where Lorens Ben lay on his back. His eyes were open, she saw. He was staring at the ceiling.

"Lorens," she whispered.

Instantly his eyes snapped closed.

She pulled up a chair by his bed and sat down. "I know you're awake. Won't you talk to me?"

She waited. After about a minute he opened his eyes. "What is there to say?" came a small, cold voice.

"Oh, lots of things," Crusher promised, reaching out to smooth his hair. He flinched away from her hand.

Trying not to be hurt, she folded her hands in her lap. "Lorens, I hate to see you so unhappy. I know what happened with Koban hurt very much, but you can't let it be the end of the world. You're young! There's so much life ahead of you; you have so much to—"

"I have nothing," Lorens interrupted her. "My mother is dead. When I was growing up in the crèche I had a father who was far away. I believed he was the greatest man in the universe. Then he brought me to Koorn, and I saw him as he really was—" His voice choked off. It was a moment before he could continue. "Shakra Ben, overseer. A bully, a coward, and even more a slave than the men he controlled. You know why Shakra brought me to Koorn? Not because he loved me. No, he wanted to make sure I grew up to be *just like him.*"

A residual spasm racked the boy's frame. He jerked rigid on the bed, and Crusher could see his furious determination as he struggled to master the trembling.

After a moment he went on, words spilling from between clenched teeth. "Then I met Koban. I thought, He's a leader. When he led the rebellion, I was glad—even though I knew he'd killed my father." He drew a ragged breath. "I'd have done anything for him. And he would have left me to be—to be . . ."

"What he did was very wrong. But you can't give up on people, just because one or two turn out not to be what you thought they were," Crusher insisted. "There are still people who love you."

"Like you?" he asked bitterly. "You only chase after me because I remind you of your son."

"That's not why," she said steadily.

"But I'm *not* your son!" Lorens raged on, not hearing her. "Anyway, you'll be leaving soon. That is, if we aren't all killed in a war with the chickens. So tell me, Dr. Beverly, just what do I have?"

Crusher's heart swelled. "For one, you have yourself. It's true that at first I saw Wesley in you, but that isn't the case any longer. The Lorens I've gotten to know these past few days is his own person—and a splendid one.

"And you also have me," she added softly. "It's true that if . . . if everything turns out all right, I'll be leaving with the *Enterprise* soon. But I'll still be your friend, Lorens, wherever I am."

His only answer was a disbelieving stare.

"Listen. When Wesley was very young, his father —my husband, Jack—was killed in an accident." Crusher swallowed the sudden lump in her throat. "When I got the news I thought I would die, too. Jack was the world to me.

"It took me years to even begin to get over it. I won't pretend it doesn't hurt, even now. But after a while, I found something out. You know what? There's a part of Jack that never died. He's in my heart, in my mind, forever. Even if I were to fall in love with someone else, I'd never lose Jack. Because I *remember*. Do you see?"

Lorens still didn't reply, but she saw that he had risen to his elbows and was watching her carefully.

"I'll tell you something else," she went on. "The same thing is true for Wesley, my son. He's not with me now, and as he gets older it's likely that our careers will keep us apart more and more of the time. But wherever he is, wherever I am, and no matter what happens, we'll always have a part of each other—in our memories."

Beverly Crusher fell silent, realizing that what she had just said was simple truth. Come what might, she could never really lose Wesley, any more than she had lost Jack. Sudden, profound relief swelled through her.

"Dr. Beverly." Lorens struggled to sit up.

"Yes?"

"Will you—" He broke off, then tried again, in a voice so soft she had to lean down to hear it. "Will you remember—"

Suddenly a sob racked his body. He flung his arms around her waist, burrowing his dark head into the fabric of her smock, the tears that had been so long held in now raining down his cheeks.

Tears sprang to Crusher's own eyes and dropped unnoticed onto his head. "Always, Lorens," she promised, rocking his small form in her arms. "Always."

Beneath the surface of Koorn, Jean-Luc Picard paced impatiently in their prison. "Blast it, Counselor!" he burst out. "Learning about the existence of a native Tseetsk population puts an entirely new complexion on the situation!" He lowered his voice. "It's the key to the whole problem. If we could only get back to the *Enterprise!*"

"Someone's coming," Chu Edorlic hissed from the mouth of the cavelet. He'd maintained a vigil there, glaring at the silent group of Kraaxaa-Tseetsk who guarded them.

More warriors appeared, ringing a tall Tseetsk in a fur robe as fine as the chief's. "Ik-kard," the newcomer called.

"Why is he treating *you* like the boss?" an annoyed Edorlic wanted to know as Picard stepped forward.

The Tseetsk dignitary put a hand to his chest, identifying himself. "Sss-kaa-twee."

Picard noticed the chain around the Tseetsk's neck, from which dangled the only jewelry he'd seen these people wear. It was a piece of black crystal in the shape of a cube, carefully rubbed and polished. He gazed thoughtfully at it.

"I believe that pendant tells us what Sss-kaa-twee does. He's a priest, a sage—the guardian of the computer."

As if in answer, Sss-kaa-twee gestured down the cavern, toward the chamber that housed the ancient geothermal tap, accompanying the gesture with a staccato speech. They followed him out of the cavelet, surrounded by the guards.

The huge square room was now filled with Kraaxaa-Tseetsk who had removed their silvery fur outdoor garments. Several of them were much smaller and rounder than their fellows—females, Picard guessed. The bird people sat on the floor in rank upon rank, leaving a large circular area around the tap open.

"Quite an audience," Picard muttered. "Are they here for a trial or gladiatorial combat or just an execution?"

Troi shook her head as the bird people's expressionless black eyes stared at them. "All I sense is intense anticipation."

The humans were led to the open space and invited to sit. Then Sss-kaa-twee, the tallest of the—priests? scholars?—stepped out. He came before the huge black cube that stood to one side of the tap and began chanting in the harsh-cadenced Kraaxaa dialect. A glow appeared in the heart of the cube.

Pictures appeared, clearly of the Kraaxaa-Tseetsk in their days of glory. Then came discord and war. "The chickens fought among themselves?" Edorlic said.

"According to one of my officers who penetrated your computers, there were several factions: Sree, Joost, Loor, and these people—the Kraaxaa."

"Huh!" Edorlic muttered. "The chickens called their language Sree-Tseetsk. Koban made us all learn a bit of it. But the ice creatures' gobbledygook doesn't sound anything like it."

They continued to watch the cube as pictures of campaigns appeared, followed by a star map with a light show of intensely quick flashes of various solar systems. At last they saw the doom of Koorn and the fate of the survivors.

"Amazing. This explains their relative sophistication in spite of their crude technology," Picard whispered.

"They still have a memory of the universe, and I can feel their reaction to their ancient enemies," Troi said.

Another priest rose to join Sss-kaa-twee. He

pointed at the humans and began a chant of his own. It was simpler, harsher, as were the pictures on the computer screen.

Of course, Picard thought. Computer capacity must be limited. There's only one cube here, versus an entire wall in the Sree-Tseetsk base. Controlling the geothermal tap must take up a good bit of memory, as must that history lesson. Further imaging capacity would be limited.

The images were indeed simple, no more than stick figures, but they were quite clear. The first was a clip from the history file. It showed a Tseetsk flier, the same arrowhead shape as the kind the human slaves used. A mutter of recognition rose from the crowd; apparently, the Kraaxaa-Tseetsk associated these fliers with their ancient enemy.

From under the streamlined flier, stick-figure humans appeared, pursuing equally sketchy Tseetsk warriors armed with bows. More Tseetsk appeared, unarmed, shorter, some of them in much smaller scale—women and children, Picard surmised. Whenever the humans in the drawings encountered a Tseetsk, they pointed their arms. Any cartoon Tseetsk they pointed at fell down and lay still. Arrows flew from the warriors. Some humans died as well.

"They don't know about the nerve disrupters," Troi whispered. "All they know is that death comes somehow from the hands of the humans. That's why they were so nervous when they were binding our arms."

"The implication of the chant is clear," Picard

said. "They're linking us with the Tseetsk who are trying to colonize this planet—and they're accusing us of genocide."

Sss-kaa-twee turned to the humans.

"It seems he expects us to present a rebuttal," Picard said. "Not an easy task with a language barrier before us." If only they'd kidnapped Data too, he thought. The android could have operated that computer as well as they did.

The silence grew longer. "They're waiting for an answer," Troi said.

Picard turned to Chu Edorlic. "You know some of the language, don't you?"

Edorlic shook his head impatiently. "I told you, I only know Sree-Tseetsk."

"Sree-Tseetsk!" cried the accusing shaman. A mutter ran through the massed ranks of aliens.

"Sree-Tseetsk!" Sss-kaa-twee addressed the computer. A set of more melodious vocables floated from the machine.

"Hey! That's the chicken word for 'translate'!" Edorlic suddenly exclaimed.

"Apparently, that's what the computer will do with what you tell it," Picard said.

"Sure, but I don't even know the chicken word for 'slavery.' So how can I tell them?"

Troi knelt on the floor and began drawing figures in the dust. "Come and help," she called.

Picard and Edorlic joined her. "This triangle is the Sree-Tseetsk flier," Troi said. "Can you tell him that?"

Edorlic pointed to the sketch and trilled a few stumbling syllables. Sss-kaa-twee turned to the

computer, which gave forth harsher Kraaxaa vocables.

Under the flier, Troi added several stick-figure
Tseetsk, arms extended. Then she sketched in a
clump of humans, arms down, several lying on the
ground.

"I get it," Edorlic said. "Their ancient enemies
came and killed us."

Troi nodded. More pictures appeared under her
fingers, these of humans bent in submissive poses,
Tseetsk over them. "Perhaps this will explain it,"
she said.

Edorlic began pointing and speaking haltingly in
Tseetsk, groping for words as the computer trans-
lated. "I said they came and killed us, to make us
work for them."

Now Sss-kaa-twee rose and began his own chant.
Images similar to Troi's picture story began to
appear. A murmur arose from the crowd.

The second scholar-priest—Picard thought of
him as the prosecutor—rose and reiterated his
images. "I see," Picard said. "Whether we're forced
or not, we're attacking their people."

Troi immediately went to work, amending her
drawing of the flier, the Sree-Tseetsk, and their
slaves. Now the human figures stood up, pointing
their arms at the Tseetsk, who pointed back.

"Okay," Edorlic said. "You're drawing the rebel-
lion. We humans are fighting against the Sree-
Tseetsk." He began explaining in his pidgin-
Tseetsk.

As he did, Troi erased the Tseetsk figures one by
one, then drew them lying down in death.

After these images were broadcast on the computer screen, the two shamans turned to the audience at large.

"Looks like show-and-tell is over," Edorlic said.

Kraax-koorn-aka now appeared in the open space, easily recognizable thanks to his scarred chest. He seemed to act as moderator while sinewy warriors stood to speak. A few of the shorter females also rose to join the discussion, until a consensus was apparently reached.

The chief spoke to his people, then turned to the computer, speaking more slowly.

Edorlic listened intently to the translation. "We live," he said jubilantly. "Sss-kaa-twee wants us."

As the tribe members filed out, the tall form of Sss-kaa-twee came toward the prisoners, flanked by guards. He beckoned them around the side of the cube.

Picard stared as he saw a wall of new images, flashing data readouts, written and calibrated in Tseetsk ideograms.

Edorlic frowned in puzzlement. "I never saw anything like this on the computer cubes in our base."

"I suspect this is a dedicated display, giving readings on some major piece of equipment," Picard said. He glanced at his erstwhile captor. "Chu, did your rebel education give you anything of the Tseetsk written language?"

Edorlic shrugged. "I can read this stuff. It's a diagnostic of the thermal tap."

He looked from display to display, then let out a low whistle. "Half of these gauges are near or in the danger zone. The chickens may build well, but even so, things wear out after a few thousand years." He snorted, adding, "I see now why Sss-kaa-twee wanted us to live. They need our help to fix the thing!"

"So they recognized the similarity to the tap you were constructing farther up the Rift," Picard said. His lips thinned as he considered. "We can only hope that Tseetsk tap technology is as standardized as their computers."

"You want to fix their tap?" Chu Edorlic demanded.

"Academy engineering classes gave me a grasp of the technology. With your knowledge of the nuts and bolts, we should be able to do it."

"And if I don't help?" Edorlic asked.

Picard gazed around at their guards. "Are you that eager to die?" he asked.

After a moment Chu sighed. "Let's get on with it."

With the rebel translating, Picard attacked the monitors, slowly piecing together the form of the tap from the functions reported.

"Apparently the Tseetsk created their own geyser, drilling a shaft down to hot rock, then introducing water," he explained to Troi. "Essentially, it's a steam engine, powered by the planet's interior heat, running a series of turbines close to the surface."

"And it's been running for more than ten thousand years," Troi marveled.

"Carefully maintained by a priestly caste," Picard added. "The problem is that many of the moving parts are finally wearing out. Control valves, turbine vanes, mounting rods—all have a finite span of usefulness."

"But they can be replaced?"

Picard nodded. "We've pinpointed the main problem spots. Now we have to get the spares."

That expedition will take us to Camp One and the wrecked fliers, he thought. Our one hope of escape lies at the bottom of that cliff—if the communications gear survived the fall. . . .

Chapter Seventeen

PICARD FELT BEYOND WEARINESS as he stared at the icy landscape before him, inadequately illuminated by Koorn's two small moons. The deal with the cave-dwelling Kraaxaa-Tseetsk had been quickly concluded. It had been a simple enough negotiation: their freedom for the necessary repairs on the geothermal tap.

Kraax-koorn-aka had ratified Sss-kaa-twee's proposal that he lead the expedition to salvage parts. Preparations had begun immediately. Picard had barely an hour's rest before the guards came to their little holding chamber. Then the first hint of trouble had arisen: Picard and Edorlic were led out, but Troi remained confined. Picard's protests were peremptorily vetoed by Kraax-koorn-aka.

"I guess the chief chicken feels the need for some

leverage, Picard," Chu Edorlic said. "He wants the woman to stay behind as a hostage."

How could he argue the point with someone who didn't speak the same language? Picard wondered. Still, he had tried, until he noticed the odd look in Troi's dark eyes.

"Spare yourself, Captain," she had said. "The chief won't be convinced." Her voice took on a deeper significance as she lowered it so only Picard could hear. "I get the strong sensation that I'll never leave. Nor will you, after the work is finished."

Not alive, at any rate, Picard realized. He supposed it made sense from the chief's point of view. The three humans knew too much—the hidden entrance, the location of the home caves, the source of power. The Kraaxaa-Tseetsk wouldn't dare let them out again.

Still, Picard had felt the stab of frustration. Was there no one on this mission willing to deal honestly?

Looking into Troi's eyes, he nodded. "I understand, and will act accordingly."

Picard shrugged into his parka. "Come on, Mr. Edorlic. We have much to do tonight."

At least the journey back to the wrecked base camp was less demanding than the journey from it. The underground cavern system had a branch that opened barely half a mile from the camp. Picard, Edorlic, Kraax-koorn-aka, and the guards marched by torchlight in reasonable comfort along a sinuous route of caves and subcaves. Again Picard found himself wondering if all the twists and turns were necessary, or if they were added to confuse the route out.

"I've seen drunken worms that left a straighter trail than these guys," Edorlic complained. "Why are they leading us around like this?"

The time had come. Picard explained about Troi's intuitions.

"So they're going to kill us after we've saved their bacon, eh?" Edorlic's face contracted in a scowl. "Guess they're typical chickens after all. We should never have trusted them."

"That would sound considerably more virtuous if it weren't coming from a man who'd kidnapped the counselor and me," Picard told him.

"Ancient history," Edorlic said. "The question right now is, what are we going to do about it?"

Picard took a deep breath. "There are two fliers lying in the gorge below the camp."

"Neither of them is likely to be in any shape to lift out of there," Edorlic objected.

"But both have communications gear," Picard pointed out. "If we can get down the cliff face from the camp ahead of the Tseetsk and get one of those sets running—"

"We can get help," Edorlic finished. He stared penetratingly at Picard. "But what about Troi? We'd never be able to fly people into that cave in time to save her."

There was a way to save Troi, but revealing that would also reveal too much of Picard's long-range plans—plans Edorlic would undoubtedly oppose.

He needed a brutal argument to convince a brutal mind, Picard decided.

"We're dealing with survival," he said, turning a hard face toward Edorlic. "I expect that you're used enough to getting half a loaf."

Chu Edorlic turned from the starship captain to the shaggy-pelted guards around them. "You know, I almost respected these chickens. It surprised me to hear that they wouldn't keep their word. But hearing you write the woman off like that . . . you *really* surprise me, Picard." Edorlic gave him a cold grin. "Even if you are talking sense."

As they left the hidden cave exit, Edorlic described the layout of the base camp shelters. "The one we'll be making for is the largest building. We cut into the cliff behind it; that's supposed to be the head of the new geothermal tap. It's also where the components for the tap are located, along with a few other things."

"Such as rope, perhaps?" Picard asked. It was hard enough, memorizing the field of action. But he also had to labor along the treacherous ledge trails, in much worse light than he'd negotiated them before. To top it off, Koorn by night was even more bitter cold than it was in its frigid daylight hours. Icy fingers seemed to probe their way into each seam of his protective clothing and around his face mask, sinking into every joint: his legs, arms, even the hinge of his jaw.

"Several hundred meters of rope," Edorlic concurred.

"Excellent," Picard said. "We'll go in, get the tap

components out of their crates, start sorting, then make our move for the rope and try for a downward climb."

"Don't you think the guards may object?"

Picard shrugged. "Use your disrupter on them."

Edorlic stopped in mid-step to stare. "You knew?"

"I'm not blind, Edorlic. I've watched you cradling it to your chest all this time. Besides, Troi told me about the way you hunched over when you stood up to surrender. We guessed you were hiding a weapon in your clothes."

"Smart," Edorlic said with a nasty grin. "You're right. I did keep my disrupter."

It had better work, Picard thought, beating his numb arms against his frozen rib cage. *I don't know how much help I'll be in a hand-to-hand struggle against these beings.*

A click from Kraax-koorn-aka brought the convoy to a halt. The ledge widened out, and Picard could see the buildings of the base camp. Could it have been only that afternoon when he first saw those smashed-in doors?

The Kraaxaa-Tseetsk chief stared inquiringly at the prisoners. Edorlic pointed to the main shelter, then traced a mushroom shape in the air with his hands.

The chief sent a scout ahead. He emerged a moment later, beckoning. Then they entered.

Inside the shelter, the guards produced and lit torches. Picard saw that molded plastic formed only three walls and the roof of the structure. The room extended much farther into the cliff face, where the workers of Gang Fourteen had burrowed into solid rock. A construction that seemed half derrick and half scaffold rose in the artificial cave. At its base was a series of rough plastic cartons—square, man-high things, unopened. Behind them were even more massive boxes of components.

Sprawled before the cartons were two men: dead.

"Forns and Jevet. The overseers who fled here," Edorlic said laconically.

Koorn's deep freeze had preserved the victims perfectly. The men's faces were twisted in terror, and their bodies bore numerous wounds, some from arrows, some from spears. Even their blood had frozen.

Kraax-koorn-aka and his men paid no attention to the stark corpses. Instead, the Kraaxaa-Tseetsk set to work demolishing the cartons. Embedded in protective foam, they found enormous turbine vanes, huge metallic housings, sections of jointing rod twelve feet long—all the components for a new geothermal tap.

Edorlic waited until the Tseetsk guards were all engrossed in freeing the machinery. Then he nodded back toward the shelter door. "The rope's in the right-hand corner, behind us," he said. "You grab a coil while I provide a distraction."

Picard grunted as he freed a coil from an untidy pile of rope. Behind him he heard the snarl of the disrupter.

Whirling, he found Edorlic in the doorway, sending another bolt into an unfortunate guard. The shelter resounded with sharp Tseetsk exclamations as the warriors dove for their weapons.

"Come on!" Edorlic grabbed the rope, and they plunged into the darkness outside. "We drove several spikes into the rock over here." He led Picard to the lip of the ledge.

While Picard set about belaying the line to one of the embedded spikes, Edorlic kept a watch on the kicked-in doorway of the main shelter. The torchlight within would have effectively silhouetted any Tseetsk who attempted to fire arrows at them. "If there's a next time, the chickens will do a much more careful job of searching us," he remarked.

The disrupter snarled again, and Picard looked up to see a Tseetsk stagger back, hit, but still alive. "You're not firing at full power?" he asked.

"Out of practicality, not mercy," Edorlic responded with a hard smile. "I don't want to exhaust the charge." His weapon snarled again. "Aren't you finished yet?"

"Ready," Picard said. His end of the rope was secure. The other end disappeared into the darkness below.

"Start down. I'll come after you in a moment. Got to prevent our friends from cutting our lifeline."

The trip down the cliff face remained in Picard's memory as a blurry nightmare version of mountain climbing. He rappelled down sheer stretches of rock and descended broken stretches with little concern for his numb hands and ankles. The rope burn on his gloves grew so bad that his half-frozen hands responded to it as a source of heat. Somehow, however, he found himself at last at the bottom of the cliff. To his left was a huge, crumpled metal arrowhead, the overturned hull of the flier that had taken him into captivity. Already a thin layer of snow covered the abandoned vehicle.

He had approached it and was circling to find the hatchway when an arrow from above shattered against the metal. Picard moved more quickly. In a moment he was joined by Edorlic. "They're climbing down after us," he said breathlessly.

They finally reached the hatch, which loomed over them about a foot above head level. "Let's check the other one," Edorlic suggested.

The overseers' escape flier lay nose down, in worse shape than the more recent addition. The hatch had been closed when it went off the cliff, but had been sprung open by the impact of its crash landing. Edorlic kicked packed snow away from the bottom of the door, hauled it open, and stepped inside.

Reaching into an emergency kit by the entrance, he fumbled out a battery flashlight. Its dim beam brought the tumbled contents of the flier into sudden focus. It was virtually identical to the machine that had brought them here: the same cramped cabin with low ceilings built for a smaller race. Bare, worn floor plates constituted most of the interior. Rough welds showed up clearly in the dim beam.

"The comm gear is up at the pilot's console." Edorlic wormed his way through debris piled against a compartment wall toward the nose of the flier. "Damn!" he exclaimed. "Something landed on it pretty hard, I'd say."

Picard glanced over his shoulder through a small opening to a pair of seats canted at a strange angle and a control panel that had been stove in by a major impact. Bashed chips and torn wires were revealed through the hole. "Let's cannibalize what we can and head back for the other flier," he said.

They ran with what equipment they could scavenge. They could hear avian cries overhead as the Tseetsk climbed down the cliff face. More arrows fell on them.

At the overturned flier, Edorlic boosted Picard up. The captain reached down to return the favor. An arrow spanged off the hull inches from their clasped hands.

"Our feathered friends are getting tired of reasoning with us," Picard muttered.

Besides being upside down, the flier was canted at an odd angle, which turned the climb toward the cockpit into a life-or-death fun-house excursion.

"I'll check the communicator gear," Picard said. "You find some working power."

Several chips had cracked, whether from the impact of the crash or from the sub-zero cold, Picard couldn't tell. He was able to replace them from the gear he'd scavenged.

He was just finishing as the flier's emergency lights came on, almost blinding after the wan beam of the flash. "Well, I've got some power on-line," Edorlic said. "How's the comm gear?"

"We'll see in a second." Picard flicked a switch, and a row of telltales blinked into life. "It seems to be in working order."

"Good." Chu Edorlic climbed the junk pile, leveling his disrupter at Picard. "I almost regret this, Captain, but I'm afraid you need to be reminded who's the captive and who's the captor. A call to Koban will bring some fliers to chase away those savages. We still need you, Picard. You're the only hostage we have left. As you said, we'll have to be content with half a loaf."

Keeping one eye—and the weapon—trained on Picard, Edorlic set the frequency on the communicator. "Edorlic to Koban, Edorlic to Koban. Do you copy?"

"Lock on."

It was a satisfied voice—and it was unmistakably Will Riker's.

"Number One!" Picard burst out.

Chu Edorlic had time for one incredulous gawk at the gear over his head. Then Picard swung his leg at Chu's knees. Edorlic tumbled face down into the pile of debris. And then he was fading in a wash of blue light.

"Number One! Are you still there?" Picard called up to the communicator.

His answer was a tightly spaced group of figures beaming in.

Moments later the Kraaxaa-Tseetsk warriors arrived to launch their attack. They found the hatch unbolted, and the blue light that had three times streamed briefly from the cockpit was gone.

Kraax-koorn-aka was the first in, as befitted his

position as chief. He had time for an instant of surprise as he found, not two escapees but a Starfleet security squad, phasers aimed. Then the stun-blast hit him, and he knew no more.

"*Enterprise,*" Worf spoke into his communicator. "We've got the one with the scar. Six to beam up."

Deanna Troi was almost as astonished as Kraaxkoorn-aka when a team of security officers, led by Will Riker, blinked into existence right outside her small cell. A quick flash of phaser-fire and the guards lay on the floor, stunned.

"Will!" Troi exclaimed. "How did you find . . . ? Did the captain—"

"We've been monitoring and tracing all rebel transmissions, on the chance of finding the kidnappers. Geordi was also able to home in on the geothermal tap, once Captain Picard was aboard to confirm that it wasn't simply one more anomalous reading." Riker's teeth gleamed against his beard in a quick grin.

At that moment a troop of Tseetsk guards appeared in the outer tunnel. Whistling the alarm, they charged. Riker's face was serious as he picked off two of the lead attackers, then tapped the communicator on his chest. "Let's end this away mission while we're ahead. Riker to *Enterprise.* Mission accomplished. Five to beam up."

Back on the bridge at last, Jean-Luc Picard sank gratefully into the captain's seat. He felt considerably better physically, thanks to Beverly Crusher's ministrations. And with the news of Troi's successful rescue, his spirits brightened as well.

"Mr. Data!" he called. "How are you progressing with a translator for Kraaxaa-Tseetsk?"

"On-line, Captain," the android responded. "The chief will now be understood."

As if on cue, the turbolift opened and Kraaxkoorn-aka entered, flanked by two husky security officers. "Murderers!" the chief raged. "What have you done to my people?"

"Kraax-koorn-aka!" Picard's voice carried over the Tseetsk leader's tirade. "I regret that you were taken aboard this vessel in such an unorthodox manner, but at the time I doubted you would give us a hearing."

The Tseetsk chief halted, staring at Picard. "You! Now you speak my language! What—"

"I have machinery here that helps me speak your language," Picard told him. "There is great need for us to understand each other, as you will shortly see."

He pointed to the entrance to his ready room. "Please wait in there with these men. You will see and hear what is going on, but I don't want you to be seen immediately."

"I will not—" Kraax-koorn-aka began, but Picard cut him off.

"I'm sorry, but I simply cannot stop to argue with you at the moment. Mr. Worf, will you and your officers escort Kraax-koorn-aka to the ready room? And make sure the viewing screen in there is on."

Worf nodded and hustled the raging bird crea

ture through a small door to the left of the bridge. As soon as the chief was out of sight, Picard called, "Bring in Drraagh and Vossted. And hail the Tseetsk commander."

Hweeksk's face appeared on the screen as the ex-overseer and the alien positioned themselves by Picard. "I am Jean-Luc Picard, captain of this vessel," Picard identified himself. "Until now I was on the planet's surface tending to . . . other business. My officers have informed me that you propose to destroy our ship and exterminate the humans on Koorn."

Feathers rustled in agitation as Hweeksk responded to the captain's blunt speech. "The slaves are in revolt, and you would help them. Elimination of the problem is the only possible solution."

"To accomplish that task, you would also have to eliminate the regent Drraagh," Picard pointed out.

Hweeksk's agitation grew. "I am aware of that."

"That knowledge troubles you," Picard went on. "I understand your cultural imperative is the survival of the race, indeed the survival of every individual. To the Tseetsk, there is no worse crime than being responsible for the death of another Tseetsk. But suppose I told you that the pacification of Koorn would require the loss of not one Tseetsk life, but hundreds—perhaps thousands?"

The Tseetsk captain ruffled her feathers in anger. "I do not think your vessel could inflict sufficient damage on mine that such casualties would result," she said. "And I do not propose to risk my people on the planet's surface. So how can you—"

"I assure you, Captain, if you continue your attempt to colonize Koorn, many Tseetsk will die. Because, although your government has installed a regent for Koorn, there is already a planetary governor there. That, I believe is the literal translation of the title 'Kraax-koorn-aka.'"

He gestured, the ready room doors opened, and Kraax-koorn-aka stepped out.

Muffled gasps came from Vossted, Drraagh, and Hweeksk. They stared at the Kraaxaa-Tseetsk and he at them, as if both sides were seeing beasts they had thought mythological.

Kraax-koorn-aka, with slightly more time to prepare himself, was the first to speak. "Greetings, cousins." Even through the translator, Picard could hear the irony in his voice. "So you're the ones who sent these bareskins out to kill my people."

Drraagh stared in fascination.

Hweeksk exploded. "What sort of wretched human trick is this?" she demanded.

"Hardly a human trick," Picard told her. "No human ever looked like that." He looked up at Hweeksk. "I'd say this was a trick the Tseetsk played on themselves by insistently hewing to a narrow view of the universe. Even at the height of your race's power, you took specialization—the narrow view—to an extreme. The result was a fragmentation of your society and a deadly internecine war.

"The founders of your new society attempted a more universal view: loyalty to all of Tseetsk-kind. Yet in fact the narrow view still prevailed. After meeting representatives of another sentient race, your solution was an attempt to incorporate them into your society as slaves, simply because they were not Tseetsk. They didn't fit your definitions, so you felt free to misuse them."

Picard pointed to Kraax-koorn-aka, everything a civilized Tseetsk would abhor: tall, male, and aggressive, with clear marks of danger on his body. "But if the humans you found were a problem for your narrow view, here is a disaster."

"He is Tseetsk," Drraagh said.

"He is nothing like us!" Hweeksk quickly returned.

"No, Hweeksk, deep down you know that he is Tseetsk, and our victim," Drraagh said. "You know the order for all the new colony worlds: eliminate all large, dangerous life-forms. The humans have been doing this as a matter of course, even though, in this case, the large life-form was killing back. Our slaves have been murdering Tseetsk—at our command!"

The notion of having participated in wholesale slaughter of their own people caused both Sree-Tseetsk to bob their heads in horror. Hweeksk lowered her eyes. "The homeworld must know of this," she finally said.

"Indeed." Drraagh turned to Kraax-koorn-aka. "In the meantime we have much to talk about. Cousin."

The Kraaxaa-Tseetsk gazed measuringly at her. His belligerence was gone, replaced by a sort of guarded composure that Picard found astonishing. "Much indeed, I think," he replied.

"I shall inform you when contact is made." Hweeksk disappeared from the screen.

Drraagh turned to Vossted. "We'll need your help, old friend. This will be a challenge for both our peoples."

"A challenge and an opportunity, I think," Vossted said, smiling. "But I can't talk for my people alone. Captain, could you contact Koban?"

"Make it so," Picard ordered.

The screen shifted to reveal the communications post down on Koorn. A tired, slightly nervous-looking Koban came into view. The unruined side of his face went deathly pale when he saw who was calling him. "Picard! What . . . Where are my people?"

"Six of your people, Koban, discovered too late that certain dangers on Koorn do not come from natural causes. The only followers of yours to survive your little game of extortion are Chu Edorlic and Lorens Ben."

Koban sank despairingly in his chair. "So you'll send them down and abandon us to the chickens?"

"I'll send them down and invite you up for negotiations," Picard corrected him. "Much has happened that you don't know about. The ice creatures your people hunted are actually Tseetsk, descended from the losing side of a ten-thousand-year-old war. Your ex-masters must come to grips with redefining their race, its future, and its relations with other peoples. I suggest that you might profit from the same examination."

"I have turned to Vossted for help," Drraagh said, stepping forward.

Vossted spoke. "But I must turn to *my* people, for *their* help. I now have the ear of the Tseetsk, but my voice needs your fire, Koban, your spirit.

"You've shown that you're willing to die for freedom. Will you live for it? Will you help me argue, teach, *lead* the Tseetsk and the humans into a new relationship? One where we'll have freedom, dignity, and the chance to renew our ties with our lost past through the Federation? Isn't that a battle worth joining?"

"Think of it, Koban," Picard said. "A chance to fight for the freedom of all the humans working on Tseetsk worlds, without shedding human blood."

Koban stared, bemused. "You're sure? The chickens—I mean, Tseetsk—are ready to talk?"

"I think your opportunity is better than that," Picard said. He smiled. "For the first time in a long history, they may be willing to listen."

Two weeks later the *Enterprise* was ready to break orbit and leave Koorn. Days before, the USS *Charadri* had arrived, carrying a Federation ambassador to moderate the negotiations. As part of the diplomatic protocol, Picard, Riker, Troi, and Crusher were making their good-byes.

"The Federation made a good choice, sending an Aurelian as its representative." Riker glanced over at Ambassador Struthio who, with her high-plumed head, stood even taller than Kraax-koorn-aka as she talked with both sets of Tseetsk.

"I think Hweeksk is already trying to figure out how to duplicate the ambassador's feather patterns," Troi said with a smile.

Picard and Beverly Crusher were exchanging warm words with Vossted when two more figures stepped out of the diplomatic crowd—Koban and Lorens Ben. "I wanted to say good-bye, Dr. Beverly," Lorens said.

"And I . . ." Koban hesitated a second, searching for words. "I wanted to thank you, Dr. Crusher, for saving Lorens." Again he hesitated, glancing at Picard. "For the last five years I felt I had to chart a dangerous course, gaining leadership, then planning revolution. Because I dared not make any mistakes, I finally convinced myself I *couldn't* make them.

"These last two weeks, talking to the Tseetsk face to face, have shown me some of the mistakes in my thinking over recent years." Koban paused again. "And they've shown me how many mistakes I made in dealing with you and your people."

"You are willing to learn, Koban," Picard said. "That's an important capacity in any commander, not letting yourself get bound up in the chains of past misconceptions."

"No. At last we're all talking about the future, for all our peoples. When I go to Tseetsk-Home, I'll be taking with me a cadre of our brightest young minds to learn Tseetsk techniques. This young man, for instance," he said, putting a hand on Lorens Ben's shoulder, "will learn Tseetsk medicine." The boy and the man smiled at each other.

It seemed that another peace had been negotiated, Picard noted.

"Yes," Koban went on, "when he earns the title

of *Doctor* Lorens, perhaps I'll ask him to take care of this." Koban's hand brushed the layer of scar tissue on his face. "For the present, Kraax-koorn-aka and I are keeping our scars for political reasons. The delegates from Tseetsk-Home are very much impressed by our fierce appearance."

"Then I look forward to the day when scars are gone," Picard said.

"Me, too," Lorens added. He looked at Crusher. "I'll remember you, Dr. Beverly. I hope you'll remember me."

"Count on it," Beverly Crusher said.

At the exit from the reception room, Riker strode up beside Picard. "What was Koban saying to you?"

"In part, it was a roundabout apology for kidnapping me," Picard said.

"It was the least he owed you." Riker's lips went tight under his beard.

"He had the grace to admit he misjudged his course of action under the pressure of command," Picard said. "That's a pressure I know you understand, even though you led better than Koban."

"That's right, Will," Crusher said. "We owe the rescue of the captain and Deanna to you."

"I was lucky," Riker said, a bit flustered by the compliment.

Picard smiled. "I think it was Napoleon who said that great commanders make their own luck." He stepped into the hall. "Now let's get to the transporter room. I want to get back to *my* command. We still have a good portion of this sector to chart.

And I'd like to accomplish as much of that as possible before Starfleet pulls the *Enterprise* off for another one of those boring political missions."

"Boring?" Riker raised an eyebrow. "You mean, like this one?"

Back in the reception room, the solemn delegates were startled by the peals of laughter that suddenly rang from the hall outside.